BLOOD OF THE WICKED

EVERLY ABBOTT BOOK TWO

K.N. BANET

1

CHAPTER ONE

JANUARY 10, 2021

I was having what I thought was a normal evening, considering my new circumstances. There was a burning in my throat that was bothering me, but I was focused on the gutted computer tower in front of me, trying to install a new motherboard, so I got on with rebuilding the rest of the computer. I was having more issues than I had planned for, which kept my mind off the burning. The mounting screws kept getting away from me when I tried to screw them in. My patience grew frayed as I lost another, hearing it ding inside of the case and get lost. I grabbed a spare with a groan.

I'll have to get that one out before I boot it up.

I was three screws in when a smell hit my nose, and I dropped my screwdriver.

Blood.

Straightening like a board, feeling a strong tug to head to the smell, I turned quickly, my eyes trying to find the source. I tried to remain still, only taking a single step toward it, as my canines grew into long fangs and my mouth watered. I stopped breathing as the burning in my throat became an inferno. Not being able to smell it made it easier to stay still. I knew if I rushed for the smell, I would be picking a fight I would lose.

I hadn't heard the door of my rooms open, but Alexius entered, a large metal cup in his hand. He closed my door and slowly walked toward me. I was shaking when he finally held out the cup.

"Calm down." He wasn't angry, and it wasn't even much of an order. It was soothing in the same way someone would talk to a scared animal.

Keeping my hand steady, knowing he expected me to show some level of control, I took the cup. I was even able to take a long drink without shaking or spilling any. The burning soothed down to something manageable on my third swallow of the rich, fresh blood, which had been heated to the perfect temperature. My heart began beating steadily, and my body felt warm. By the fourth swallow, the burning was mostly gone, but I knew it would be back before long.

It always comes back. It always burns.

"Thank you," I finally said, my thoughts clearing as I finished the entire meal and put the cup on the table. Not a drop was left.

"You never came for your second meal, so I brought it here," he explained, picking up the cup. "You shouldn't miss feedings. We've had this discussion."

"I'm sorry." I waved at the computer on the table. "I was working on—"

"We've had this discussion," he repeated, pinning me with a dark stare. In the two and a half months since I was brought here, Alexius had given me that look more times than I could count.

"We have," I agreed, looking away from him. "I got distracted, and it won't happen again."

"Don't make promises we both know you won't keep. You will do this again. I've never met a young vampire so willing to starve because they would rather do something else," he said, shaking his head as he turned away to leave. He stopped at the door and sighed. "I will repeat this for good measure because you're still young. *Nothing* you are doing is more important than feeding when you need to feed. The *only* exception is making sure you are protected from the sun, and since you are securely in my home, that isn't an issue. You have alarms for when it's time to feed. Pay attention to them. Also, it's time for your lesson. Meet me in the library."

"Damn it," I mumbled as I watched him leave. He left my door ajar, a clear sign ignoring his schedule wouldn't fly. Wake up, eat, spend four or so hours doing whatever I wanted, then eat again. After the second meal, I had to spend two hours with him, talking about being a vampire and part of the supernatural community, which was even bigger than I had realized. After that, I had two hours to do whatever I wanted again before I needed to feed. After that last meal, I had whatever free time was left to enjoy before I passed out wherever I happened to be.

This wasn't the first time I accidentally missed a meal. I grabbed my phone, checking for the alarms I kept. It was going off and had been for twenty minutes, but I had silenced my phone.

"Well... crap." Shoving it into my pocket, I left my

suite. When I had moved in, Alexius told me he was preparing a guest room, and I had been under the impression I was getting a single room. I'd been wrong. I had three rooms that were completely mine—quarters, a suite, whatever someone wanted to call it. A sitting area, a small kitchenette I never used, and an expansive bedroom. All of it was light safe, with no windows or access to the outside world.

I went down the long main hall, casting a look at Alexius' door. He only had a single room, which made my living situation strange, but he never brought up the reason I got a suite while he only had a bedroom. Farther down the hall, I passed the garden, seeing a few flowers in bloom under the moonless night. I looked at them for a minute, glad to know there was at least something alive in the house where I lived.

I certainly wasn't.

Shoving my hands into my pockets, I continued the long walk to the library. It was one of the rooms farthest from my suite and the other bedrooms. I passed the study, which I wasn't allowed into, leaving me with the impression Alexius used it to get away from me. I passed the armory and the gym; I was allowed into both but never went. Physical activity had never been my strong suit as a living, breathing human, and I wasn't prepared to have that proven true as an immortal.

I'm still an out-of-control vampire. I don't need to add a sharp object and my natural physical ineptitude to the equation.

Finally, I reached the library, which was at the beginning of the separate wing of the mansion. There was the living side and the working side. The library was in the middle, leaning toward the work side. Alexius was pulling several books from the shelves and putting them on the only table in the center of the room.

Everything about the house made it clear he was the only person who lived here. I was used to an active nest with dozens of people around to deal with, but now I was in a world that catered to only this man and his desires. He wanted a library, but it only had books he wanted in it and space for him to sit with maybe two other people. The gym only had a set of equipment for one person. The garden was small and intimate, and I didn't know who cared for it, but it had plants that bloomed at night for the vampire who couldn't see the sun anymore. Even my suite had once been for guests, not someone who lived here, but someone passing through.

"So... What am I learning today?" I asked cautiously as I went in and closed the door behind me.

"We're going to discuss a new control technique, then move on to something else. It's been nearly three months, and you're not as controlled as I thought you would be. I can't safely take you around humans yet. It's becoming an inconvenience not to allow the staff down to do their duties."

"Oh..." I grimaced as I sat. Guilt and shame raced through me as I thought about my reaction to the blood he brought into the room. It had taken everything for me not to jump him the moment the scent hit my nose. I had stood there, waiting for him to bring it to me, which was an improvement. "We've already gone over a bunch of techniques. I'm trying all of them."

"There are a few more that may help," he said, not looking at me.

"I don't know what I'm doing wrong."

"You're not doing anything wrong," he said, frowning as he turned to me with a book shoved under his arm and another in his hands. "While I would prefer you not to skip meals, that wouldn't account for your lack of control. It's possible I misjudged the time you would need based on the blood that Turned you or your personality. These things... are different for every vampire, and anything can affect how quickly or slowly one adjusts to the need. If I sired someone tonight, it could take them a decade before they could safely go out. I'm too old and too powerful. It's been proven that both things make the need to feed stronger and control harder to maintain, but after I had..." He walked to the table and put the books down. I didn't know why he'd trailed off.

We both knew how I had become a vampire, and there was no going back. I wasn't particularly sour about it... most days.

"After I gave you Edwin's blood, I had hoped his blood was weak enough to make your adjustment quick. I probably miscalculated, and you're moving at the same speed he did. That doesn't mean this lesson won't be useful, and you can't gain control earlier with it and everything else I've taught you."

"I did really well that first night," I remembered wistfully. I had accepted the delicious drink, then been able to have a conversation and think about other things when I had blood around. When I woke up on the second night, I had practically attacked Alexius for the cup he had brought me.

"You were in shock that first night," he pointed out as he sat down across from me. "I knew you would backslide, but I expected you to quickly get control."

"Sorry I haven't lived up to expectations," I mumbled, staring at the books on the table.

"I should have set reasonable ones," he muttered, opening a book on the table. "Now, these texts don't actually have the control technique I want you to attempt. They're for you to read in your free time. They're just stories about some of the more ancient vampires. Good things to know, stories many vampires talk about to get a point across. Some of our history."

"What else could there be?" I asked, pushing my hair back as I ignored his explanation about the books. I had a feeling they were going to be dry reads. Everything in the library was dry to read. If I wasn't forced to sleep when the sun came up, the books Alexius kept would be a great way to get sleep. "I'm meditating every day. I'm trying to ignore the burn. I've tried counting until I can focus, which *never* works. I've learned how to freeze instead of attack, but that doesn't really solve the problem. I shake like a leaf—"

"Pain," he said simply, cutting me off. "We haven't tried pain."

I blinked and looked up, my entire body stiffening as he pulled a knife from the table. I eyed the knife, then him, his dark eyes telling me nothing. The knife slid across the table and stopped in front of me as I stared at him in horror.

"Particularly, we haven't tried small amounts of self-inflicted pain. I'm not talking about mutilating yourself, but pinching yourself or poking yourself with the tip of something sharp. Those things often give vampires something else to focus on to break free of the need to attack whatever source of blood they've found. It's a slight shock."

"Oh."

"I've waited months to bring this up because I don't particularly like telling you to hurt yourself. That's why I'll add that this is just a suggestion and nothing more. The knife is yours if you want to try it."

"Yeah... I don't think so..." I said, reaching out to push the knife away, letting it slide across the table back to Alexius' side. "I'll try pinching if I'm desperate, but I'm not going to accidentally stab myself."

"Fine." Alexius shrugged, taking the knife off the table. I couldn't see where he put it, but I was glad it was gone. "We'll proceed with a normal lesson. I want to review vampire law to make sure it's sinking in. I'll ask you things, and you'll answer. Then we'll spend a moment expanding and discussing why it's one of the laws by which we abide."

And here I thought when I graduated from college, I would never have a pop quiz again.

"Okay, I'm ready."

"What is the first law of our kind?"

"Keep our secret from the human public. They know of the myth, but we have to keep it a myth because we hunt their kind. We feed the myth, so they can't learn the truth about our kind. We're one of the few supernaturals who exclusively prey on humanity on a large scale. Other species are much smaller than our own. To maintain the secret, we're allowed to employ humans to help with things we can't do because of our limitations, but we have to have protocol and security measures established to keep our staff from exposing us." I smiled as Alexius nodded. "That one is easy. It was my entire life before this."

"Of course, but it's good to establish some confidence in you before I give you anything harder." He gave me a small smile, promising this lesson wasn't going to remain easy.

I should have kept my mouth shut.

2

CHAPTER TWO

Two hours later, I rested my head on the desk as the clock in the library chimed with the time. It was three in the morning, though it was my afternoon or evening with the nighttime schedule I was forced to take. Alexius had grilled me for two hours about the laws of vampires. There were some strange ones, ones I was certain I'd never see play out, but others were easy.

"We're done, yeah?" I asked, staring at my feet as I pressed my forehead into the table.

"One more," Alexius said, not getting up from the seat across from me. "Who are we not allowed to Turn under any circumstance?"

"Children," I answered immediately, not lifting my head. He was ending on an easy one, and I was grateful. He'd put me through a pop quiz worse than any college exam I'd taken. "It's frowned on to Turn someone who is elderly but not illegal. Turning a child is a death sentence."

"Why?"

"Children don't grow up. There are two ways it's a problem. We're locked in the physical state of our last moment, with only some variations like our weight. Our mental state can change as a vampire, but a child won't mentally become an adult. The brain isn't developed enough. A toddler will always be a toddler." The idea of an immortal child disturbed me, especially now that I knew just how bad the burn was. The need to feed was extreme, and I struggled not to attack when I could smell blood. I couldn't imagine how a child would adjust to this sort of life.

Things don't become laws until someone does them. Someone had once done it. Who thinks to Turn a child? Sounds like a nightmare.

"Good. Now you can go. In two hours, I expect you to be in the small sitting room for your last meal. Please don't miss it."

"I won't," I promised, getting up. I had the odd sensation of wanting to yawn but being unable to. Grabbing the two books he'd put on the table earlier in the evening, I left him there. I was ten feet down the hall when he caught up and walked beside me.

"Is there something else?" I asked, giving him a curious look as we passed the gym. He didn't normally walk with me, so there had to be some reason he was stalking me tonight.

"Yes. It just occurred to me. Have you contacted your human friends or your brother since I brought you here?"

"No," I answered quickly, shaking my head. "Why?"

"You should. They know about vampires and are already subject to the geas. If you get under control, you could even have them visit and maintain those relationships. Maybe... it could help motivate you."

Like motivation is the problem. I want to be in control, damn it. I'm just not.

"I'll think about it," I mumbled, a complete lie. I had made my mind up about my human family and friends the first week, and nothing would change my decision

I don't want them to see me like this. They think I left and don't want to be contacted after everything that happened in Maine. It's better they don't know. Maine was traumatizing enough to justify it. They don't need to know I didn't survive.

"Good." He nodded once, then kept walking, leaving me in the hall by myself.

His footsteps disappeared, and I knew I was alone. My eyes welled with tears as hopelessness ran through me.

I was living in a dark basement, trapped underground until it was safe to leave. Not safe for me but for everyone else. I was the monster I had worked so hard to stop in Maine, and even Alexius, the ancient vampire, didn't know how to make me better.

It's only been two and a half months. I have eternity. It'll be okay... right? I just need to... stay busy.

Wiping my eyes, I went back into my suite and back to work on my new desktop. I had lost my work rig and my home computer. Alexius had apparently burned the entire mansion to the ground after he got me out of there, and he never told me what happened to my computer from my home in Maine. I had already built a replacement for the work computer, and it was set up at a desk in an office Alexius cleared for me, but I wanted a personal computer for my suite. It took months for the parts I needed to come in, thanks to a chip shortage plaguing everyone. Stock was limited everywhere, which meant I had been fighting against bots and scalpers to get the graphics card I needed for the computer.

The problems I was having with the motherboard earlier weren't so troubling now. I had it mounted in fifteen minutes and retrieved the screws that had gotten away from me, putting them in a little baggie and throwing it into a drawer. I always kept the spares just in case.

Sadly, building the computer wasn't as calming as it normally was. The entire time, I was bouncing a leg, bothered by something. I was finished with the computer by the time I really thought about what was wrong.

Life sucks. That's it. My life is miserable.

I nodded, satisfied with that conclusion.

I mean, I should be grateful to be alive, but who wants to live in a basement forever and never get to leave? I might not like going out, but it feels as if I'm in a cage. A cage with someone controlling my entire life from when I work to when and how much I eat.

I picked up my tower, unsurprised with how easy it was to lift. The towers used to be nearly too heavy for me, but now I could lift them with ease. Controlling my physical strength was one of the first things Alexius and I worked on, and I had figured it out quickly. I didn't like breaking things, so I had learned how to stop breaking them.

Too bad that logic hasn't worked for the whole eating

people thing. I don't like to hurt people, but I can't seem to get any sort of control over my bloodlust.

Plugging in the power, then the monitors, mouse, and keyboard, it was ready for testing. I hit the power and felt a burst of joy to see it turn on. The LED fans lit up and began to spin. The signal to the monitors was working, and I grinned everything worked.

"Success!" I sat down at my little desk and started the necessary installs needed to get the computer into working order. Operating systems were important. The next hour was spent stress testing the new computer, monitoring the CPU temperature as I went. I was immensely satisfied with my work when my meal alarm went off. That glorious feeling was chased away by the blaring telling me I needed to head to the small sitting room for my last meal of the day.

Time to face Alexius again.

I rubbed my face as I walked out. Facing Alexius wasn't really the problem. He wasn't really a problem. He was a quiet man, studious and stiff but not uncaring or mean. He could be a bit cool, but I was thinking that was just his normal personality and not anything against me. He liked schedules, and he was trying to help me. He had been trying to help me when he fed my dead body Edwin's blood and made me into a vampire, a reward for helping him discover that his only son had been murdered. How and why he did it were the only reasons I wasn't furious with him.

As I stopped in the archway of the sitting room, I had a recurring thought.

There are definitely less attractive men to be stuck with. I didn't lose on that front.

It was stupid and girlish, but Alexius was one of those men who fell into the category of tall, dark, and handsome. Bronze skin from the Mediterranean and dark brown eyes, though the shoulder-length black curls were gone. He'd cut it back in November into a short modern style, very short on the sides and styled on the top. He was broad and muscular and held himself as if he ruled as a king or a god.

No. A warrior. He looks as if he could go into battle at any moment.

He was wiping down two glasses, his hands steady and practiced, thorough like he was cleaning a blade in another life. He seemed focused, and that was always my favorite way to see him. Focused, but preferably not on me.

He didn't seem to notice me, so I kept enjoying the view. Considering I had no one else to look at, I tried not to feel guilty about staring at Alexius so much. I watched as he put the glasses down on top of the minibar in the room, then put the hand towel away. He turned to see me in the archway as if he knew I had been there the entire time.

He probably did. He misses nothing in this house.

"You don't need my permission to enter, Everly," he said blandly.

I quickly walked in, folding my arms over myself. If it still could, my face would have flushed. It did when I had fed recently, but after four hours, it was probably a very light pink, something I hoped he wouldn't notice. I couldn't help it.

Hope he doesn't realize I was ogling him.

"Um…" I didn't know what to say, so I went to find a seat. I felt like a guest, trying to decide where my host wanted me to sit, so I didn't take his place. I had been in the small sitting room every night for at least one meal, but it was always like this. Generally, Alexius let me know where to find him, and the small sitting room was a common choice, close to the bedrooms and his study. There were plenty of seating options. Two armchairs by the fireplace were nice but felt too intimate when Alexius and I sat there, leading me to be a stuttering idiot when he tried to have a conversation. I chose the other side of the room, aiming for the love seat and couch positioned around a coffee table. It had space to breathe.

"You seem off tonight. Is something wrong?" he asked as he pulled out the blood bag that would be our meal tonight.

I had no idea where the endless supply of blood bags came from, but there was always one when I needed a meal. I went through three a night, which was enough to beg the question if I was ever ready to ask.

"No, not really." To me, tonight wasn't much different from any other night. I heard the beep of a little microwave he used to heat the blood and knew it would be warm and ready soon enough. The burn in my throat exploded into an inferno again.

"You would tell me if something was wrong, wouldn't you? Or are you trying to pretend something is okay when it's not?"

The first question hadn't caught me off guard, but the second did.

"Yeah, I would tell you," I lied, looking at the table instead of him.

He didn't reply as the microwave dinged. A moment later, I heard the bag punctured, and the scent of blood filled the room. I stopped breathing and closed my eyes, trying to focus on staying still, but my hands were shaking as I listened to it poured into the glasses Alexius had prepared. I felt each footstep rattle my bones as I tracked his movement across the room. Finally, hearing the clink of glass on the coffee table in front of me, my eyes flew open and I stared at it until he sat down. He gave me a single nod, so I grabbed it from the table and started drinking, not stopping until I drank every drop.

"Well, you have been showing improvement about waiting until you have permission," Alexius commented as I put the empty glass down. It was practically clean again. I felt my heart pound in my chest as it tried to move my meal through me.

"Yeah, but that's not all control is," I said, staring at the empty glass. "Once I start feeding, I can't bring myself to stop."

"Yes, but that's something..." He shifted a little, moving his legs until he appeared to be comfortable with them crossed. "That might take some... physical training."

"Like someone forcing me to stop when I feed on a human. Jacob used to do that to other vampires."

"He was strong enough to do it. Not every Master or Mistress is, but thankfully he was, considering his goal with his nest." Alexius looked away for a moment and sighed. "Back on topic. I want you to be steady with the scent of blood before I let you feed on a human. It still brings out your predatory instincts too strongly. Your eyes turn red the moment you scent it, which doesn't bode well for keeping our secret in public," he said with no emotion on his face.

I desperately wanted to pick his brain. I wanted to know if he thought I was as much of a failure as I felt. He'd said he thought I would make a good vampire the night I had woken up after being Turned, but I felt as if I was shaping up to be a pretty piss poor one and was running out of faith in myself.

I think I ran out weeks ago.

I didn't want to ask, though, didn't want to hear the disappointment he probably kept to himself, so I diverted back to the conversation he clearly wanted to avoid.

"When are we going to work on Jacob's murder again?" I asked, trying to keep eye contact with him. "I want to get to work on what we were planning."

"When you're ready to work on it, which will involve visiting other vampires and dealing with humans, neither of which you are ready for." He took a sip of his meal, the rich blood coating his upper lip. He casually licked it off like it wasn't a big deal.

I didn't get to watch Alexius feed on most nights. He only needed to feed once a week, if even that often. My heart raced a little faster as I remembered the first time I had seen him feed—from me, his fangs deep in my thigh, his head between my legs as he used some sort of magic to make the experience all too enjoyable instead of painful.

"Don't concern yourself right now. Focus on learning about what you are and how to live with it," he continued as if I wasn't totally focused on him like an obsessed stalker. "I noticed you were working on another computer. Didn't you already build one for your office?"

"Yeah, but I wanted a personal computer for my suite," I explained, finally breaking my stare from his lips. "Something I can... put games on or something. Something that isn't for work. Not that I really need a reason to build a computer. It's something I really enjoy doing."

"We all need something we enjoy on the quiet evenings." He leaned forward. "You know, I'm certain there are several computers around the mansion that could be replaced."

"Oh, yeah, I've seen the old ones in the offices for the staff." I snorted, remembering the bricks I found in there. I had met none of the staff in person because they were banned from the basement until I was ready, but I spoke to them over the little wall-mounted microphones Alexius had installed around the mansion. He used them to talk to the staff but never to get hold of me.

"Do you think you can give them something—"

"Yes," I said quickly. "Absolutely."

"Truthfully, I'm surprised you haven't already," he said, a small smile forming. "Based on your excitement, I bet you've been considering it for some time."

"I haven't, but I'd never turn down the chance," I replied, smiling back. After a second, I realized he had inadvertently given me a chance to escape awkward dinner conversation. "I'll start making plans. I've been ordering spares of nearly everything, so I could probably get started in a couple of days if I order the rest before the sun comes up." Standing, I picked up my glass and took it to the bar. "Have a good rest, Alexius."

"You as well," he called softly.

CHAPTER THREE

A couple of days later, I woke up at sunset and stared at the ceiling, trying to find any motivation to move except for the aching burn in my throat. I knew it would be more of the same today as it was every day, which made it hard to get out of bed. I had thirty minutes to find Alexius and get breakfast, and I was always hungriest when I woke up. Showering quickly, I threw on something comfortable to wear for the day, going for a hoodie over a tank and jeans. I found Alexius in the small sitting room once again, wearing a black t-shirt and dark jeans, casual for him. Normally, he wore button-ups and slacks. The only thing consistent about his wardrobe today was the loafers he always wore. I never saw him in socks or with bare feet. It just never happened.

"Mail has been delivered," he said as I walked in. "Let me prepare breakfast, then we'll sort. You've received a number of packages." He pointed to a small table at the side of the room, where a pile waited to be sorted. The mail was dropped down a chute when it arrived upstairs, so the human staff didn't have to come down and run across me at any point.

"They all made it?" I grinned as I looked over the packages. "Good. I can start upgrading the other computers." Trying to stay focused on the brown boxes as Alexius heated the blood and poured it, I remained still until he brought it to me. I drank quickly, then went to wash my glass, not wanting to drag out breakfast longer than it needed to be. Alexius waited patiently for me to finish the clean-up, then we began to sort.

I stacked ten packages to get them back to my room in one go. Alexius flipped through some letters, pausing at a postcard with a deep frown.

"What is it?" I asked, curious because no one had ever sent a postcard to him.

"I don't know," he answered, turning it over in his hands. "Do you know anyone from Alaska?" He held it out.

"No..." I said slowly as I took the postcard. Fairbanks, Alaska. There was no message written, only the address for his home here in Savannah, Georgia, without a name. There was no return address, either. Someone had put a stamp on a blank postcard and sent it. "Do you?"

"Most vampires avoid Alaska. We don't keep nests up there. I can't think of anyone I know who would go there for any reason."

"Why? Isn't it dark for like half the year?"

"The other half of the year is too sunny all the time, and it's the busiest season. It stands out to be the one person who isn't enjoying the sunny days," he explained. "So, we avoid Alaska as a permanent home. At one point, a vampire tried to start a winter resort for our kind, but it didn't work out. Most vampires settle into one hunting ground and don't want to leave it undefended for half the year, which makes winter homes up north even less likely. Nests don't like when their vampires go missing for several months. There are many reasons."

"Oh. Yeah, that makes a lot of sense... kind of." I hadn't considered it like that. Turning the postcard over again, I frowned at a dark brown spot on the photo, blending in with the picture. As though on autopilot, I brought it to my nose and inhaled deeply. The burn in my throat reacted to the scent, but only a little. The blood drop was too old and dry for it to be anything worthwhile. "Alexius, there's blood on it."

"Let me see."

I gave it to him, and he sniffed it as well, frowning deeply as he caught the same thing I did. I watched him reexamine the card before shaking his head.

"I'll look into this further," he said softly, tucking it into his back pocket.

"Should we like... check for fingerprints or something?" I asked as I stared at it shoved haphazardly into his pocket. It also gave me a chance to see how nice his jeans...

Stop. Stop ogling the mysterious vampire who controls your life, Everly.

"It would have been passed around by postal people. Too many people would have touched it by now. I'll reach out to some friends and see if anyone is playing a little game with me. It's been known to happen. If I need anything from you, I will ask." He picked up the rest of his mail, which I knew was mostly spam Rupert liked to annoy him with. I didn't understand the joke, but I saw Alexius sometimes smile at the garbage sent down the chute for him.

"Well, okay. Let me know," I said, put out by his shutdown. Picking up all my boxes, I balanced them precariously and walked out, barely navigating around him. I was nearly at my door when I heard him chuckle. I tried to get one hand to open the door but nearly lost my tower.

"Damn it," I muttered in annoyance as he came into view. He put one hand on my leaning tower to steady it while he reached to open my door for me with the other.

"There you go," he said, clearly amused.

"Thanks," I said, getting into my suite as quickly as I could while he held the door. I put everything down and started opening everything, knowing he was still there, watching me.

I really didn't like when people hovered, never had, but now it wasn't just anxiety from being watched and possibly messing up in front of someone. Now I thought about Edwin hovering over me at my desk, demanding that I cover up my mother's murder. Now I thought about how he did it to intimidate and scare me. My face grew hot, and I stopped moving, slowly looking at Alexius.

"Is there something else you need?" I asked, finally driven by my growing anxiety and an undercurrent of fear that had no place in my new life.

Edwin is dead. Alexius promised me he was dead. He has to be dead. He's not the one at the door.

"No, I just wanted to make sure you had everything...

handled," he said, then quickly closed my door, leaving me alone in my suite once again.

I relaxed and went back to my packages, getting out the parts I bought. Luckily, the cases used for the current computers were somewhat recent, so I only needed to buy new internal parts like better motherboards, CPUs, and graphics cards. I had gotten replacement fans, too, knowing the older computers didn't have the airflow I liked in computers.

Waiting twenty minutes before I dared leave my room, I went to get the first computer I planned to upgrade from Rupert's office. He was the main butler for the house, so to me, he had to get the first upgrade.

Not like he can use it until they're allowed down here again. For that to happen, I need to stop being a ravenous monster. The least I can do is make sure they have nice things when they can finally get back to work, since I threw off their entire schedule and life.

I went to work, gutting the old computer, falling into a serene place, focused only on the task in front of me. It was peaceful, better than the meditation Alexius had me do. Better than drinking blood. Machines were complicated like people, but I could take them apart and learn every little nuance, which I couldn't do with people.

Given half a chance, I would take Alexius apart in a second. Maybe then I'd understand him well enough to make this living situation work. Right now, it feels as if I'm always an outsider, and...

I pushed away the thought of loneliness and focused once again on what I was working on. The night ticked on. I only stopped when my alarm went off, and I found

Alexius in the garden for my midnight meal. It went the same way it always did, with my downing it as quickly as possible.

"Do you think I can skip the lesson tonight?" I asked as I washed the glass. He was sitting at a little table, books already stacked for me to read. He even had one open and was reading it while I fed and cleaned up.

"Why?" he asked without looking up from his reading.

"I just really want to keep working on the computer for Rupert. I can finish one a night, maybe two, if I really put my mind to it."

"Come sit down. The lessons are important. The computers will still be there—"

"Alexius, two visitors have arrived at the front gate," Rupert said over the intercom. "Good evening, Everly. I hope you're having a lovely evening."

I smiled a little, hearing the human. I beat Alexius to the microphone and hit the button.

"Hi, Rupert. You're not normally up this late. I was just asking Alexius to let me play hooky from our lesson time tonight. I'm working on something nice for you."

"Oh, that sounds fun—"

"Who is it?" Alexius demanded, putting his hand over mine to force me to keep the button held down.

"Who else would it be? Isaiah is here to check in, and he's brought another vampire I don't recognize." Rupert sounded exasperated. "It's always Isaiah. No one else calls on you."

"Isaiah…" It clicked for me. "Oh. The Tribunal… the Master of the Tribunal!" I felt a rush of fear. The Tribunal was the shadowy supernatural government that ruled practically everyone who wasn't human. There were five species on it—vampires, witches, fae, werewolves, and werecats, their rare cousin I had learned about only recently. "Why would he come here? Do I need to change?" I had no idea what the protocol was. I certainly wasn't up to entertaining the ruler of the vampires. "Alexius! Tell me what to—"

Alexius put his free hand over my mouth when Rupert chuckled.

"Let them in and send them downstairs. No need to wake up anyone from the staff. I'll entertain them and figure out what they want."

"Yes, sir."

Alexius pulled my hand off the button, and I heard Rupert disconnect from the intercom, off to do the task Alexius gave him.

"You don't need to change. You're dressed decently, and that's all he's allowed to expect of anyone here. Isaiah doesn't dictate how my household presents itself. He knows I won't keep any protocol for him," Alexius explained as he removed his hand. "He's a good friend and has been since he was a very young vampire and before the Tribunal even existed, or nests, for that matter. We hadn't been that organized when he was Turned. Further information you should know." Alexius paused, his expression thoughtful. "He's also the Master of the New York nest, the one that helped with everything from Jacob's nest when I needed to bring you here. He knows about you. I'm certain half of the vampire community does at this point, but that's neither here nor there. Just know he's possibly interested in how this has been working out. Normally, I welcome his visits." He didn't seem very welcoming of it tonight, though.

"Do you want me to prepare anything? Drinks or..."

"You won't be preparing drinks," he said, giving me a look as he finally stepped back and gave me space to move as if he suddenly remembered he'd accidentally pinned me against the wall. "You'll need to welcome their arrival with me. Let's go."

He started walking, and I rushed to keep up with him. His strides were longer than mine, so I had to move if I didn't want to end up ten feet behind him and leave him waiting on me at the main door. There were three ways in and out of the basement, but one acted as the front door. I had never passed that door, never even seen beyond it. While I was desperate to leave the basement one day, I knew better than to test Alexius. If I did anything that put his human staff at risk, I was dead. He'd made that clear the first night.

My heart was racing, stronger and faster than it had in months. Being recently fed made it react to my anxiety worse than normal.

"I hate that my anxiety feels like it came back since I Turned," I said to myself, nervously rubbing my hands together.

"You're being fed regularly," Alexius said softly, staring at the door. "Right after you Turned, you had just been brought back from the dead. You weren't healthy yet. You are now. There's no reason to be anxious with Isaiah, though. He's good-natured. Not as nice as Jacob, more political, and certainly more cunning, but he doesn't hurt anyone who isn't his enemy. I'm not his enemy. You are an unknown, so he'll be curious but nothing more." Alexius gave me a look, assessing me with those obsidian eyes. "Well, he might be more than a little curious. Being an Orphan, you might pique his interest more than most."

We waited ten minutes as Rupert greeted the visitors upstairs and brought them to the basement entrance. Alexius opened the door to two men waiting. I took my chance to see what was beyond the door. It was a room with another door that I heard click as someone locked it. Probably Rupert to make sure I didn't try running for freedom.

That's underwhelming.

The room was decorated like a fake porch, with a mat to wipe your shoes and potted plants on either side.

"Isaiah." Alexius pulled the door open wider. "Come in. It's a pleasure to see you."

"Don't lie to me," one said, laughing as he walked in, stopping only three feet from me on the other side of the hall. He was tall, taller than Alexius and his companion. He had dark brown hair styled as though he should be in a bank, wearing a suit that said Wall Street. The suit was perfectly ironed, crisp as if he never sat down. He unbuttoned the blazer and threw it over his shoulder. "We both know you don't like when I show up without warning you, especially with someone you don't know." His British accent made him sound regal.

"Oh, I know who you brought," Alexius said, his words less friendly. I didn't know why he was tense. "To what do I owe the pleasure of seeing you and your youngest son?"

I blinked, looking at the second vampire who was still outside the door. He had blond hair, bright blue eyes, and looked as if he walked out of a magazine, a gorgeous model who broke hearts of all varieties. He wore a matching navy suit, and when he caught me studying him, he smiled. I flushed, looking down at my feet, which made me realize I was barefoot.

Great first impression to make with the ruler of all the vampires. The weird ginger girl Alexius keeps barefoot and locked in his basement. Fantastic.

"I was hoping to stop in and check how this new... arrangement was working out for you," Isaiah said, amused. "With further thought, I decided to invite Corban to join me so your new vampire could meet someone closer to her own age."

I looked up at him, eyeing the Master of the Tribunal before looking at Alexius again. His expression was unreadable.

"Of course. Socializing is good for a young vampire," Alexius finally said with an undercurrent of annoyance. "Come in, Corban. It's been a long time, a decade, at least. You must be keeping busy. You've been a vampire for... two hundred and fifty years, yes? Isaiah must have set you up with your own nest by now. A nest does keep people busy."

I did my best to keep my mouth closed because I had never heard Alexius talk to someone like that. He was smiling as Corban came in, showing his fangs which shouldn't have been down visible since there was no reason I could find for the aggression. Isaiah stepped closer to me to give Corban space, and I stepped back, trying not to get too close to the newcomers. I didn't know them, and Alexius didn't seem happy about them. I glanced at Isaiah, his brow now furrowed as he stared at Alexius and Corban.

Clearly, there's more going on than I know. Maybe Alexius will explain later.

"You're right. I'm in charge of the Boston nest now, have been for eight years," Corban answered, seeming unfazed by Alexius, but I saw him move close to Isaiah's side, putting distance between him and Alexius in the now cramped hall.

"Let's move to a sitting room and catch up," Alexius said as he closed and locked the door. He moved past Isaiah and Corban but slowed next to me. He gave me a look, and I didn't need to be told he wanted me to follow him.

4

CHAPTER FOUR

Alexius led us to the larger sitting room, where I rarely went. The smaller sitting room had an intimate and homey feel, but this one was clearly for larger groups. One side of the room had four couches in a square around a table. There wasn't a fireplace, but there were several smaller tables with two or three chairs. The bar was larger, holding not only blood but a variety of liquors.

Alexius grabbed the back of my shirt to stop me from heading to the couches and kept walking to the bar. I followed him, confused. Isaiah stopped by the couches while Corban took in the room with interest.

"Have a seat. I can't offer you blood for several hours because Everly just fed, but I can get you something else to drink," Alexius said as he went behind the bar, grabbed a bottle from the shelf, and poured the amber liquid. When he put it back in its place on the shelf, I read the label, a scotch I'd never heard of.

"I'll have a glass of wine," Isaiah said with a smile,

settling on a couch and stretching out. Corban picked a different couch, a bit more composed.

"I'll take whiskey if you have it."

"Oh, he'll have it," Isaiah said, chuckling.

Alexius poured their drinks and handed me the glass of wine for Isaiah. As I held it out to him, Isaiah looked me over. I was positioned so he couldn't see my feet, but I knew he would have already caught that I was barefoot. I was just trying to save myself from being any more embarrassed. When his eyes met mine, I was paralyzed. His fingers brushed mine as he took the glass.

"Thank you, Miss Abbott," he said before leaning back again.

"You're welcome," I said, trying to find my voice. It came out shaky and quiet. I retreated to the closest couch and sat down, pushing my feet under the coffee table. Alexius brought his scotch and sat down next to me, too close to ignore, and extended an arm over the back of the couch, trapping me beside him. Something about it screamed possessive or protective, I couldn't decide which, but both were weird. In the months I'd lived with him, he hadn't been either with me.

"Are you going to get anything to drink?" Corban asked, and it took me a few seconds to realize he was talking to me.

"Oh, I'm not... I'm not thirsty," I answered, shoving my hands in my lap. Alexius made a noise that had everyone looking at him.

"Let's get proper introductions out of the way. Everly, this is Isaiah, Master of New York and of the Tribunal, where he sits among the other leaders of the supernatural world." He pointed, a bit rudely, at the excessively tall man. "He works closely with Maria. Between them, they rule all the vampires of the world. In my home, you can call him Isaiah, but in public, call him Master Isaiah, for he is the Master of us all. This is Corban, his youngest son and Master of Boston." To Corban, Alexius was even ruder, shoving a thumb in the vampire's direction. "I don't care what you call him so long as it's not Master. You owe him no deference."

I nearly sputtered and saw Corban narrow his eyes on the back of Alexius' head as Isaiah chuckled.

"Isaiah has had five children. His bloodline is one of the strongest in the world, with over one hundred members who work as a tight-knit unit. There are nine nests in North America under the control of his bloodline and six internationally, including London and Berlin."

I tried to catch everything Alexius was saying as Isaiah and Corban both nodded in greeting.

"Isaiah, Corban, this is Everly."

There was a long silence, so I gave them a little wave, which made Isaiah grin.

"Everly... a beautiful name." Corban smiled at me, and my face flushed again. "I'm glad Isaiah invited me. He's only spoken a little about you, telling me there was a young Orphan living with Alexius, but nothing else."

"She's Miss Abbott to you. I asked your father to keep information about her quiet. I don't want too many people knowing about her until she's prepared to face them *because* she's an Orphan." Alexius growled softly, and I didn't understand what his problem was. "Which is why I don't appreciate this visit, Isaiah. What are you doing here?"

He's been keeping me a secret?

I wasn't sure if I was okay with that or deeply concerned by the prospect. I was leaning toward deeply concerned.

"I'm here on something I think humans call a welfare check. You took in a new vampire, one who will gain attention no matter where she goes or what she does. Considering she's an Orphan, she warrants... an eye on her. Plus, when was the last time you brought up a young vampire? Have you ever actually done it properly? You Turned Jacob so long ago, no one knew what to do with a new vampire. I would know because no one knew what to do when I was Turned."

"Isaiah..." Alexius sounded like he was trying to warn off the other vampire.

"What has he educated you on so far?" Isaiah asked me, ignoring Alexius. "Do you know the situation you're in right now? How it happened? He hasn't kept that from you, has he?"

"I have lessons on vampire culture, law, and physiology every night. When we're not covering those topics, he gives me lessons on the Tribunal and their role in the supernatural world, along with the other supernatural species we share the world with," I answered, swallowing my nerves to speak clearly. "I know how I became a vampire. I know who Alexius is and what he does as a... job for vampires."

"Then you know more than I thought. That's good."

"Well, I'm glad everyone knows what's going on

except me," Corban said, chuckling dryly. "Miss Abbott, do you think you can tell me the story of your new life?" His smile was flirtatious, turning his charm up to a blinding degree. There was no subtlety to it. "I bet your story is very intriguing. I would be interested in hearing it."

"She worked for Jacob's nest as a human. Edwin orchestrated my son's murder and framed it as a suicide. He drove the nest into the ground when he gained control and killed her mother, who was head of the household and was trying to stop the rampant killing. Everly reached out to me and was the one who helped me discover the truth about Jacob's death. In retaliation for discovering and telling me, Edwin killed her before I could get there. I used his blood to Turn her," Alexius answered before I could open my mouth, snappy with Corban again. "Now you know."

"Oh..." Corban sipped on his whiskey, his eyes on me. "A tragedy then. My condolences for your mother, Miss Abbott."

"Edwin's dead now, so it's okay," I said, unable to stop the words. Corban's eyebrows went up as Isaiah leaned forward. The only person who didn't react was Alexius. "I mean..."

"You don't have to tell them anything you don't want them to know," Alexius said, his arm still behind me over the back of the couch. He sipped his drink, then put it on the table. "Or justify that statement."

I was blushing again. I could feel the heat on my cheeks. My heart had never stopped racing, but now it was noticeable again, pounding in my ears.

"Of course she doesn't," Isaiah agreed. "Why don't we let her give Corban the grand tour of your home while we talk privately, Alexius? Do you mind if my son and I stay for a couple nights? I would very much like to see a normal day in her life. Maybe I'll be able to offer some advice about helping a new vampire."

"Stay downstairs and make sure you show him the emergency exits," Alexius said to me. "When you're done giving him a tour, send him back here and do whatever you please with the rest of your evening."

"All right." Standing, I shuffled out of the sitting area, knowing Corban was following as I left the sitting room.

"There's no reason to be so nervous," the vampire said as I led him down the hall. "We're not here to do anything. Isaiah was feeling nosy. Alexius is one of his oldest friends, and you're interesting."

"Why do you call Isaiah by his first name?" I asked as I stopped in front of the garden. I'd been disarmed by their questions. "He's your sire, which makes him like... your father, right?" That was always the way Alexius talked about it.

"As an Orphan, I guess it wouldn't make sense to you because you don't know what it feels like. Using those sorts of terms depends on the vampire," Corban answered, staring out the double doors. "More often than not, vampires don't feel parental toward people they Turn, and offspring don't feel like children. Often, it's just a strong sense of loyalty from the offspring to the vampire. From my understanding, Alexius is one of the few vampires who looked at his relationship with his offspring in such a manner."

"But there's a bond—"

"There's a bond, but it elicits the need to obey and connect as a unit, not the emotion of love," Corban said, cutting me off. He gave me a sweet smile. "Two very different things. A sire and a father aren't the same thing. Isaiah is the vampire I owe my loyalty and obedience to because he sired me to his bloodline, but, no, he's not my father." He tilted his head to the side. "It must be so odd not understanding something every vampire knows instinctually. You don't feel it at all."

"No, I don't." Shaking my head, I waved at the garden. "Let's start the tour. This is the garden, the first room in the house I saw." It was a little bit of a lie, but it didn't seem appropriate to say Alexius' room had been the first. "I don't know the names of any of the plants, but they all bloom at night. It's very pretty when the moon is full."

"Yes, this must be the infamous garden," Corban said, nodding as he looked over it. "Are we allowed to go in?"

"Yeah. We were just finishing up a meal in the garden when you arrived. I don't think we're allowed to take clippings, so please don't damage anything."

"I would never. The gardener would kill me," Corban said, walking out.

I watched as he inspected the different plants and gently touched the petals of the few blooming flowers. Watching him gave me a chance to think about what he'd said.

Why did he call it infamous?

When he came out, he seemed thoughtful.

"We can continue. Thank for letting me enjoy that for a moment," he said as he dusted his hands off.

Leading him down the hall, I pointed out the different rooms, including the gym and the library. He examined the library as thoroughly as the garden. As we passed the study, I made sure he knew no one was allowed there. I showed him the two emergency exits as Alexius had asked me to.

"It must be lonely here," he said as we walked back to the sitting room. I was trying to move quickly, but Corban was strolling as though he wasn't in any hurry. "Only you and Alexius. I was Turned in Isaiah's nest and stayed there for over two hundred years. His nest is active at all times. There's no such thing as a quiet moment with over a hundred vampires living in one place. I believe when I left, there were nearly two hundred."

"He keeps his entire bloodline there?"

"No!" He laughed. "Isaiah's bloodline has spread out all over the world into dozens of different nests. He doesn't need to keep all of us with him all the time. He would rather we go out, make our own names, make our own allies. When he needs something, he calls us in, and we report and offer everything we have to him. Most of the vampires in his nest are his personal allies or vampires he's taken in to shelter and keep an eye on from a number of different bloodlines."

"So, you all come to his beck and call just because he asks?"

"That's the deal we made with him." Corban shrugged, and it looked like a practiced move. An attempt at casual and easy-going, but there was something fake about it.

"Are all vampires like this?"

"Not everyone manages their blood the way he does. Only a few bloodlines are as cooperative or unified. Isaiah's bloodline is rather exceptional, and I'm grateful to be a part of it. If someone is Turned in his bloodline without his permission, he summons the vampire who did it and the new, then judges them both on their worth and the reason for the Turn. He won't let anyone unworthy be one of his bloodline. He also doesn't tolerate disobedience. The moment someone steps out of line, they're dealt with."

"Definitely not a family then," I mumbled, trying not to be judgmental and failing. "Seems... cold."

"His control over his bloodline is how he rose to power. He won't let anyone jeopardize that." Corban didn't seem all that bothered, but I didn't like it. The idea of killing the weak for personal power just rubbed me wrong.

I could finally see the sitting room and stopped.

"Well, this is where I leave you. Have a nice evening." I smiled at him as I gestured to the sitting room.

"Why don't I come hang out with you, and we let the two old ones catch up?"

"Alexius wanted you to return to the sitting room," I reminded him. I didn't like his use of 'hang out.' It felt too modern for a vampire I knew was over two hundred years old.

"He did," Corban agreed, sighing.

The moment he was out of sight, I retreated, heading back to my suite. I had purposefully not shown Corban any of the bedrooms. I didn't want to tell a stranger where I slept.

5

CHAPTER FIVE
ALEXIUS

A lexius watched her disappear with the power-hungry brat on her heels.

"What game do you think you're playing, Isaiah?" he snapped the moment he knew they were out of earshot.

"Corban wanted to meet the new Orphan, and I didn't see any harm in it," Isaiah said with a shrug.

"Don't try that with me. You want to play matchmaker and set your son up with a lover who can't be forced to betray him," Alexius growled. "And you're doing it to my vampire without my permission."

"It crossed my mind a young Orphan may be a good match for one of my offspring," his friend admitted. "But meeting her, I can tell it's a long shot. She's too skittish for someone with Corban's level of charm or any of my children, really. He'll spook her before he woos her, probably already has. I could tell the moment I saw her."

"Yet you sent him off with her," Alexius hissed, pointing at the empty archway Everly had left through with that brat staring at her ass.

"It was clear you needed one or both of them out of the room for a moment. It will give her something to do and let us talk. It even gave you the chance to excuse her for the evening. Alexius, I've known you for a long time. You think I missed the possessive power plays you pulled with him?" Isaiah chuckled. "You purposefully pointed out the faultiness of my excuse to bring him in the doorway where she would hear it. You wanted her to know I was bending the truth. You wanted her to know something was amiss."

"Lying," Alexius growled, not in the mood for his friend's wordplay. "Of course, I made sure she knew something was amiss. I'm her teacher, her mentor. I'm supposed to educate and protect her until she can do those things for herself. Beyond that, I am also her employer once she's ready to work. I don't put my people in harm's way."

"A little bit of matchmaking is harmless," Isaiah said with patience that made Alexius want to strangle him.

"Your matchmaking might seem harmless for a moment, but I won't let one of your children seduce her into the political schemes they play and get her killed. I can name a good number of vampires pulled into the same trap by your children."

"Fine," Isaiah said, throwing his hands up. "I won't try it again."

He's accepting his defeat all too easily...

Too late, it dawned on Alexius what Isaiah's game had really been.

"Damn you."

"Figured it out?" Isaiah laughed. "I told you the

purpose of my trip was to check in on you, her, and this new arrangement. Clearly, I was going to test some boundaries to see how you really felt. Corban comes on the strongest of all my offspring. He would have been all too flirtatious and charming for you to ignore. Possessive and protective... Alexius, you know better. She's practically your offspring."

"She isn't, not even a little bit. There's no bond," he said, shaking his head. "She's just another vampire. I might have given her the blood, but it wasn't *mine*."

"You never really explained to me why you did it," Isaiah said, clearly musing on his own question, trying to figure it out. "You like her. You're too protective of her for there to be nothing about her that intrigues you. Something about her must have spoken to you. I guess there are two questions I want answered. Why did you make her a vampire, and why did you make her an Orphan?"

"I offered her a job before Edwin killed her," Alexius said, picking up his drink and leaning back to be comfortable. Thinking back on the moment was uncomfortable, but for Isaiah, he would remember it. Isaiah deserved the whole story, which Alexius had left out of the final reports because it was unnecessary. He hadn't wanted the world to comment on his personal choices.

"She's educated and proficient at things I am struggling to keep up with. She understands modern technology better than anyone in my household. She would have been a useful human to have in my employment. The plan was for her to send me the information, then leave the building, get in her car, and drive away. I would have met her before dawn after it was done. One of Edwin's offspring found her trying to leave, and it fell apart from there. When I arrived, Edwin was just finishing the act. He drained her and dropped her body on the marble floor." Alexius could still see her lifeless body slamming to the ground. "I felt guilty. She wouldn't have been in that position if not for me."

"Guilt over a human? That's new for you," Isaiah murmured. Alexius was deeply offended by that comment, and it must have shown on his face because Isaiah lifted a hand in apology. "Normally, when you have to use a human to help with these situations, you don't Turn them when they die, and we both know they have before. Humans are fragile. There's a reason we're all glad we're not humans anymore. Other vampires feel that much guilt, but you never have. You compensate the family if they have one or give them a proper burial, but never this."

"She learned the truth about my son, something you had failed to do," Alexius said, picking up his drink again. "You, Maria, and so many others... you all believed my son would kill himself. I knew it was never right, but there was nothing I could do, no way I could prove it. Part of me even wondered if what I was feeling was truth or just wishful thinking. She found the truth, though. She had the skills to find the information I needed. That service alone was enough to warrant immortality."

"But you didn't make her your offspring. You made her an Orphan," Isaiah pointed out, rounding back to that particular point.

"I promised myself a long time ago I wouldn't have any children besides Jacob," he reminded his old friend. "Everly was not someone for whom I was willing to break that promise. Being an Orphan will be advantageous for her in the long run, much more advantageous than being my child." Alexius sighed heavily, remembering his thoughts.

I could fix it. I couldn't bring Jacob back from dust, but I could save her.

"She deserved immortality, but she had already made it clear she was uncomfortable with the idea of control of the bloodlines, answering to people like that. I gave immortality to her in the only way I could, a way I knew she would appreciate, then took responsibility for it. It's not as if I Turned her and dumped her on someone else to train and teach."

Isaiah liked to think, to mull over information from every angle before he came to a conclusion. That was the real reason this conversation had taken months to happen. Alexius was slow to speak about his personal life, and he considered Everly personal. Isaiah was slow to act on new information until he processed it. Isaiah had probably spent the last few months processing the truth of what happened with Jacob and his nest and how it ended with a new Orphan in the world.

I knew he would come, eventually. There was no way I could get him to stay away from an Orphan vampire for long. A few more months would have been welcome, though.

"Is she having control issues?" Isaiah finally asked.

"Have you seen something since your arrival that concerns you?" Alexius asked in return. He thought she

49

had been rather controlled. Nervous, but that was to be expected.

"No. Orphans always have control issues compared to other vampires," Isaiah explained. "Rather, it takes longer to gain control. I already know the answer, but I want you to confirm it."

Alexius sat up, narrowing his eyes as he thought about the interesting piece of information.

"I've never heard that before," Alexius said, surprised there was *anything* about vampires he didn't know. He was among the ten oldest of their kind who still participated in the world.

"There's never been a reason for me to tell you of my personal knowledge about Orphans," Isaiah countered. "Answer the question."

"Yes, she does," Alexius said, giving Isaiah the confirmation he wanted. "To be honest, I thought my estimation was wrong about how long it should take her based on Edwin's blood."

"You probably were right if that was the only factor at play, but she is what she is. Orphans have control issues for a long time compared to other vampires of similar situations. I have some very solid evidence if you want to discuss it." Isaiah stared at him for a long time, and Alexius knew he was being judged. He could only nod at Isaiah's offer. There were some topics Alexius believed Isaiah could be wrong about.

This wasn't one of them.

"You should have reached out to me sooner. You can be a fool sometimes."

"I would have reached out in a few months if there

was no improvement. I didn't want to rush her, though I have somewhat failed at that. I've been slowly introducing her to new control techniques to give her more options instead of overwhelming her with all of them at once. I only just introduced the use of pain to her, pinching herself and such."

"Not just about *that*," Isaiah snapped. "You clearly haven't told her much about me, or she may have been more enthusiastic to speak to me. You could have told her when Rupert told you I was here to see you, but you didn't."

Alexius tried not to wince. Isaiah was right. Alexius could have told her more about Isaiah before he allowed them in, but he'd been distracted, trying to reason out why Isaiah had dropped in at this very moment with one of his children in tow.

"This is why I've come to check in. I knew I would need to test some boundaries to get all the facts." Alexius felt chastised. "I'm going to stay until I'm positive this is going in the right direction."

"An extended stay is very much unnecessary," Alexius said quickly. The last thing he wanted was Isaiah breathing down his neck.

"She might want me to stay," Isaiah countered. "And you need to be focused on what *she* needs and wants."

"I am," he protested. "But you don't—"

"I am the Master of the Tribunal, one of two rulers for our entire species that have fought bitterly to attain and maintain our positions at the top. Every vampire's wellbeing is my responsibility, something I take seriously, much to the detriment of other supernaturals. Alexius, you are a dear friend and a valuable member of this community, but you have never trained a new vampire, not truly. Consider your position in our world and our friendship a boon because if you were anyone else, I would have come here the moment I learned she was an Orphan and not your actual offspring. I would have swooped in and claimed her. There hasn't been an Orphan in the vampire world not taken on by myself or one of my family in over seven hundred years. You know how seriously I take this."

He wanted to fight Isaiah, but he knew how committed Isaiah was to this.

"Fine. One week and Corban is not allowed to stay," Alexius snapped. "The time can be extended if we come to an agreement, but Corban is non-negotiable. I want him out of my house at sunset, and he's not allowed to be in her quarters."

"I thought you would see things my way," Isaiah said, finishing his wine. "I only waited this long because it was you. Corban will leave promptly after sunset and head home. He won't try anything without my permission... or yours. He doesn't want to die."

Alexius ran a hand through his hair but couldn't respond. He didn't want to admit it, not yet, but he was in over his head. He thought the fiery, resilient woman would make a great vampire, but there was something smothering her, and he had no idea what it was. If it was him, he needed her to tell him, but she didn't tell him anything. Gone was the passionate woman who yelled at him, and in her place was a shaking leaf.

That's why he was relieved, even if he didn't like it.

Isaiah would be able to see something he couldn't. Relying on Isaiah to find the problem annoyed him, but Isaiah was the only vampire alive he'd ever allow to help him with this.

I'll let him observe her for a few nights, then get his opinion.

"Let's change the subject," Isaiah said, standing to refill his glass of wine behind the bar. "I've combed through everything from Portland and looked into all my contacts, all my advisors, and those connected to them."

"And?"

"None of them have obvious connections to Edwin. The problem lies with how we decide who will lead a nest when openings are presented, or we approve the foundation of a new one. We keep a running list of vampires who are ready to take over nests or begin new ones based on their age, experience, and reputations. A vampire needs extensive recommendations from several other nest Masters and Mistresses, and they have to want to, which not every vampire does. That keeps the list short, more than anything else. Edwin had been on the list for half a century. He was due. I had skipped him for Corban to take over in Boston because I would not put one of my sons in anything but a prime location. Boston was a great chance for Corban. Maria had been angry because it was nepotism. Several vampires were a little upset, actually." Isaiah chuckled. "It was nepotism, but really, what were they going to do about it?"

"Six years ago." It clicked for Alexius. "Five years before Jacob died, my son took in a vampire named Oscar, newly Turned and unstable, with no one claiming him as their own. He grew obsessed with Everly after Edwin took over. I killed him when I arrived in Portland. We learned later, he was Edwin's offspring and spy, a plant in the nest. Oscar helped him with killing Jacob by feeding information back to his sire about when Jacob would be vulnerable."

"Edwin must have been an easy target for whoever wanted to kill Jacob because he was desperate for his own nest. He was harboring a criminal as a lover without anyone knowing, one you and Jacob had both been outspoken about," Isaiah said, shaking his head as he lifted his freshly filled glass. "Edwin knew he would be a prime pick for a new nest, and the people behind it helped orchestrate an opening."

"Which means it probably wasn't any of your advisors," Alexius said, concluding the chain of thought he knew they were both on. "An outsider who knew Edwin was due, probably because of the fuss made with Corban's position in Boston. They weaseled into the situation, either knowing about Camilla or learning about her when they looked at Edwin's dealings to evaluate his usefulness." Alexius put his elbows on his knees, letting his mind piece together the little things. "Edwin already didn't like Jacob, probably on principle."

"He never made that impression on anyone I've spoken to. What did he say to you?" Isaiah asked as he walked back.

"A number of things. He thought Camilla was perfect. Called Jacob and I relics. We were forcing vampires to live as half of what they truly were. Things of that nature. Nothing new," Alexius answered. Isaiah said something, but Alexius wasn't listening. His old friend realized the conversation was over and settled for him, so he let the room go silent.

Alexius only left his thoughts about what happened in Portland when he heard Everly and Corban close by.

"Well, this is where I leave you. Have a nice evening." He could hear her politeness, diplomatically sweet.

"Why don't I come hang out with you, and we let the two old ones catch up?"

Alexius curled his fingers together tightly as Isaiah covered a smile with a hand.

"Alexius wanted you to return to the sitting room."

Good move, Everly. Remind him I am the most dangerous vampire in the building. I dictate every move he's allowed to make, and you are mine to protect.

"He did." Corban's sigh was one of annoyance but not defeat.

I'll have to fix that.

6
───────

CHAPTER SIX

I went to the small sitting room for my last meal of the day, finding Alexius already there but neither of his guests. Before I walked in, I glanced at my feet, reminding myself I had put on socks, and no one would see my bare feet again.

"Are Isaiah and Corban joining us, or have they left already to find shelter before dawn?" I asked once I was satisfied socks would be okay. I sat down on the love seat as he waited for the bag of blood to heat.

"Isaiah and I discussed it earlier. He'll be staying for a week, possibly longer, to see how you are coming along in your new life. It's not a test of your progress, but a judgment he's trying to make of me," Alexius explained, staring at the microwave. "I haven't trained a new vampire since I Turned Jacob, and he's keen to make sure I'm not doing anything that may be detrimental to you." Alexius smiled a little when he turned to me, and I noticed his fangs as his lips pulled back to reveal his teeth. "Corban will leave at sunset."

"You don't like him, do you?" I crossed my arms as I leaned back into the soft cushions.

"No."

"Why?"

"He's one of Isaiah's children," Alexius answered as if that explained anything.

"I don't really... understand," I admitted as the microwave dinged. I stopped breathing and looked away, so I didn't have to see the blood, waiting patiently for the sound of Alexius putting it down, but that never happened. I slowly looked to see him holding it out to me and didn't breathe until I was holding the glass. The rich smell invaded my senses, causing my fangs to drop. I drank without stopping, trying to get every drop before I handed the cup back.

"Is that how she always feeds?" someone asked. I jumped off the couch, startled as I turned to see. I should have recognized the thick British accent. Isaiah was leaning in the archway, frowning at me.

"Yes," Alexius answered. "I take it you are done with your work calls?"

"It wasn't really *work*. I told my nest to manage themselves for a week and only contact me in case of an emergency, then decided to be nosy. I heard talking and could smell the blood," Isaiah explained. "Came to see if it was mealtime or just something for the youngling. Alexius, will you be feeding?"

"I fed two nights ago," Alexius answered. "Do you need a glass?"

"I wouldn't mind one, but it would be an indulgence, and I know you don't like that."

Alexius shook his head as he took my glass back to the minibar.

"You know I don't care if you live on a perfect schedule," Alexius said as Isaiah left the archway and came into the room. "With friends, a *little* indulgence isn't the end of the world. I'm the safest vampire you could indulge with, as you know."

"A little indulging for everyone else, but never you, right?" Isaiah smiled, but at me, not Alexius. "He rarely feeds off schedule unless he needs to be certain his strength is at its fullest. Alexius is very controlled."

"I know." It was one of the easiest things to figure out about the brooding man I lived with. "Controlled, controlling, a bit cold, and blunt. Oh, can't forget full of self-loathing. Those are five things I've learned about Alexius, and some of them I figured out when I was still human." As soon as the words rolled off my tongue, I wanted to take them back.

"She has a tongue, and she knows how to use it!" Isaiah said, shocked and pleased, as he sat down beside me. Alexius didn't say anything. "Controlling and a bit cold, you say?" He extended an arm over the back of the love seat, making the position we were in seem familiar. I was immediately uncomfortable. "Tell me more."

"Oh, no, I—"

"Here," Alexius growled, suddenly on the far side of the love seat, holding a wine glass of blood for Isaiah. Isaiah grabbed it and took a sip, savoring it as though it was the wine he'd had earlier in the night. Even though I had just fed, watching him enjoy it made me want it. I stopped breathing, hoping it would stop me from wanting it.

"You have a good preserved supply. Normally, the bagged stuff is stale," the vampire commented. "Has he told you I'm staying for a short time?"

"We were just talking about it before I fed," I answered, trying to inch away from him, casting a look at Alexius, hoping he would give me an excuse to get up and move. Alexius sat across from us, looking at me with dark eyes but said nothing. "You asked if I always fed like that. Why?"

"Alexius, do you want to tell her, or should I?" Isaiah said, staring at the blood in his glass.

"Isaiah is like you... or rather you are like him. He's an Orphan."

My mouth dropped open as I looked at the vampire in a new light.

"I'm the first recorded Orphan of our kind," Isaiah elaborated. "That's why people say it's *my* bloodline," Isaiah said, still staring at the blood in his wine glass, swirling it slowly. "My sire committed suicide after he began my Turn. He was dust before I finished. Alexius and Jacob had known him and took me in after I woke up, and they put together what happened. We've been friends since I was a boy. I didn't stay with them very long, but they were the first two vampires who helped me when I woke up and realized my great-grandfather had killed himself."

"In Rome, before Julius took control," Alexius added, and my eyes wanted to pop out of my head. "If he had stayed human, Isaiah was primed to join the Senate."

"Thank goodness I didn't because Julius took control not five years later."

"A sad day for Rome."

"Yes, it was."

"So, the British accent is fake," I said, finally finding words to say. It was a really stupid thing to point out, and my face heated as I realized I had just blurted it out.

"I could use one of the many American accents if you would like," Isaiah offered with a wide grin. "I moved to New York from London in the nineteenth century. I've been considering going to an American accent since then. Maybe I will, but there are just so many to choose from. I don't think I could pull off a Southern accent. What do you think?" When I didn't answer fast enough in the three seconds he gave me, he laughed. "I know dozens of accents and more languages. I enjoy learning them. I switch up every few centuries, trying to match the humans for secrecy reasons and to annoy people around me."

"He was South African for a decade."

"I don't really... care," I finally said, moving away from him a bit farther. "I just..."

"We stunned you. I know," Isaiah said with a softer smile and gentleness that disarmed me. I could only nod. "One of the reasons I want to stay isn't just to monitor Alexius. I want to answer any questions you may have about being an Orphan. We're not like other vampires. We are vampires, but there are some oddities. Alexius explained that part, correct?"

"Yeah, when I first woke up. I don't have a bloodline that can control me."

"That's the major part, the part everyone focuses on, but there are a few quirks. In fact, earlier, I needed to tell him something he didn't know." Isaiah grew more serious. "Time and time again, I've seen this play out. It took me a century to feel confident with feeding on humans without someone watching over me to stop me from killing them. Now, most don't face the challenge for as long as I did. It's a trend we've seen through all vampires. As time has gone on, vampires have been able to control themselves more quickly. I expect it might take you... one or two years to feel as confident as I was in a century, at the most, three. Alexius, if he had reached out to me sooner, would have been able to tell you when you first Turned, but he ran off with you and left me to clean up the mess in Portland. I've been busy."

"There was nothing else I could do in Portland," Alexius retorted.

"She deserves to know why it took three months for her to get basic information."

"You could have written an email the moment you knew I had an Orphan in my care, which you knew the same night I initiated her Turn."

"A cold, impersonal email? To speak to a new vampire *you* are caring for?"

"This didn't need to be an event."

"She's going to be one of the most talked-about vampires in the last century because of her association with you."

Rubbing my forehead as they continued, I decided to stretch my legs. The moment I was off the couch, they stopped and stared at me.

"So, I just have to work against this longer than most vampires?" I asked, refusing to indulge any of the topics they had been bickering about. I didn't want to play the blame game or think about how I would be talked about because I was living with Alexius and, hopefully, working for him sooner rather than later.

"Yes," Isaiah said, nodding, his focus on me again.

"Will I have to stay in this basement the entire time?"

Don't say yes. I'll throw myself into the sun if I have to stay in the basement for the next year... or two.

Oh God, what if it ends up being like five years?

Yeah, seeing one last sunrise would definitely jump up on the list of things to do.

"No." Isaiah laughed. "Why? Has he kept you locked in the basement since you..." He trailed off, and the laughter died. The humor fled his face as he looked in Alexius' direction. "How vicious were her attacks?"

"She was summoning claws without realizing it for a couple of weeks," Alexius answered, lifting his hand and doing it. Chills ran down my spine as I saw his nails grow into the long, dangerous claws Edwin had terrified me with. He looked at me as he turned them back into human fingers. "This is what I mean. It was quite amazing to see from a vampire as new as you."

"Ah..." Isaiah nodded slowly. "That changes things. Three years would be a better estimate if she does that as young as she is. I don't like that you've kept her down here, but if she did that, I understand your reasoning."

"My staff is elderly," Alexius said. "They wouldn't survive a bad bite if she got hold of them."

"No, they wouldn't," Isaiah agreed.

Isaiah looked at me in a new light. The weight of his stare was enough for me to drop my head. I looked at my hands and wondered if I really could summon those claws. Alexius was right about one thing; I didn't remember doing that. I could remember jumping for him, trying to claw the cup from him. I would have done anything to get the blood. Learning to freeze instead of attack had been a month-long struggle, and it was still *hard*.

I felt like a monster again. The only difference was it wasn't my failing. It was inevitable I was a monster.

"It probably has to do with Edwin being a blood bonded lover to a much older vampire. They could have been together for ten years," Isaiah said softly. "We forgot to consider how much of Camilla's blood he might have had in his system, both in the long term and at that moment. She was roughly five hundred years older than him, and he was just under four hundred. We knew she was approaching a thousand. She was never particularly powerful, but she was cunning enough to escape you for... at least a couple centuries. Age only made her more slippery."

"Camilla was sentenced to death five hundred and twenty-two years ago. It was... August," Alexius answered.

I knew who Camilla was. She had been Claire to me, but I had learned her real name right before Edwin killed me. It had been just one of the secrets buried in Edwin's emails on his private computer.

"She was always ten steps ahead of me until Portland. I didn't know it was her until I had her and Edwin cornered in the mansion. It was bold of her to think

Edwin could promise her security when none of her other lovers ever succeeded in that endeavor. Normally, she left them by the time rumors started flying. She was gone by the time I arrived to kill whoever she left behind."

"A disease of a vampire, that one," Isaiah said with disgust. "Either way..." He turned back to me. "Generally, a vampire doesn't bring out claws in their first few years. Using any of the shadow magics, especially those that create a physical transformation, is a massive draw on energy. Using them normally requires a feeding sooner than what a vampire needs. Herein lies the problem with trying to theorize how long a vampire might need to learn control. Each vampire is a unique combination of many things."

"So... all this plays a part in why I can't control myself," I said, nodding as that made sense but clearly made finding an answer harder. "And you can only guess."

"I think you'll be able to rejoin society sooner rather than later, so long as you continue to freeze instead of attack." Isaiah shrugged. "But yes, educated guesses are all we have for every vampire. I'm usually right. Give it three years, and I bet you'll be feeding on humans without needing a babysitter. I'm willing to put money on it."

Three years of needing supervision when I fed. Three years of being too dangerous to go out alone. Three years of being unable to control my own urges.

Three years was a long time.

"Everly?" Alexius' voice tried to cut through my

internal dialogue, but I didn't reply. Before I knew it, he was grabbing my chin and forcing me to look up, so I was staring at dark eyes.

"Sorry, I was just thinking," I said, pulling away before he could say anything.

"Why don't we stop this topic for the night?" he said, turning his back to me and putting himself between Isaiah and me.

"Yes. There are better things to talk about. Have you started her physical training? This is about when I would begin testing someone for their natural abilities with our magic, but clearly, she has some natural instincts."

"Why don't you and I continue the discussion privately?" Alexius suggested. "We should let Everly enjoy the short time she has before the sun rises."

"Oh, that is coming close, isn't it?" Isaiah nodded. "Yes, it would be best to draw this to a close for the night." He smiled kindly at me. "You have a wonderful rest, Everly."

"You, too," I said, nodding to both of them before retreating.

"She asked me about why she was controlled when she first woke up," Alexius said once I was out of the room. "And why she lost that control by the end of the first night."

"You explained to her that many vampires will backslide in the first few days, right? Especially when there's shock involved. The rapid adjustment of the mind to realize the new urges will keep them alive instead of food, the rising instincts of a young vampire."

"I did, but I don't think it helped ease her conscience."

"Yes, you have a guilty one. She wants to go back to normal, but this is her new normal. You said you rushed her earlier. What did you mean by that?"

"I... I thought she would be in control in a month," Alexius admitted. "I misjudged the blood, what she is."

"Sometimes, you are a complete fool, Alexius," Isaiah said, louder and clearly exasperated. "No wonder—"

I locked myself into my suite so I didn't have to hear them anymore. I wasn't annoyed they were talking about me because that was why Isaiah was staying. I was annoyed they *needed* to talk about me.

Three years.

I cleaned up my work area before changing for bed. Without bothering to check the time, I got into bed, resolved to lie there until the sunrise forced me to sleep.

There was too much on my mind to sleep before sunrise, but there was too much for me to think about to do anything else.

7

CHAPTER SEVEN

When sunset came, I moved quickly to get up and make myself presentable. I had more energy tonight than in weeks and knew it was because there was company in the mansion.

It's not like I know Isaiah or Corban all that well, and normally, I hate meeting new people, but...

I threw my hair into a ponytail to get it out of my face and even tried to do a typical day's makeup, something I had stopped doing a few weeks into my new life in the basement mansion. The burn in my throat felt as if I had burning coals shoved into it, but I did my best to ignore it until I made my way into the small sitting room. I took a quick look around the room and decided I would rather bother Alexius at the minibar than sit alone with Corban and Isaiah. While I was excited to get out of bed and do something different today, that paled compared to actually dealing with the guests.

"Right on time," Alexius said. "Good evening."

"Good evening." Walking to the bar, I couldn't smell

the blood yet, but I knew it was coming. The microwave was already going, which meant it could be any second. Alexius eyed me but didn't send me to sit down. I knew I was doing something he generally didn't like. He liked when I was seated.

In the end, my attempt to use him as a shield from the guests didn't work. Isaiah got up and came to my side, his hands in his pockets.

"We don't bite," the old vampire said with a smile.

"I know for a fact that you do, and I would prefer to stay off the menu," I retorted, and once again, I was left wanting to shove the words back in my mouth. Isaiah laughed, but Alexius' small smile caught my attention. The only good thing about the situation was I hadn't fed yet, making any blush very light if it was visible at all. My face didn't feel nearly as warm as it should have.

"You'll never be on the menu, don't worry. Feeding on you wouldn't be worthwhile. Wouldn't do anything for any of the vampires in this room." Isaiah's smile turned mischievous, and I wondered how this man became a ruler of the vampires. "Well, it wouldn't do anything for the bloodlust. Another type of lust—"

"That's enough," Alexius said, his words all too calm —bone-chillingly calm—but it silenced Isaiah. They exchanged a look before Isaiah sighed.

"I won't tease too much," the vampire finally promised. I swallowed the lump in my throat as Isaiah once again turned his eyes on me. "A quick tongue but none of the confidence to back it up. A troubling combination for a vampire."

He walked away as Alexius waved for me to follow

him when the microwave beeped. I didn't breathe as I went to the couches. Instead of sitting by his son again, Isaiah picked the love seat, which meant I had to choose —sit next to Corban or next to Isaiah.

I decided on Corban. Isaiah was coming on a bit too strong for me today. I didn't sit close to Corban, aiming to sit as far from him on the couch as I could. When Alexius brought food, he looked at me, Corban, then Isaiah, who chuckled. Alexius eventually sat down next to Isaiah.

"Corban, I hope you have an easy trip home," he said, leaning back in the love seat and stretching his legs out. It was the same way he sat when I had met him, looking like a god from times before human memory. It didn't matter that he wore modern clothing or had cut his hair short. He still had that presence.

"I will. I'll be home before midnight."

"I'm glad to hear it." Alexius smiled.

I finished feeding, then left the couch area to wash out my glass, and the entire time, none of them spoke another word.

"All right, I'm going," Corban said with a snap. "I'd forgotten how much of an asshole you could be, Alexius." I looked up to see him standing. He met my stare, sighed, then shook his head. "Good luck with your new life as a vampire, Miss Abbott. You'll need it with these two shadowing your every step. Isaiah, call me if you need anything."

"Of course." Isaiah reached out, and Corban shook his hand as he passed his sire. He didn't look back or say goodbye to Alexius. Apparently, calling him an asshole was the last thing Corban wanted to say to the vampire I lived with.

There was a long silence, no one saying anything as I went to sit down, now having an entire couch to myself while Isaiah and Alexius were on the love seat.

"You never explained why you don't like any of Isaiah's children," I pointed out.

"My children are political sharks, willing to do anything to get two steps ahead to maintain their power and further their own reputation, as well as mine. They know their actions reflect on me. They are ruthless because they know I want them to be. In fact, I purposefully find humans who ride the fine line of being conniving political operatives and strong allies with a sense of loyalty. Such a rare type of person but a very good one to have at your side," Isaiah explained, smiling. "They're not always easy to like, though, if someone doesn't care for politics and schemes.

"As for why Alexius has forced my son to leave while I get to stay..." Isaiah smirked. "Corban is looking for a lover to stand by his side in Boston. Until he has someone committed to being with him, someone he can trust who won't be exploited by others, other vampires will attempt to fill the role by getting into his bed and using it for their own means. Being so close to the Master or Mistress of a nest comes with privileges, as you must have seen with Edwin and Camilla."

"Yeah..." My answer came automatically while my mind was acting like a record with the rest. "He was here to... see if I would..."

"An Orphan who can't be controlled by someone

more powerful through the blood? It's appealing in a lover."

My stomach dropped. I had known something was off about Corban. He'd been fake with me, and learning he had a double meaning was unsurprising, but I hadn't expected that sort of double meaning.

"He was hoping to seduce you, regardless of whether you have any interest in that sort of life," Alexius muttered, shaking his head.

"Eww, and you brought him here?" I turned my disgust to Isaiah. His humor at the situation was gone.

"Consider it another lesson about what you are. Many vampires won't trust you because they won't know if you're loyal to anyone but yourself, but just as many will want to use you for their own means." Isaiah reached out and patted Alexius' shoulder. "He wouldn't have whisked her away in a single night or even a week. He would have let you get her through her control issues and education while he positioned himself to be the person who caught her once she branched out on her own. It would have taken a decade for him to get her to Boston, but I think you've well and truly chased him off."

"Getting involved with his children can and will get you killed," Alexius told me, ignoring the Master of the Tribunal. "I don't normally allow them into my house. They don't have a standing invitation to call upon me the way he does. If Corban reaches out and contacts you, please tell me, and I'll handle it."

"Unless you want him to," Isaiah said, leaning forward to put all his attention on me. "Tell me if you want his number or email. I'm certain if you push a little, he might come back and fight for you."

"No, thank you," I said, trying to be polite when I really wanted to tell this vampire he could go stand in the sun. Only remembering who he was and the position he held stopped me from snapping at him. Part of me couldn't believe this vampire was ever in charge of anything. He didn't act like a ruler.

"You're lucky, Isaiah, that I know you have her best interests in mind," Alexius growled.

"What if I had fallen for it?" I asked, looking between them. "I mean..."

"Is he even your type?" Isaiah laughed. "Alexius wouldn't have let you fall for it. He would have told you how he felt about Corban, about who he is, and who he reported to. You would have stepped back. You don't seem like a young woman who likes the limelight, and Corban would have put you at center on the political stage. Furthermore, he would have realized early on that you're ill-suited to his lifestyle and let you off easy. He wouldn't pick a lover unequipped to handle the life he lives, not even if he fell madly in love with you. I knew you were safe from falling for him the moment I saw you... and saw Alexius' reaction to his presence."

"You are..." I bit my tongue, hoping it was enough to stop me from saying anything. I retreated to the life I had lived for years before the massive upheaval of becoming a vampire had brought. "I hope you'll excuse my absence, but I have work I need to get to."

"Aren't there lessons to get to?" Isaiah asked as I stood up.

"After midnight," Alexius answered. "She gets the first half of the night as free time." He nodded at me, silent permission to escape. I was nearly out of the room when he continued speaking. "She might have stayed and talked if you hadn't admitted to letting Corban come to scope her out as if she were a prized cow."

"It was safe! She needs to know people are going to attempt to use her. If she lived in my nest or in one of my offspring's nests, like every other new Orphan does, she would get small tests and lessons all the time. She needs to be aware, and your job is to make sure she is prepared for *everything*, Alexius. It was a lesson I knew you wouldn't be able to give her, so I was proactive."

I stopped in the archway, turning back. Alexius was standing and shook his head. I left, heading for my suite to get straight to work. If I worked fast enough, I could finish up the second computer from the day before and get started on the last one before my lesson with Alexius. A lesson I was now dreading because Isaiah would be there.

What felt like minutes later, Alexius came into my suite, closing us in together. He even locked the door, a loud click that seemed to echo in the room. I looked up from what I was doing and saw him stop on the other side of my worktable.

"He really has your best interests in mind," he said, running a hand through his hair. "But Isaiah can be... a lot to deal with. He tends to take control of whatever situation he's in and do things his way because he believes he's always right. He has a strong personality, but you handled him rather well, considering the circumstances."

"Did I? I don't know how to talk to him. I almost said something I shouldn't. That's why I left. I don't know *how* to handle him," I said, shaking my head. Going back to plugging in small wires while I thought about the Master of the Tribunal, I kept talking. "He brought a guy to... check me out. Treated me a prized cow, like you said. That's disgusting."

"I won't make excuses for him, but if he believes it was futile and would have never worked for Corban, then he's telling the truth. Isaiah doesn't lie to me. He's not foolish enough to..." I looked up for a second when Alexius didn't continue. "You called him the most powerful vampire in the world. He's not. He's a political mastermind and knows how to manipulate people into playing the roles he needs them to play, but he's not the most powerful vampire in the world." He put his hands on my table, his dark eyes locked on mine.

"He's not in the top ten or even the top twenty or twenty-five. I am physically more powerful than him. Others are magically more powerful. I could beat him in a fight, and he knows better than to lie to me. In two thousand years, he never has. To others... all the time, but not to me."

"He's politically the most powerful vampire in the world," I said, knowing it was the truth. "If he's not, he's probably tied with... Maria, the Mistress of the Tribunal. Right?"

"Yes, but in my home, that's not something you need to concern yourself with. Here, he's just Isaiah."

"Still... knowing Corban was here to see if I was good enough to be his lover makes me feel *dirty*." I didn't pause what I was saying, but there was no ignoring Alexius' low growl. "And Isaiah let it happen on purpose while laughing as I... sat next to Corban." Groaning, I dropped the small wires before pushing away from my worktable.

"Tell him how he made you feel. He will apologize. Not well, mind you. Isaiah doesn't *like* apologizing, but he will."

"You know, when they got here, I realized something else was going on and should have put it together sooner. You were trying to warn me. Corban wasn't really close to my age."

"I'm glad you picked up on the undercurrents of that greeting, but don't hold this against yourself. You don't know the internal politics of our kind, but you'll learn with time."

"How can you stand it?" I demanded. Alexius seemed like someone who *hated* political machinations and schemes. "He's one of your oldest friends."

"You have to know Isaiah." Alexius looked down at the computer, and I gave up. "Isaiah is a lot like you if that will help you understand. Good with putting the little pieces together to create a machine."

"We're not—"

"Yes, you *are*. Let me explain."

8

CHAPTER EIGHT

I waited impatiently, crossing my arms as Alexius looked at the motherboard I already had mounted in the open tower. I was working on getting new fans mounted and plugged in when he came in.

"He just uses people instead of... computer parts." Alexius waved a hand over the open tower. "And instead of making a machine like this, he made a political unit that reaches the entire globe, with hundreds of people as the cogs that keep it moving." He lifted a stick of RAM. I knew he didn't have any idea what he was holding, but I was grateful to see he wasn't touching anything more expensive. "When a part breaks, he quickly finds a suitable replacement. Sometimes, a part doesn't need to break before it finds itself replaced, though. He'll replace it because he's found something better, just because he can. That's what you do, isn't it? You aren't destroying these machines. You are looking at all the parts, finding the old pieces, and putting in new ones as replacements to increase the... overall efficiency."

"The parts of a computer don't have feelings. I can't insult the RAM. I'm not trying to make it do anything it wasn't made for," I countered, even though Alexius' elaborate metaphor was really well done. I grabbed the RAM from him, though, and put it down out of his reach. "It's a tool."

"In Isaiah's mind, so are we, and yes, that is callous. You know what each of the pieces here does. With every new person he meets, he must figure out what type of piece they are and if they might fit in a place." I opened my mouth to say something awful, but Alexius lifted a hand. "He recognizes that we have feelings. He'll apologize if you tell him how you feel."

"Fine," I bit out. A moment later, I decided to interrogate Alexius more since he was in a talkative mood. He'd clearly come to talk to me, and I needed to take advantage. "Why do you think he cares about my best interests? He doesn't even know me, other than the Orphan thing, which seems pretty shallow right now."

"Isaiah does everything for the success of the vampire race as a whole. There are individuals he doesn't like, but he will always put them over another supernatural, so long as they aren't criminals. He believes he can do his best for vampires so long as he sits at the top. As long as his rules are fair and he continues to work in the interest of vampires, I've never involved myself too deeply in his schemes or tried to stop him from playing games with those around him. *Normally*, he respects the distance I keep." Alexius played with a loose wire sticking out of the tower as I studied him and listened. "My life has never been interesting. Jacob and I were both good at finding our roles and staying in them, which made him content to leave us be. My life is interesting now."

"Because of me?"

"Not you... entirely. I became interesting when Jacob died. There isn't a vampire alive today who has known me without my son. In fact, Jacob was the driving force behind many of my connections. He was charismatic. I am not."

I snorted. "No, you're not." He gave me a look, but his small smile let me know he was okay with that comment.

"Back on topic. He meddled with us because we're both interesting to him right now, Everly. I, an ancient who has lived a very steady life for thousands of years that has suddenly been disrupted, and you, an Orphan vampire like himself who I created. Clearly, he's trying to judge us both to see how we will be useful for the vampire community in the future. He also feels a particular... endearment to other Orphan vampires. That's not shallow. I hadn't thought about it when I gave you Edwin's blood. I didn't much care about the repercussions of what I was doing when I used Edwin's blood to Turn you."

I ignored that last part and went back to the root of the conversation.

"Let me guess. We're even more interesting because you're training me, and I plan on working for you," I said, sighing heavily.

"Absolutely."

"I don't like being interesting," I admitted. "I like being ignored, someone in the background. It worked really well for me for a long time."

It kept me safe for a long time. The moment the spotlight was on me, I ended up dying and becoming a vampire. If that's the sort of stuff attention will bring to my life... no, thank you. One time was more than enough.

"I'm sorry to say it, but it needs to be said. That part of your life is over. No one will ever let you live in the background anymore. Isaiah is a crash course in how many people will be looking at you, judging your every decision, and wondering what move you'll make next. They'll all have a need to figure you out, to understand where you go on the invisible structure that is our culture."

I had been disturbed when I learned Alexius had been trying to keep me a secret, but now, I was grateful. He didn't need to say it. I could put the pieces together. He had been trying to save me from the spotlight for as long as he could.

Because he doesn't like it either. No one lives alone like this is if they're even remotely comfortable with attention.

"Maybe I can become boring, blend in with the crowd, and they'll ignore me," I pondered. "Like you're able to."

Alexius actually chuckled. The deep, robust noise reminded me he had real feelings. He didn't always make that clear.

"You think it couldn't work?" I asked, crossing my arms.

"No. You could never blend in, and your logic is faulty. I didn't escape the sight of the vampire world by trying to. Attempting to disappear is probably the worst thing you could do if you actually want to be left alone. It just makes everyone curious about where you went or what you're hiding. I escaped their sight because I became someone they didn't want to look at. Not many want to meddle with the vampire who kills them when they step out of line. They all know about me and choose to look away."

He had a fair point, and his dangerous smile made me nod silently instead of trying to continue the conversation.

"I'll leave you alone until your next feeding time," he declared, stepping back from my table.

"Um… you can watch me finish this," I said, waving at the tower on the table. "I might have more questions about Isaiah and… stuff."

His eyes narrowed, but he nodded, grabbing a chair from the stack I made at the side of the room. I had little use for the dining chairs that went with my worktable. They had just gotten in my way.

I went back to work on the computer as Alexius sat down. I normally hated hovering, but something made me want him to stay tonight. The minutes ticked by in silence as I finished mounting the fans and plugged them in, then went to work on the CPU.

"I hope he's been helpful even though he's upset you," Alexius said, breaking the silence. "While I am old and know a great deal about vampires and the life ahead of you, he holds a unique perspective."

"Yeah, he has," I said, thinking about it as I answered. "He knows more than I could dream, so anything he knows would be useful, like your lessons. I would be stupid to miss them. I just don't think I like him all that much, so he needs to be *really* helpful if he wants me to play some part for him."

"I'll be certain he knows that." Alexius stood, ready to leave.

I paused what I was doing to watch him walk to the door and unlock it. Mind-bogglingly, he had a small smile. I didn't know why he would smile to hear I didn't like one of his oldest friends, but it was there.

"I'll be in the garden if you need anything. Your lesson will be in my study tonight, so meet me there for your next feeding."

"Your *study*?"

"Yes. Is there a problem with that?"

"N-No..." I quickly shook my head. Alexius frowned away that mysterious smile. He didn't move for what felt like an eternity, then he was gone, closing the door behind him. I was left with my silent machine, with its parts that needed to be replaced.

I finished the build and put it aside to carry back to the office before dawn, then started on the next computer, gutting it first. Every one of the work computers the human staff used was the same.

They must have bought pre-built computers. They were probably more expensive than they needed to be with the hardware they had. That upcharge is criminal.

It was a distraction but a pleasant one. It had taken me over a month to pick up my favorite hobby after I had woken up in Savannah, Georgia, but now it was the only thing I did all night. I had books to read, shows and movies I could stream, but I always found myself fiddling with a computer. My mom would have laughed if she had seen me. In the same building as Isaiah, Master of the Tribunal, and Alexius the Hunter, each probably having hundreds, if not thousands, of interesting stories they could tell me...

I could practically hear her.

"There are two ancient beings in this house who want to answer every one of your questions and teach you... and you're just playing with your computer, like always. Don't say it. Don't say computers are easier than people. People are not hard. You just won't get out there."

But they are, Mom.

Chuckling, I wiped my eyes before I could keep going. It had been a long time since I had heard her voice so clearly. I worked until my phone started going off and hissed at it as I turned off the alarm. I caught the date and felt like something hit me in the side of the head.

January thirteenth? My birthday is in less than a week. When did that happen?

I was staring at the date as I left my suite. The idea of my birthday approaching bothered me, but I couldn't put my finger on why. I shoved my phone back into my pocket as I stopped in front of Alexius' study. As I waited for the door to open, Isaiah came strolling down the hall, adjusting his blazer, playing with the sleeves to smooth invisible wrinkles, as though he didn't see me.

I stepped out of his way, my back hitting the wall. He caught the movement and stopped in front of me. He studied me, then looked at the study door as he turned his back to me.

"You try so hard to be a mouse," he said as he entered the study without bothering to knock. Alexius was already inside, and we made eye contact. He waved me to follow Isaiah as the Master of the Tribunal held the door open, looking bored.

Or annoyed. What did I do to annoy him? And what the hell was that comment? I'm not trying to be a mouse. I was trying to be respectful by not being in his damn way.

"Tonight's lesson will be on protocol," Alexius said, sighing heavily. "Come in. I've forgotten the blood, so I need to get it." He stood slowly, stretching as he did.

"A lesson you should have given her weeks ago," Isaiah said, clearly condemning Alexius for failing.

"Why? It's not like I use it," Alexius retorted. "Why would I make her? It's an exhaustingly boring topic, which only people who feel the need to feel good about themselves enforce. And they only ever enforce it with people they wish to belittle."

I couldn't stop my gasp and figured Isaiah had the same problem because he hissed at Alexius.

"I do not *belittle* people with protocol. It teaches people how to act without embarrassing themselves. She needs to know it."

"She won't be using it in my home," Alexius said, and I wondered if they were continuing a previous argument.

I kind of wish we would. Protocol makes things easy.

"It's not about your home. You're in charge here, and I don't care what you do here, but if she's going to work with you—which is an idea I find idiotic and insane—then you will have to take her to places to meet people. People who will demand she follows every bit of the protocol, knowing they can't force you to do it. You can't shelter her from that."

"I'm not trying to shelter her," Alexius snapped. A moment later, he was out of the room, moving faster than I thought possible. The study door slammed shut, leaving me alone with Isaiah.

"He's coming back, right?" I asked, pointing at the door.

Isaiah shrugged and sat down.

To pass the time, I looked around the office and took it in. The centerpiece of the room was a sleek black desk, modern in style, with clean lines. It was surprisingly simple. The bookshelves on the left side were the same. On the right side, there was a black electric fireplace inserted into the wall with a shelf acting as a mantle. The mantle held a few knick-knacks, but I wasn't close enough to inspect them and didn't want to be nosy with Isaiah watching me.

The real centerpiece of the room was a nondescript black frame with a portrait of two men, faces I knew all too well. Alexius and Jacob were posed together from the waist up. It wasn't a large portrait as I would have expected. Probably only eleven by seventeen, it was thought-provoking how small it was.

Actually, Alexius doesn't seem like the type to have a five-foot portrait of himself on the wall, so the small size kind of makes sense.

I crossed my arms as I studied it. Jacob's blond hair was falling over his eyes as he smiled broadly. I knew the smile. It was joyful and humored as though he had just finished laughing. Alexius was trying. A small smile I had seen a few times was there, but there was something in his brow, an exasperation with something. The picture only emphasized how different they were.

I wish I had seen them together.

"Yes, you missed a good thing. A truly beautiful pair those two could be together," Isaiah said from his seat. "Jacob made Alexius... alive."

"I didn't realize I said that out loud." I looked over my shoulder at the vampire who was constantly studying me.

"It was clear what you were thinking. You knew Jacob. You knew how he could be. Do you see him as the son of Alexius?"

"Truthfully? No, I don't *see* it. They're so different." I shook my head, but looking at the painting, I had another thought. "I *believe* it, though. That's the look of a father who got dragged into a picture he didn't want to take and a son who knows he won a battle, and it's all in good fun."

"Then you see them better than most ever could."

9
_____

CHAPTER NINE

A lexius came back, and he brought blood. I fed quickly but wasn't allowed to leave to clean the cup. Instead, the protocol lesson began in earnest while Alexius threw the cup into the trash as if he couldn't be bothered with it.

Truthfully, while Alexius glowered behind his desk, I was looking forward to this. Protocol gave me something I didn't have. Protocol was how to act, when it was appropriate, what to say and do.

"Now, while you don't live in an established nest, Alexius is your Master. I know he hasn't given you his blood, even the inconsequential amount normally used between a Master and those he rules." Isaiah shrugged. "Don't take offense. He's never given his blood to another vampire."

"This isn't a nest, and I am not the Master of anything." Alexius crossed his arms as he leaned back in his chair.

"There is more than one vampire living here, and one

of you is in charge of the household. Therefore, politically, it is a nest," Isaiah retorted. "The protocol of you as the Master of the nest where she resides is better than her being a lone vampire with no reputation, no money, no permanent address, no—"

"I understand the point you're trying to make," Alexius snapped. "Fine. If the world needs to think of it that way to respect her, I shall play the role, but it is *not* official."

"Maybe you should let me do the lesson alone with Everly." Isaiah smiled. He was doing rather well at keeping his cool, which really surprised me. Alexius clearly hated everything about this lesson and Alexius was scary. "You know the protocol. I know why you don't want to be considered the Master of a nest, but it's better for her, and it barely inconveniences you."

"Of course," Alexius muttered, standing. "I said it was fine. I'll let you do this lesson. I don't have the stomach for it this evening." He left silently. I watched him go, wondering if I had heard his footsteps before. It was an easy thing to think about while I was terrified. I didn't want to be alone with Isaiah. Not at all. With Alexius around, they bantered or argued, but now the Master of the Tribunal's entire attention would be on me with no buffer.

It was easier to think about the silence of Alexius' departure.

Is that how he sneaks up on me? Does he always walk that lightly?

"Why does he hate it so much?" I asked, staring at the

closed door, hoping the question kept Isaiah from diverting his entire focus to me.

"Is this a lesson on protocol or the vampire you live with? If you want to know about him, just ask him."

Oh, look, it's the same advice Alexius gave me earlier with Isaiah. Just, you know, talk.

"Protocol. I'm sorry. Why is it important that Alexius is my... Master?" I felt uncomfortable using that word. The idea of someone being my *master* sounded like something that would have made my mother blush. I fought the urge to let my mind wander down that path. This wasn't the time or place. I grew up with this terminology, but as a human, it felt separate. Now, it felt weirdly intimate. Alexius wasn't just the Master of a nest —he was *my* master.

"He'll take responsibility for you, and if you screw up, no one is going to annoy him to punish you unless the offense is particularly egregious. If you misspeak, misstep, many will ignore it. Everyone knows how Alexius can be about protocol, and they'll expect you have been... uneducated on it and having to learn on your own. You'll truthfully disarm them by being perfect while he's a blustering idiot. Remember when he introduced us? He told you I must always be called Master Isaiah unless we're in his home. He was giving you a lesson. I am the Master of all vampires, whether or not they like it. That includes Alexius, though he lives somewhat outside the rest of society and has privileges many could only dream of."

"It's because of what he does, right? He's the Hunter,

as everyone calls him. Just his name scared everyone in the nest."

Yes, let's keep the conversation on Alexius.

"He's one of five vampires willing and powerful enough to do the job, and yes, it is partially because of that. He was the first, which adds to his reputation. The other reason is there are few vampires out there powerful enough to kill him who would find it a worthwhile endeavor. If he stepped out of line, I would have a hell of a time trying to find someone willing to bring him back in line or kill him. As your Master, his reputation and everything else about him will add a layer of protection to you. A very good one, actually. In sheer power, he will outrank nearly every vampire you ever meet. When you decide to leave his household, you'll go into the world as his protégé... his *only* protégé. He's never had another. Everyone will want you in their nest... if they think you're house trained, at least."

"Which is controlling my blood lust, understanding protocol, the laws, and everything," I assumed.

"Exactly, and obedient, which will always be a question because of what you are. That's up to you, though. Everything else is on the shoulders of those who take on the task of educating you. I know Alexius will cover everything except protocol. Now, you know it as a human in a nest. You made yourself invisible. You probably understood feeding on human staff is inappropriate unless the human signed up for it, and so forth."

"It kept me alive for a little while," I whispered, looking away.

"Did it keep you alive the night your mother died, or did you just get lucky?"

The question was bold. I turned back to him, the words ringing in my ears. He sounded professionally curious, and his eyes seemed to take me apart piece by piece.

"Yes. Following the rules, knowing how to talk to Edwin, to keep my head down, to... disassociate—kept me alive. I didn't really have another option. I was summoned to the mansion in the middle of the night, and Edwin wouldn't let anyone else handle the problem." As I spoke, my anger with his rude, awful question grew.

"I was led into his office, and if I hadn't fallen into the rules of how I was supposed to behave, I would have been in hysterics because no one thought to tell me I was going to bump my foot into my mother's body. No one told me I would see her blood splattered all over the wall or that I was about to commit the heinous crime of covering up her murder. That I was going to wipe away every bit of evidence, so no one ever knew the truth but me. Yes, Isaiah, you could say that protocol kept me alive that night. And it kept me alive every day as I desperately searched for a way to help the other humans working there and get justice for her."

"I see I touched a nerve—"

"She's been dead for less than six months," I hissed. "Of course you did."

"I know," he said, not reacting to my anger, his cool professionalism still at play. "It was to let me drive home the point. Protocol can keep you alive with other vampires as well. If there ever comes a time when Alexius

93

and his reputation can't do it, you can lean on the rules, and they will keep you as alive as you and I are. I still have scientists working out the puzzle of our... *status* among the living or the dead."

"Then start teaching it and stop asking me personal and upsetting questions," I demanded. All I got was a frown, which lasted a long time, the silence stretching into minutes.

"I see," he finally said, his words so soft, I nearly missed them. I was certain I only caught them because I was staring at him and saw his lips move. "Did you forget somewhere in the last ten minutes that I rule the vampires? Well, co-rule."

"No," I said quickly, my anger running from me.

"You go from hiding against the wall, unable to knock on the door, to biting and fierce. You remembered in the hall, but you have forgotten since we've sat down."

"I'm sorry—"

"Don't be. It's curious," Isaiah said, finally cracking a smile.

"You don't act like you rule the vampires," I said, trying to avoid his stare. It was the same thing I had said to Alexius, and I stood by it.

"Yes, it's one of my charms. I find it easy to make people comfortable, lull them into a false sense of security, then get them to talk to me as if I were a friend. It lets me see through the outer shell of a person into who they are. Almost no one gives their truth through the first impression." Isaiah chuckled. "Alexius also knows I can't really turn it off."

"Can we get back to the lesson?" I asked, finding the shift in conversation uncomfortable.

"Of course. Now, when you meet another Master or Mistress, Alexius will always introduce you to them, and they will introduce anyone they have brought. Take how I tried to introduce Corban, though Alexius cut me off, then introduced us to you and you to us. He might hate protocol, but some of it is common sense, and he's been around for so long, he does it naturally. It only makes sense since he is in charge of you and should introduce you to any guests who may come see him."

"Yeah, that's common sense. So, do I wait for him, or do I introduce myself if he's not around?"

"Introduce yourself if it's necessary. Your official introduction should be Everly Abbott, serving Alexius the Hunter of Savannah. They'll get the picture. You also don't have to use a last name. The older you get, the more you'll change it, and it gets hard to keep up with which name you should be using. Don't change your first name too often. For example, I changed mine about a thousand years ago, though some will still use my original name if they know it. I'll answer to both, but my original name... fell out of fashion and stood out more than anything." He smirked. "Few people are named Servius Vitus anymore. I picked Isaiah. It had a nice ring to it."

"No, I don't think there many running around with... authentic Roman names anymore," I said softly as my mind went into a slideshow of history. "So, it worked while the empire was around. Eventually, the empire fell, the names went out of style, and you had to switch. You didn't get lucky with a name like Maximus, which could have become Maxwell or an easy variant."

"Want to know the comical part of my original name? My great-grandfather wanted his human descendants to remain human. Servius means to preserve. Vitus means life. In the end, he was the vampire who sired me. I am, in fact, preserving life in a way."

My jaw dropped.

"Protocol lesson number three... don't react," Isaiah said, reaching out faster than I could see. His touch was gentle as he pushed my mouth closed. "That is the same as when you were human. You'll be around many who have lived... interesting lives, which will become less so as you get older and begin hearing the stories. Never react. A shocked expression, a laugh, or anything else that might betray how you feel about a situation could be seen as an offense. If someone is dead, you don't cry or overreact. You give your condolences and move on... unless you're trying to get into bed with someone. Then you try to position yourself as someone who can comfort—"

"I don't need that half of the lesson," I said quickly. "I don't need to know how to act to manipulate people. I don't like that."

"That's life, Everly." Isaiah shrugged. "Let's continue our lesson."

I listened and asked questions, keeping them on topic. We went through introductions, how complicated or simple they could be, depending on who was there and what the occasion was. We dove into how to feed on certain humans, where and how much could be taken.

That part worried me the most because I didn't know how to stop feeding once I started. Isaiah calmly reminded me Alexius would never let me do anything that anyone could find a fault in, and I had to trust that.

Which was easy. Alexius would have to kill me if he thought I was a lost cause. Considering he made me a vampire, and I lived in his house, I didn't think he would let me even toe the line.

Then there was discussion about the different properties a nest could own and how protocol changed. That one really stumped me.

"Jacob only owned the mansion and a small cabin, but he went there alone."

"Normally, he did, but I could always visit him while he was there," Isaiah countered. "So could Alexius, which is why you never saw the dusty old man at the mansion."

"I know Alexius and Jacob were close, but... you must have been really close to him, too."

"I know you knew him and respected him, possibly loved him a little, which is why I'll tell you this. Besides, someone else will probably tell you one day. He was my closest friend." Isaiah smiled sadly. "He was kind. He knew the difference between wisdom and intelligence and had both in spades." Isaiah cleared his throat. "And for two hundred years after I became a vampire, I was honored to be his lover, and he mine, regularly exchanging blood, living together, and talking about our plans for the future."

"Oh..."

"We were better friends in the end, but yes, we were close." Isaiah sighed. "Back on topic. Jacob, due to his ambitions, or lack thereof, didn't keep many of the regular establishments major nests have. Every major city in the United States has at least one club or bar that is actually run by vampires for vampires, a blood club. The rules are strict. Humans must survive the night and either not remember what happened or think something else did. There are ways to fool the mind of a drunk human, but those aren't the lesson tonight.

"A blood club has different protocols than a residence on a normal night. You don't need to announce yourself to the Master or Mistress, who may or may not be in attendance. You do need to tell your name to the vampire in charge that evening in case there's an incident, and you need to be found later. Blood clubs are safe havens for travelers who need to feed in a secure place. They're also places for parties of a more informal nature and no guest list. You probably won't see a blood club any time soon."

"Why?"

"Alexius doesn't like them and won't go near them unless it's work-related. Neither did Jacob, though Jacob understood their usefulness. He believed they invited people to lose control, feeding in a room full of other vampires. If someone isn't completely ready for the experience, losing control could be easy, but to account for the risks he saw, there have been strict rules established. Owning and operating a successful and accident-free blood club is often the pride and joy of many who run nests."

"So, having an accident when I'm visiting someone would reflect poorly on Alexius and me."

"Accidents still happen, and normally, they're swept

under the rug. It would be more embarrassing for you than it would be for others. You serve Alexius. You can't have accidents."

"But doesn't every vampire have one, eventually? Alexius said that once. Jacob used to preach it. An accident doesn't mean someone is bad or anything. It just happens because of what we are. I don't want to have one, but—"

"Certainly, but you're Everly, serving Alexius the Hunter of Savannah. He doesn't have accidents. He hasn't since I met him over two thousand years ago. If you killed a human from a temporary loss of control, it would be considered *his* failure, and Alexius has *never* been involved in something like that. It would be talked about by everyone. So, again, remember Alexius will be with you every time you feed on a human for some time and will never let you kill anyone. He just wouldn't. I wouldn't if I was around. Any powerful vampire witnessing you losing control would stop you. Dead bodies are a problem, as you know. So, don't worry too much about it unless you're alone, which won't happen until he's certain you can handle it. By then, you'll be fine."

"Yeah..."

Isaiah stood and stretched, though I knew he wasn't sore. Soreness never happened as a vampire. It had taken me two days to figure that out. Or at least, I hadn't gotten sore and had never heard of anyone complaining about it.

"Well, that is enough for tonight. You seem to pick it up quickly, and I have a book you might like to read. I wrote it ages ago with some other vampires to help beginners. I brought a copy for you. It can't leave this home under any circumstances for obvious reasons, much like the other books in Alexius' library."

"Oh, thank you. I guess you knew I wouldn't have any idea, huh?"

"Yes, and with Alexius as your teacher... Well, let's say you're doing better than I expected." Isaiah chuckled, then walked out as I stood up. I grabbed the door before it could close and saw Alexius leaning on the opposite wall, arms crossed, his obsidian eyes boring into me.

"She's all yours again, old man," Isaiah called from down the hall.

"How was the lesson?" he asked me.

"Educational," I answered stiffly.

"That's good."

Just ask him.

"Why do you hate protocol?" It flew off my tongue as though he would answer because I asked. There was a shred of bravery, but not as much as I thought I would need. This was Alexius, the man who had answered all my questions when I had been a human, exposed secrets about their kind when I was desperate, and offered me a job.

Who fed me vampire blood after I died and made me one of them, giving me a second chance at life.

He moved around me into his study. Turning to watch him sit down and kick his feet up on the desk, I grew more embarrassed about my intrusive question with each passing moment, watching as he put his arms behind his head.

"It's tedious, and people abuse it, as people abuse

every sort of power structure. Those on top get everything they need and want in excess and leave others suffering, even if they don't need to. Protocol forces silence from those on the bottom of the social hierarchy while they are the very people who need to speak up if things are unfair. It's been a recurring theme I have seen from humanity and supernaturals for centuries. I have a distaste for it. It's the moral reason I refuse to have a nest and why Jacob knew better than to leave his nest to me. I refuse to take part in the practice of dominating and controlling others endlessly. Once you're trained, when we're not working, you'll have more freedom than most vampires. I have to be controlling now because you're at a vulnerable time for yourself and a dangerous one to those around you, but I don't like it. Once I can give you freedom, you will have it."

"There are other reasons?"

"I have a dangerous occupation that I enjoy but could put others at risk, so I don't want too many relying on me for their safety. Fewer people around me mean fewer people to keep safe. An official nest has at least ten vampires and two or three business holdings, with few exceptions. A nest would also be a time-consuming endeavor that pulls me away from work. Lastly, it could lead to a conflict of interests if I have to execute a vampire I like. Unlikely, but possible. It's not a risk I want to take."

You're taking it with me, aren't you?

"Thanks for explaining," I said and shut his study door.

10

CHAPTER TEN

Over the next three days, my head was filled with more information than Alexius had ever given me. Every topic Isaiah decided to teach, Alexius disliked. Protocol was only the first. Next was a beginner's guide to vampire politics. After that, we delved into more politics, with Isaiah focusing on the laws between vampires and other supernaturals. There was no feeding on other supernaturals without their express permission, but it went deeper. He went into how vampires and fae avoided each other after some "regrettable" incidents. We didn't finish that topic before the sun rose. By the beginning of the fourth night of his visit, I wasn't nearly so excited to get out of bed, amazed I was even there. It took me ten minutes to realize why.

I didn't remember going to sleep in my bed.

I passed out in the study, didn't I? He kept me until dawn. Oh God, which one of them brought me here? Did they change my clothes?

I threw the blankets back, grateful to see I was still in what I had worn the night before.

At least whoever it was didn't go that far. I'll just be... grateful one of them did. Better than waking up in the study and Alexius waiting on me to get out of his way.

Rubbing my eyes, I went through my morning routine, then found Alexius and had my first meal. He said nothing as I cleaned up but raised a hand as I put the cup away and went to leave.

"We're going to do something different tonight," he said. "Isaiah feels the need to make his lessons longer than you can stay awake, so I'm moving your lessons to the beginning of the night."

"What does he want to teach me tonight?"

"Oh, tonight... He won't be teaching you anything tonight. You'll notice he's not here right now because he still believes he'll have the second half of the night with you. I didn't tell him I was making the change."

"Um... did I miss something?" I asked as Alexius gave me a small, and to be honest, incredibly sneaky smile. Once again, I was the person in the room who didn't know the full story, the only one who was missing some sort of subtle context about the situation.

I hated it. I didn't know if it was a 'me' problem or if it was just the way Alexius and Isaiah were together. I didn't know if I could learn to catch all the little things going on between them. They were jumping around, changing things, talking about things I had no idea about, that I couldn't see.

"I was offended on your behalf that he kept you until

the sun rose. Isaiah would have many ways to talk himself out of it, so I'm going to punish him without telling him. He came here with the expectation of having access to you, to teach you, and watch me to make sure I was doing everything exactly the way he wanted it done, but last night was a step too far. There was no reason for him to potentially embarrass you or put you in a position that could make you uncomfortable by keeping you until the moment you fell asleep without control."

"So, you're going to take away access," I said, nodding as I saw Alexius' little game. "Look, as long as it gets you in trouble and not me, I don't care. I didn't really like being kept until the sun came up. I was... really confused when I woke up this morning and wasn't in the spot where I went to sleep."

"Ah, I moved you. I didn't think you would be comfortable sleeping in my study. I hoped waking up in your space would be preferable. Next time, I could leave you—"

"No, it's fine!" I lifted my hands as he rubbed the back of his neck, his mood shifting to uncertainty I had never seen from him. "You made the right choice. I'm glad it was you, really, and thanks for not... trying to change my clothes or anything. I'd prefer if no one saw me naked when I'm unconscious."

His hand dropped, and he studied me, the uncertainty fading away to a small amount of confusion, and if I was reading his face right, embarrassment.

"I've seen..." He stopped, and I went wide-eyed.

"Oh, that's right," I mumbled as I remembered what

he was clearly trying not to remind me of. He'd handled my body while I Turned and woke up naked. I hadn't just woken up naked; the first time I fed, I was naked in *his* bed and hadn't even realized until he told me to get dressed. "Yeah..."

"I wouldn't change your clothes now, clearly," he said, clearing his throat. "There's no reason to put either of us in that position."

"Thank you," I said, looking at his shoes, hoping my beating heart would stop racing. Embarrassing conversations so close to feeding were the *worst*. I waited until it stopped altogether before continuing.

"So... what am I learning tonight?" There was one thing to look forward to. As a teacher, Alexius was shaping up to be more respectful compared to Isaiah. Alexius never held me longer than he promised. He didn't keep me up until the sun rose, and I couldn't stay awake. While Isaiah taught me things I could use going forward, Alexius was just... easier. Not *easy*, but I knew him a little. I didn't second guess with Alexius because he never seemed to have ulterior motives that left me guessing.

"I think tonight might be a good night to test and begin training your physical abilities."

Damn it. Anything but that. Why?

"I know it's been hard locked away like this."

This will not make it any better.

"The lack of physical activity was purposeful for the first two months. I didn't want to train you and your instincts while you didn't have control over the initial blood lust. Dealing with you untrained was easier and, honestly, safer for both of us. You haven't attacked for blood in some weeks, so I believe tonight might be a good time to start."

Fuck.

"Okay. I haven't really... seen what I can do with a new, uh, body yet. Well, it's not new, but um... vampires. We're faster than humans and stronger."

"We are, and you've done a good job adjusting to those changes. Now it's time to test them with full awareness. Come with me. You remember where the gym is?" He waved for me to follow him, and I was left trying to catch up as he walked out of the sitting room. "And no, you won't get into trouble. Neither will I. He's clearly being lazy by not coming to the first mealtime of the night, and he'll recognize I have outplayed him for being foolish with your wellbeing."

"It's really not that big a deal, is it? I mean, it's not as if he did some great damage by talking until I passed out. It was rude, but..."

"Isaiah is normally smarter than to keep a young vampire up until sunrise. I wasn't there. I had gone to the gym and lost track of time. I found you an hour after the sun came up. Isaiah had just left you there for me to find. It's not that he did harm, but he did something I consider rude, and now he must pay for it."

"I wish I understood how you two think," I said, shaking my head as we walked. "It's as though I only hear half the conversation every time one of you brings up the other. Even when you're both in the same room, I don't know what's going on. There's so much subtext."

"We've had years to understand each other as well as

we do, and it is really... constantly trying to outmaneuver each other. Sometimes, it's fun. Other times, it's necessary. With Jacob gone, Isaiah knows me better than any other person on this earth. It's equal because I know him better than anyone as well. I also have the advantage of knowing his background, having been around him since he was a boy."

"He told me a bit of that. About how you and Jacob took him in right after he was Turned because his sire..." I didn't finish. It felt like a deeply personal thing I shouldn't repeat. "He also told me about his relationship with Jacob. They're not two men I could see together."

"They were... good but young," Alexius said softly. He didn't slow his pace, and we were coming up to the gym. "Isaiah was still growing into the man he is now, eyeing power and talking about how he and Jacob could rule everyone if they put their minds to it. Jacob wanted something else out of a relationship and out of his life. Neither of them took another steady lover after that, though, for their own reasons. Isaiah won't and never will because of his position. There's not a man or woman alive or dead he would trust beside him now that he sits on the top. He barely tolerates Maria on some days, and she barely tolerates him just as frequently. He has flings, people he'll trust for an evening or two, but no more."

"And... and Jacob?"

"Never found true love. He wanted to find someone he believed he would love for an eternity, someone I wished every day he would find, but I knew he was looking for the impossible." Alexius looked down at me, stopping at the gym door. "But he found love in what he did, and he loved those he cared for. From the oldest vampire in his care to the youngest human, he loved all of you. It fulfilled him in a way I think a lover never could have. Jacob was a caretaker at heart." Alexius sighed, his head turning to the side. "I failed his memory by refusing to take over to disband the nest. I was so predictable, which only led to more despair in a situation already hard on all vampires."

I opened my mouth, ready to tell him it wasn't his fault, but I didn't really believe it. Jacob had asked Alexius to take over the nest in Portland, Maine, in his will. Alexius had refused, paving the way for Edwin to take power. That had led to the deaths of more humans than I could count, including my mother and Shane, a friend and coworker.

"We can't change the past," I finally said.

"I'm the last person you need to say that to," he said, reaching to open the gym door.

"Everyone needs a reminder sometimes."

He gave me a long look, then went into the gym. I followed dutifully and looked around. When I had first moved in, there had been one set of every piece of equipment. Now there were two treadmills, but aside from that, nothing else had changed. The floor was still a laminate or wood, like in a school gym. Half the room was empty, an open activity area, while the other half had all the equipment, most of which I had never touched in my life. The left wall was still covered in mirrors, which I never understood, no matter where I saw it. There was a massive mat rolled up in the corner by the mirrors. Beside it, on a blank tan wall, was a set of brown cabinets with doors which I assumed held more torture devices.

Like jump ropes or something.

"Question." I waited for him to turn to me before asking. "If we're stronger than normal humans, why do you have normal gym equipment? Wouldn't all this be easy to use?"

"Yes and no. You might run faster as a vampire, but cardiovascular strength and endurance must still be exercised to get better. We're stronger naturally, but you're not more muscled by becoming a vampire, are you?"

"No..." I was about ten pounds heavier, though, which was a good thing. As a human, I had been a beanpole.

"Exactly. Yes, the weights you'll use are different, but you still need to train. Most vampires neglect this because blood keeps us healthy and relatively strong, but they're only achieving half of what they could be."

"I always thought we were... frozen. I mean, I've realized that's not completely true, but how much variation are we talking about?"

"If you stopped feeding for a month, you would starve, much like a human or any other supernatural, with I believe only one exception. You would drop weight, lose muscle mass, the typical issues that come from not eating. You would then need to feed and slowly recover what you lost."

"There's... a type of supernatural that doesn't need to eat?" That was one of the most interesting things I had heard yet.

"That's not the discussion. We need to make you strong. You and I will see the worst of our kind, and I want you to have every advantage. That's why you've been on a strict feeding schedule. If I wasn't planning to train you, I would let you feed twice a day, not three times."

I rubbed my throat.

Only twice? My throat would burn so bad if he made me wait all night for a second meal.

"So, you've been trying to put weight on me. I mean, I understand why; I just didn't know I could."

"And it's working," he said, going to the cabinets. "I hope you haven't..." He looked back at me as he opened one of the cabinets. "It's not unattractive. You're not overweight or—"

"It's fine," I said while putting a hand over my face. "It's a good thing. I didn't know I could gain weight as a vampire, that's all." My tiny ego didn't know whether to burst with joy or to feel bruised.

"I know many people can get uncomfortable with their weight—"

"Alexius."

"Yes, we'll get to the lesson," he said, pulling stuff out of the cabinet. "We'll start simple."

I helped him roll out the mat, expecting push-ups and sit-ups. We did both but also squats, lunges, and more. He directed me through a workout that would have left me on the ground as a human. By the end, I knew one new thing for certain.

Vampires could, in fact, get sore.

"Now, we'll move to the treadmills. After, I'll give you a lesson in hand-to-hand combat," he said, leaving me on the floor after the last round of crunches. He'd done the entire workout with me and seemed to be just fine while I could barely move.

"Alexius!"

That had me sitting up with ease. Isaiah's roar echoed around the gym, ringing in my ears. Alexius stopped walking, then bolted for the gym's door, flinging it open.

11

_____

CHAPTER ELEVEN

I was able to get to my feet by the time Isaiah walked into the gym doorway, his eyes on Alexius.

"I need you in one hour to see Maria and the werewolves. Callahan and Corissa have demanded a meeting, and from the initial information, it's not good," Isaiah said without even looking in my direction. "I'll meet you in your study."

"Everly, go take a shower," Alexius ordered, looking over his shoulder. I pushed myself to my feet, but there was no way through the door. I inched closer, but neither of them moved. Alexius, the wall, and Isaiah, the skyscraper, were effective at blocking someone's exit.

"*You* need to go take a shower," Isaiah said, poking him in the chest. "Callahan and Corissa will find you offensive, and you're the only one here that's going to meet them tonight."

"I can't leave her here," Alexius snapped. "Not even for ten minutes. You know that."

I clasped my hands in front of me as Isaiah looked around him at me.

"I expect silence. Try to be invisible. You've had a lot of practice, and I need you to do it tonight. It's nothing against you. Callahan and Corissa are the two Alpha werewolves of the Tribunal. I govern with them. They won't expect or appreciate a new face, especially an untrained, inexperienced, and uneducated one. I went over some of our relationships with other species. Did we get to werewolves?"

"We didn't, not last night. We went over fae and witches because vampires run into them the most. Alexius once told me we don't have any fights with the werewolves, and we always do our best not to start one."

"That will have to work. Keep your head down." Isaiah nodded, thankfully satisfied. He stepped out of the way, and Alexius took the cue to do the same, but I wasn't able to get through the door yet. He grabbed my wrist to stop me.

"No need to wear anything special. Decent slacks and a nice blouse will suffice."

"Hell, you could get away with jeans, thanks to the timing of this meeting," Isaiah muttered. "I hate when we do fast meetings. No one is ready, and one side has all the cards."

"I'll aim for business casual," I promised, and Alexius let go. I headed toward the bedrooms, and he followed. I heard Isaiah following as well.

"Isaiah, tell me what you know."

"I don't know the region yet, but by account, somewhere in the range of ten people are dead. A small homestead wiped off the map. The werewolves are involved because one of the packs found the town earlier in the evening, but there was no sign of the vampires. The pack Alpha reported it to Callahan and Corissa, who are bringing it to us."

They stayed on my heels, which allowed me to hear. Out of energy and between feedings, my body had no reaction to the information, but my head was spinning.

"You'll have to send someone out," Alexius growled. "I'll give what advice I can on the situation when we know everything."

"Of course. I wasn't considering sending you. I want you for this meeting."

"You have me. Find out whatever else you can before I get to my study."

"I will. Maria knows you're coming. She was glad to hear I was here. She doesn't know about Everly joining, however. I need to call her back and let her know. She might know more by now."

"I'll stay quiet," I promised.

"Quiet is good, but the problem isn't you speaking out," Isaiah said. "They have heartbeats, real, consistent, and reactive heartbeats. They'll pound in your ears, letting you know they have the blood you need to feed. When was the last time you heard one of those? Have you ever? The problem is an untrained vampire who might lose her cool."

I looked over my shoulder, trying to think, but couldn't form a sentence before Alexius answered.

"I've kept her too far from the staff for that to be a risk," Alexius said softly. "But they smell like animals, and I don't believe they'll come to a meeting with vampires while they're bleeding. She'll be fine. I'll keep her at my side."

"It will have to suffice," Isaiah said, stopping. "Get ready quickly. If we can arrive a minute early, it looks good for us."

"Of course." Alexius put a hand on my back, forcing me to speed up to his natural pace with his longer legs.

"Alexius, I have no idea—"

"You'll be fine. Don't bother wearing makeup. Werewolves can smell it, and some of them don't like it. Only a light perfume if you insist on wearing any. They have the strongest sense of smell in the supernatural world, and they'll find it offensive. Generally, people will use artificial scents to cover up their natural smell. From you, it'll annoy them and make them look at you closely."

"I'll be with you and Isaiah. They'll look closely no matter what I do," I said. "Why can't I stay here?"

He didn't answer until we were stopped outside my room.

"I don't know if your control is good enough to keep you from trying to leave," he answered honestly. "You might truly believe so, but I have to take every precaution. You won't be able to hurt anything but our political position if you join us, which I don't care about. Here you could kill three elderly humans."

"I wouldn't..."

"It's not that I believe you will but would rather not take the risk and find out. Yes, they will be interested in the young vampire with me, but I don't work for them, and I don't work against other supernaturals. I never have. I'm not a threat to them. In fact, I'm useful to them because I deal with problems that come from vampires. So long as you do nothing that could disrespect them, they'll just see you as a young vampire I've taken in, and there won't be any questions."

"Okay." I was already trying to find the headspace I used to live in. The dutiful, quiet human servant—don't make eye contact, don't comment.

"I will tell them I employ you, and I am training you. It will make you just as useful as I am and offer you some cover to be there. It's the truth, something Callahan and Corissa will appreciate. Now, I'm going to ask something different than Isaiah did. If you believe you need to speak up at any point, I'm always willing to hear your input. It might be inexperienced, but it's not entirely as inexperienced as you or Isaiah believe. You've had an encounter with these vampires from a perspective that can't be replicated by a vampire, and you have technical skills I find useful. I'll ask Isaiah to provide a laptop that will work in the Tribunal offices, so you can do fast research." He opened my door and pushed me into my room. "Go get ready."

He shut the door on my face, leaving me overwhelmed and confused. Showering as quickly as I could, I tried to do my hair, going for a tight bun, then got dressed. I went with no makeup or perfume, deciding not to risk offending anyone tonight. When I was back in the hall, no one was around, so I headed for Alexius' office.

"Alexius, don't play with fire. She can come but—"

"She works for me. Get the laptop," he snapped as I entered the study.

Isaiah turned, seeing me in the doorway first, and sighed.

"Fine. There will be one in my office. You'll have to give it back, though. It's my personal laptop."

"If you're not comfortable with me on your private devices, I can go get one." I was talking fast, my nerves finally leaking through. "I know I've bought one since I moved here. I haven't set it up—"

"It wouldn't work," Isaiah explained before I could finish, clearly irritated. "The Tribunal's domain is a pocket dimension created by the Tribunal witches and fae, and only the members of the Tribunal have permanent keys to it. We're going to my Tribunal offices inside the pocket dimension. As a member of the Tribunal, I can open a door directly to my office from my location at any time. I can take both of you, but none of your devices will work properly. I would need to get the fae involved for that, and the last fucking thing I'm doing is getting the King or Queen of the fae up to make sure your laptop works because Alexius demands it. You'll use mine. You can do a guest login and just play on Google, type notes, or whatever Alexius wants." He made a gesture. "Get in here and close the door."

I shrank as I moved farther into the study, shutting the door behind me.

"I didn't know."

"He's in a mood, but it's not with us." Alexius' face was blank, and his words were devoid of emotion. "Neither of us was expecting you to go to the Tribunal so soon, so we hadn't explained the domain of the Tribunal yet. Most supernaturals never see the domain of the rulers, but working for me made it likely you would, eventually. That's no one's failing, just poor circumstance."

I could only nod. Alexius moved, and suddenly a cup was in front of me.

"Feed. We're going into Isaiah's office first. It's secure."

"Maria will be joining us," Isaiah added. "We'll have fifteen minutes to talk before we're expected by Callahan and Corissa."

Drinking eased the burn in my throat, but it wasn't satisfying. I was full, and the burn was gone, but those were the last things on my mind.

"Consider this your first day on the job," Alexius said as he took the cup and put it on his desk. Out of the corner of my eye, Isaiah hissed softly as he put his hand on the closed door.

"Eight centuries and they still haven't figured out a way to make it less painful for vampires?"

"You think Maria and I have asked the *fae* or the *witches* to make this painless?" Isaiah raised an eyebrow back at us. "No. We suffer in silence, Alexius. You know that. Knowing *them*, they did it on purpose. We have bad blood with both."

"Of course."

Isaiah pulled his hand away from the door and opened it. I couldn't stop my gasp of surprise. Beyond the door wasn't the hallway I was well acquainted with, but an office of rich wood furniture paired with muted colors.

"But..."

"Magic," Isaiah said, then walked through. It looked completely normal, but I let Alexius go first. I had seen magic before when a witch did a geas on me, removing my ability to tell others about vampires. This wasn't just a little magic, though, like an invisible spell. This wasn't manipulating someone's emotions to feed on them without fear. This wasn't anything like what I had seen before.

This was *magic*.

Going in slowly, looking around, I wasn't finished getting over the awe when another door flew open, and a beautiful, regal woman stormed in. Long black hair fell over her shoulders when she stopped in front of Isaiah's desk. She wore a perfectly tailored suit, white as snow in every detail. The only color was the manilla envelope under her shoulder and her brilliant red eyes.

"They're particularly cranky tonight, Isaiah. Whoever killed those humans must have killed someone close to the pack. This pack must be close to Corissa or Callahan."

"Do you know where it happened? Maybe the pack has an Alpha on one of their councils. That would complicate things."

"No. They sent pictures of the bodies, though," Maria snapped. "Definitely a handful of out-of-control vampires. No idea who it could be or where they came from."

"Let me see them, please," Alexius said, extending a hand. Maria held it out without a word. I inched closer to Alexius to see the pictures. It was a morbid interest. I had seen plenty of dead bodies before, more than I really should have, and had nailed the sense of detachment long ago, which had helped me as a human. Now, I could see Alexius was the same way, and he was looking at them to discover new information. This was work to him, and whatever was in those images wasn't shocking but pieces of a larger picture.

Seeing him made me want to work. Seeing what he was seeing and trying to understand what information he would get from it would help me.

"Oh, you must be the Orphan," Maria said, reaching out. I stepped back, dodging her hand. I hadn't intended to get her attention, trying to see what Alexius wanted, and I didn't want to be touched by a stranger. It broke my focus and killed my nerve to see the pictures, so I took an extra step back, retreating farther while she stared at me. Her hand sat in the air for a moment after I stopped before she folded both in front of her and studied me.

"Skittish, aren't you?" Tilting her head to the side, she stepped closer.

"Nervous, Mistress Maria," I clarified.

"She's a little mouse, just like I said," Isaiah added, moving to Maria's side. "She'll misstep tonight, but it won't be intentional. She just needs practice with the new social rules she has to follow. Everly, introduce yourself."

I knew a test when I heard one but also knew Isaiah didn't believe I was a mouse. Keeping polite eye contact with Maria, I called on the protocol Isaiah had just taught me. I didn't have the chance to say anything, though. Opening my mouth, someone else began talking.

"Mistress Maria, meet my protégé, Everly Abbott, once a human of Jacob's nest in Maine. She's under my protection until she's ready to join our society on her own, and she is my employee until she decides otherwise.

She's here to listen and learn while hopefully offering her unique perspective on the killings being reported," Alexius said quickly, clearly trying to get through formalities as he closed the envelope. He held it out to me, his long arms able to stretch the distance I had tried to make. I grabbed it as he watched me with his back turned to the two ruling vampires.

"I want you to consider these images and come up with your own theories about how this group of humans died. If the images are unsettling, you're more than welcome to leave it for another time. Just give them to Isaiah for his review when you're done."

"Yes, sir," I murmured. He gave me a small nod before turning away from me. Somehow, with his small movement, he blocked my view of them.

Or their view of me. Did he do that on purpose?

"You're correct, Maria. It was at least three or four vampires. Any less wouldn't have been able to feed on so many. There's simply too much blood," Alexius continued. "Isaiah, you can have the images from Everly when she's finished."

"Are you sure a delicate girl like her should look at images like that?" Maria asked, craning to look around him. I dropped my head and stared at the envelope, ignoring her as I opened it.

"She's not delicate," Alexius responded. "She's nervous, but she's not delicate."

"What did she do for Jacob's nest?" Isaiah already knew the answer, but he posed the question. It made me think about why he would do that, which blocked the sheer horror the images should have brought. I realized he was playing with everyone. Maria must have had little information on me, which put Isaiah at an advantage. He was also forcing Alexius to reveal information instead of giving away what he knew.

"Technical support of some sort. I don't truly understand all the details. It handled technology I don't use."

I'm just going to show you one day. Clearly, explaining it isn't sinking in. His lack of understanding was almost endearing, though. It wasn't a lack of respect. He'd wanted to hire me for my expertise, he just didn't understand what it was.

"I handled the automated features of the building and the digital security of the nest, which ranged from personal electronic devices to our camera system. If something was caught on camera, it was my job to clean up the footage and leave no evidence for potential humans to stumble upon." Looking up, I met Maria's gaze. I had been proud of my work for years and continued to be proud when it all went to hell with Jacob's death and Edwin's arrival. It had stained my soul to do it, but I had done a damn good job. "I've seen dead bodies before. This isn't as shocking as you would think. Thank you for your concern, though." I looked back down, ignoring her surprise, and finally focused on the pictures.

Whoever this family had been, they were unrecognizable now. There was too much blood around the images to piece together more than the sex of most of them. The bite marks were clear. Each body had several, and whoever took the pictures had tried to angle the camera to get every detail they could. There were multiple pictures of each body and the rooms they were in as a whole. The blood splattered on the walls sent chills down my spine, remembering Edwin's office with my mother's blood. I tried to focus on one thing about each room. The building reminded me of a log cabin. The furniture was rustic. Two of the rooms were bedrooms. The kitchen and living room also made appearances. In the kitchen, I saw a family photo. Leaning into the picture, I was pretty sure I saw someone who looked like a victim.

"This was their home," I whispered to myself. "The vampires were outsiders. Or related. Or broke in."

"We don't have enough of the facts yet, but it was the home of at least two of the victims," Alexius agreed. "The pictures in the home give us that much. Good catch."

I couldn't find anything else beyond the second person he had mentioned living there, a picture in a small hallway I could see from a picture of the living room. I had assumed it was everyone, but he was smart. He'd only counted those he could verify, something I tucked away to remember for later. He didn't make any assumptions like I had.

"I'm done." Closing the folder, I walked it to Isaiah, who gave everything inside a fast look. I moved to Alexius' side, who moved a little closer once I was there. There was barely an inch between us, thanks to him.

"No wonder they're upset. This is messy. We have..." He checked his watch. "Five minutes until the meeting."

"We can go now." Maria crossed her arms. "In fact, I would prefer it. Being ready for their condemnation makes us look strong and will work against their potential idea we're at fault. We need to clean this up, anyway, and I need Corissa willing to give me all the information."

"Then let's go," Isaiah said, closing the envelope. He handed it back to me, then grabbed something off his desk and put it in my hands as well. I only saw it was a laptop before he and Maria started walking out of the room. Alexius followed them, and I was left trying to catch up, a feeling I was getting used to.

12

CHAPTER TWELVE

Alexius held doors open for me until we entered a conference room. It was surprisingly *corporate* for a bunch of ancient beings who ruled supernaturals all over the world. There was a long table in the center, legal pads and pens placed out for people who might need them, and an overhead projector.

"We couldn't get a more... comfortable room?" Alexius asked as he stood beside me. "Isn't this the room where Investigators brief the Tribunal about their current projects?"

"Yes, but this is where Corissa and Callahan wanted to meet us," Maria said, finding a seat. Isaiah sat beside her, not giving us a second glance. Alexius pointed a few chairs down from the Master and Mistress, then sat between Isaiah and me.

I quickly set up, opening the laptop and logging in as a guest while Alexius went back to reviewing those images. Deciding against using the laptop to take notes of this meeting, I grabbed a legal pad and pen before anyone else arrived. I was moving fast, trying to be settled before the werewolves arrived. Alexius closed the folder suddenly, and seconds later, the far door opened.

I could *feel* they were different. Even though werewolves lived openly among humans, I had only had a single run-in with them. They had never settled in Maine, and I had been human at the time. This feeling had to be rooted in being supernatural. I tried to dissect it as four people slowly walked in and found seats. There was a sense of ferality. I could tell they were wild animals and not to be toyed with, the same way most people knew the difference between a domestic dog and a wolf. They walked with steady purpose, less poised than Isaiah, Maria, or even Alexius. Unlike us, they felt like a unit, a group ready to fight and die together. That energy made me wary.

The only woman in the group glanced in my direction as I watched them. She had a cool expression that made me think she saw through me or thought she was above me. Her brown eyes should have seemed warm, but it took me a moment to realize they weren't brown at all. They were amber, the eyes of a wolf, not a human. I didn't know why she was staring at me, but I was captivated.

She must be Corissa.

She smiled, but it didn't seem friendly. Like her gaze, it was cool and knowing, scratching my nerves in another way. It terrified me.

"Drop your eyes," Alexius whispered to me.

I did, my hands shaking a little, something I hadn't realized.

"This must be the new vampire Maria told us would have to be in attendance," the woman said in a tone I couldn't decipher.

"Yes," Isaiah confirmed. "Alexius wouldn't leave her behind, and I knew his expertise would be too valuable for him to miss this meeting. He'll be able to give us the best way to solve this problem."

"Of course. I'm well acquainted with your hunter," she replied. "Thank you for coming, Alexius. It's no harm for her to be here. Many people make the same mistake. It's rare a young supernatural of any type meets a member of the Tribunal, and most supernaturals don't have an issue with eye contact the way werewolves often do. I wouldn't have attacked her."

"I knew you wouldn't, but considering the situation, it's best not to lead anyone into making a mistake just because you can." Alexius seemed bored. I finally lifted my head to look at him. "She's a young enough vampire that remaining seated when you arrived is a positive, and I would appreciate if you didn't test her. She's here to assist me."

"My apologies," Corissa said, but she didn't sound apologetic.

I grabbed my legal pad and pen, ready to take notes, hoping to distract myself from the attention.

"Let's leave the little bloodsucker alone and get on with business," a man growled. He was positioned beside Corissa, and she smiled a little at his harsh words.

The little bloodsucker. Suddenly a supernatural yet still dismissed as if I'm insignificant.

"We'd be more prepared for said business if you told

us what was going on," Maria snapped. "Maybe if you had given us more information, Alexius would have felt more comfortable leaving his assistant at home because this meeting would have been faster."

"We've been trying to respect the privacy of the vampires, considering your status as a hidden species. We wouldn't divulge more than necessary in case of a leak," Callahan retorted.

So, you took pictures? Those are the easiest to leak. Rumors and hearsay are easy to fight, but a picture is worth a thousand words.

"We wanted to finish our own investigation and have all the details to present you at once. Don't tell me how to handle business. We wouldn't have this business if you did a better job of maintaining control over your monsters."

As though a signal had been given and it was a well-practiced performance, the Tribunal members began to bicker. I put my pen down and watched, fascinated that we were supposed to be in a meeting to talk about the murder of several humans, but they would rather bicker about how they had treated each other getting to this meeting. It seemed so counterproductive. Worse, I had a feeling the use of picture evidence of the killings as the only information given to Maria was part of the game, this performance. A massive security risk, just because they could.

Eventually, I realized it would never end. I leaned back in my seat, looking around the room until I was needed.

"Stop playing politics and move along," Alexius ordered. "I don't want to be here all night."

I went wide-eyed as an unnatural hush fell over the room. I could feel the weight of everyone staring in our direction and gave a fearful look to confirm that feeling. Everyone was staring at us.

"Look here—"

"Incidents like these happen," Alexius continued when Callahan tried to say something. "They've happened for centuries and will continue to happen. I clean them up and stop the vampires responsible. As is the case of werewolves going through the Last Change and killing dozens. You send a pack or your own werewolves to stop them, but we all know it will happen again." That made Callahan close his mouth. "We all have our flaws, and there's no changing them. Either tell me about this incident and why you find it so important, or drop this charade of anger and let it go. Anything else is a waste of my time, and if this continues, I will leave, and you can send me a report when you're ready for the words of an expert."

"I always hate when you come to these meetings. Politics are important, and they're ritual," Corissa commented lightly.

"I'm here to do my job," Alexius retorted. "And my job *isn't* to play politics, nor is it to wait on any of you. Let me repeat: If this is going to continue, just let me know when you're ready for an expert. I will read a report if you want to send one and offer my advice."

"Always the same with you." Sighing, she waved a hand, and the other two werewolves stood. They hadn't said a word during the bickering and maintained that silence now. One played with the projector while the other pulled down the screen. The room went dark, but my eyes adjusted quickly. The projector was turned on, and a collage of the murder images appeared.

"The situation is abnormal, which means it's a problem. Thanks to the relative closeness to the local pack and its overall location, we believe there's something more happening here. First, two of the humans in the family were directly related to the Alpha of the local pack. He's rightfully taking this as an attack on his pack and him. Second, it's the Fairbanks Pack, and there are no vampire holdings in Fairbanks, the state of Alaska, or most of northern Canada or Siberia, which means someone had to have traveled there to commit the attack."

They can't be connected...

"Alaska? This happened in *Alaska*?" Isaiah was talking before I could finish collecting my thoughts. Looking down the table, Maria appeared to be trying to solve a puzzle that left her stumped, but I really felt like there was another piece to this, and it came from Alexius.

"We don't have vampires in Alaska. None of our kind would tread into those areas. There's no strategic advantage," Maria said softly, drumming her fingers on the table.

"Alaska," I said softly, my mind turning over the possibility there was something else going on here. It lined up too well. "Alexius, do you remember the thing you got in the mail? A postcard, wasn't it?" I tried to keep my voice down, a whisper, not wanting to disturb the thoughts of anyone else trying to understand.

"The postcard from Fairbanks... I had the same thought," he agreed, standing as something close to confidence filled me. Everyone was looking at us, but it didn't bother me this time. I was too focused on this weird coincidence and Alexius' agreement. "I looked at it more closely after settling Isaiah and Corban in that night, but there was nothing special about it. Isaiah, can you get me back to my home quickly?" He was rubbing his jaw, not looking at anyone as he walked away from the table. Isaiah got up and grabbed the door, his confusion all too clear.

"What are you two going on about?" the Master of the Tribunal demanded as Isaiah grabbed the doorknob and pulled it open, revealing Alexius' office.

I need to know more about how that works.

"The night you arrived, I had received a postcard from Fairbanks." Alexius walked into his study, opened a drawer, and pulled out the postcard. When Isaiah closed the door again, Alexius continued to explain as he held up the mysterious postcard. "I was meaning to look into it further because it's such an odd thing for me to receive, but your unexpected visit and Everly's training took priority."

"Well..." Isaiah crossed his arms and looked back at the werewolves. "This makes things interesting."

Alexius continued back to the table, flipping the postcard around in his hands. He stopped but didn't sit down, staring at the card with an intensity that made me want to open his head and read his thoughts. Since I couldn't do that, I tried to do my job, keeping my eyes on him and blocking out everyone else. No one else was doing or saying anything, so I did.

"Can you still smell the blood?" I asked, pushing myself to stand. He didn't stop me from touching the postcard. Turning it to the right side, I pointed to the spot on the picture. It was old, making it dry and brown, useless to me as a vampire. The scent was strong enough scent for me to catch, though. It blended in with the mountain scene on the postcard, but I knew it was there.

"No, it's actually too faint to me." He lifted the postcard and inhaled deeply, nodding. "There it is. Too old to decipher anything, but it adds a layer of mystery."

"What if it's one of the humans who died?" I asked. "Could anyone tell if that was the case? The timing of this seems... too close not to be related, right?"

"To your first question, it couldn't be one of the deaths we're here to talk about tonight. The timeline doesn't match." Alexius shook his head, then stopped. I followed his gaze, and Corissa was staring at us, standing with her arms crossed. "But the werewolves could see if it matches anyone they know. As to your second question, I agree. This must be related. First, Corissa, do you think a werewolf could identify a person from a drop of old blood? You have the best sense of smell of the supernatural world, but this could be a challenge for anyone. I've never asked for something so small. I know werewolves prefer shirts or something more... personal and frequently used that would carry potent scents."

"We could," Corissa confirmed. "I can take it to the Fairbanks pack. It's not a large pack, only forty-seven members. It wouldn't take longer than a day for each of them to see if they knew the scent. However, you are correct about the challenge it would present. The postcard is potentially contaminated with the scent of dozens of people, which could be unreliable or make it exceptionally difficult for any werewolf to pinpoint exactly who the blood belonged to. I can't smell it from here. Callahan?"

"No," the male werewolf said, his eyes predatory as they looked at us.

"We can investigate both the postcard and the murders in Alaska at the same time. Alexius, I'm going to assign Javier to the case. I can pass it along to him—"

"No," Alexius said. I frowned at Alexius then directed it at Isaiah as he walked closer to us. From the look on Isaiah's face, he knew something I didn't, maybe something no one else in the room did.

"You haven't taken a case since Jacob died, especially not one involving other supernaturals," Isaiah whispered, leaning to say it in Alexius' ear. When Alexius didn't respond, Isaiah continued with more urgency. "You have a new vampire to train, and she *needs* your focus. Let Javier handle it, Alexius."

Alexius didn't reply as he held out the postcard to me. I took it, trying not to seem weird by snatching it too fast or too slow. He reached out and closed the laptop. Everything he did was slow and methodical. He fixed the blazer he was wearing even though nothing was wrong with it, then looked over the room, even studying me carefully.

"No," he repeated in the silence as everyone waited

once he looked at Isaiah. "Clearly, someone wants me to go to Fairbanks, Alaska. Corissa, Callahan, I would like the contact information of the Fairbanks Alpha. I'll begin my investigation when I land in Alaska—"

"Excuse me, but you don't decide if you take a case," Maria said, turning to us. "Let Javier take it. Isaiah is right. You haven't taken a case since Jacob died, and you have..." Maria eyed me, and I resisted the urge to step behind Alexius to block her view. "Miss Everly to train."

"Actually, I do. You can still send Javier, but there's nothing you or Isaiah can do to stop me." Alexius met her gaze until she narrowed her eyes. "I'm going because you can't take this postcard from me."

"Fine," Maria said with a sigh as she looked at the werewolves. "Alexius is on the case. I hope it suffices to say this will be resolved."

"I'll forward his information," Corissa said, smiling. "I am glad to see the best of the vampire hunters is back in action and willing to take on this situation. My condolences about Jacob. We had heard he died but had no idea where to send a card or flowers."

"Suicide. It was a tragedy, but the older we get," Maria said, her eyes distant.

"Of course," Callahan agreed solemnly.

"He was *murdered*," I corrected, pressing my lips together as anger hit me. He hadn't committed suicide. Someone has taken advantage of him and dragged him into the sun without any sort of defense, killing him and leaving nothing behind. I wasn't going to let anyone believe Jacob, of all people, would kill himself.

"And there's her misstep," Isaiah murmured.

"We'll step out and prepare our end of this investigation," Corissa said quickly. "If Alexius would like to get to Alaska quickly, the Alpha in Fairbanks will be notified that Alexius will arrive before the end of the evening. I'm certain the pack would like an investigation to begin soon. I know I certainly would."

"I can coordinate with you," Maria agreed. "Alexius?"

He was silent as Isaiah studied him. Isaiah shook his head and sighed in the silence.

"Everly and I will be ready in one hour," Alexius finally offered. "Thank you for expediting the travel. She's not ready for planes."

My jaw dropped as I looked at him.

I'm going? He's taking me to Alaska to help?

He didn't elaborate. He pointed at the closed door. Isaiah was still shaking his head as he opened it. Alexius didn't pass through, looking at me expectantly, waiting for me to mentally catch up. I went through the door first, with him right behind me.

13

CHAPTER THIRTEEN

I was still stunned silent as Isaiah spoke quickly with Maria, then came back into the study and closed the door. Alexius was fiddling with things at his desk while Isaiah cast me a long, hard look, then turned to glare at the ancient.

"Leave her with me," Moving to the desk, he leaned on it and stared down Alexius. "You could get someone hurt or killed if you take her, and you know it."

"I don't know that. In fact, now that she has gotten past her aggressive phase, I believe a small population while focusing on work might be the perfect exposure she needs with humans. She didn't even consider feeding on the werewolves because she was focused on the environment we were in and the situation unfolding. That's a good sign and not something I could have tested in any other situation without risking fragile individuals. She won't be far from me for the case. There won't be a time when I would willingly let her leave my sight."

"You come up with some damn good excuses," Isaiah

hissed. "Tell me the real reason you're willing to drag her all the way to Alaska without asking her if she wants to go."

"If I left her in your care, would you let her come back or stay here?" Alexius asked, his hands pausing on the papers he had been shuffling around. "Or would you whisk her away to your nest, claiming it would be easier, then lock the doors?"

Isaiah leaned back, putting his hands in his pockets. They stared at each other for a long moment as I got over my shock, which turned into annoyance.

I'm like a toy they're fighting over.

"Maybe," Isaiah answered. "Maybe not. Depends."

"Anyone going to ask me?" I demanded, spreading my arms in exasperation. Stepping closer, I tried to get their attention. I was an adult, and while I understood there were some things I couldn't control in my life right now, who I lived with was one of them I could.

Isaiah turned to me so fast, I had to take a step back.

"Now might not be the best time for you to speak," Isaiah warned, but he smiled, and it wasn't cruel or mean. "Young vampires. They just don't understand."

"Everly, would you like to stay here with Isaiah or come with me? You can also decide to live with Isaiah in his nest if you choose," Alexius asked as Isaiah was finishing what he was saying. He was patient while Isaiah was condescending.

"I'm going to Alaska because I work for you," I answered, crossing my arms. "When I was Turned, that was what I decided to do, and I'm going to do it. And no, I won't be living in New York in Isaiah's nest."

I also wanted to get the hell out of the basement, breathe fresh air, move, and see people. I was going to Alaska.

"Perfect. Pack a work bag, whatever you need to do your job as you feel might become necessary. I haven't had the chance to teach you what to pack for clothing in these situations, so I'll help you with that, and it will be your second bag. Isaiah, you can hover, as you so enjoy, but please stay out of the way," Alexius finished looking at Isaiah, who hissed softly.

Scooting toward the door to pack, I didn't want to draw their attention, but I also didn't want to miss any of the conversation.

"I rule the vampires, yet I have you to always remind me my position only goes so far. You're always on your own program, Alexius."

"Someone has to keep your ego from growing too large," Alexius retorted, but I saw a small smile forming. "And I wouldn't be nearly so effective at my role in our society if I let you put too many leashes on me. There's a reason I am more effective than any of Maria's people or the rest of yours."

"I *know*," Isaiah bemoaned. "Go get ready—"

"One more thing now that I've gotten you off the topic of Everly. We have an hour, which is plenty of time to prepare. Why didn't Maria know about Jacob's murder?"

I froze at the door.

"Ah, Everly's misstep. You shouldn't have corrected them, you know." He was talking to but not looking at me.

"He was, though," I said, wondering how I had

possibly messed up. "It disrespects his memory to let people believe—"

"He's dead. His memory doesn't have feelings to disrespect." Isaiah turned slowly, his eyes cold and calculating. I couldn't forget Isaiah's history with Jacob, but I also couldn't believe it because of the look in his eyes.

"I understand the werewolves. Why didn't Maria know?" Alexius asked again. "She could have helped with the investigation. She still can. I won't rest until I know who orchestrated Edwin into the position to kill him. I won't stop until they all burn in the sun."

"Because she's not our *friend*, Alexius," Isaiah snapped. "Because I spend my days constantly watching to make sure I don't misstep and give her a reason to send others after me. The same thing I do to her. We're allies for our people against the outside world, but we both would rather find someone we like more to sit in the other chair, preferably someone we could control. It's been like that since the Tribunal was founded eight hundred years ago."

I rarely saw it, but there was a flash of anger from Alexius. He curled a hand closed in a fist. Isaiah continued his spiel, though, ignoring or missing the change in Alexius.

"Do you really think I would tell her that my closest friend, my only acknowledged lover, and the most ... *revered* vampire on the planet was *murdered*? On our watch? Do you really think I would expose that weak flank? I don't *care* about the werewolves. What would they do with it? Nothing. But *Maria* knowing Jacob was

murdered makes *me* vulnerable. It makes *you* look weak."
He pointed at Alexius. "Alexius the Hunter, one of the
deadliest vampires of our entire society, couldn't keep his
son, the only member of his bloodline, *alive*. The son he
loved above everyone and everything. Sure, tell whoever
you like now that Maria knows, but I certainly wasn't
going to expose *that*. For either of us, Alexius. I wasn't
going to put us in that position. After two thousand years,
the last thing I would do is make you look vulnerable.
You have just as many enemies as I do, if not *more*."

"So, you'll ignore her usefulness because of your
desperate need to be in power. Isaiah, I expected
better—"

"I'll ignore her usefulness because I can figure out
who killed him without her, and I'm going to. If you think
you are the only person who doesn't taste blood over his
murder, you are sorely mistaken. I'm just smarter about
these things. I won't jeopardize everything in the process
because that could get hundreds of others killed. It would
get my *entire* bloodline killed. I'll have my cake, and I'll
eat it, too. And who knows, maybe Maria did it, but don't
you *ever* imply that I'm..." Isaiah hissed. "Go. Go to
Alaska. I can't fucking look at you anymore."

I jumped out of his way so he could storm out of the
office. He didn't slam the door, but he didn't need to.
There was no missing the dark, furious expression on his
face. I remained silent as Alexius walked around his desk
and stopped in front of me. He stared at the doorway, his
standard, unreadable expression keeping me from even
guessing at his thoughts.

"Let's get ready to leave... and thank you for standing

up for Jacob's memory." He turned those damnably dark eyes on me. "It was unnecessary, but I do appreciate it."

"It was... nothing," I mumbled. I had spoken out because I cared. I hadn't thought about how Alexius would feel about it. My heart beat steadily when it shouldn't as he shook his head.

"It was more than nothing."

I was the first to move, heading for my room, unable to handle the stare anymore, and was grateful when he went the opposite direction. Once in my room, I collected everything I could think of. I didn't have my old bag anymore, but I figured replicating it was a good place to start. There was no telling what I would or wouldn't need for something like this. As silence surrounded me, I was finally hit with nerves.

I'm going to Alaska to solve the murder of a human family. And Alexius... he'll probably want us to stay there until we kill the vampires who did it, right? I've never actually killed someone...

I made a stack of things—the new laptop I would have to set up quickly, a few blank USB drives if I needed to pass along files, a blank SSD in case I needed more space, and a small kit of tiny screwdrivers and flatheads to open electronics was always useful. Some devices couldn't be opened by tools someone could buy at a hardware store, but if I ran into any of those, they'd probably brick if I tried to take them apart.

I was pleased with my stack of things when Alexius walked in. He dropped a bag on the table for me. Saying nothing, I loaded it up. Once I was done, I looked up to see he had a full bag slung over his shoulder and another empty one in his hand.

"This is for clothing," he explained. "Only pack for three or four days, with some replacement items. If we need anything after that, we'll make do. We could use a laundry, buy new clothing, or begin a rotation of wearing older clothing. I pack light and expect the same from you. There's no telling what might come up, and being burdened by several suitcases isn't wise."

"Of course. Yeah, that's... that's fine." I had figured as much. He looked at my bedroom door, then back at me. Opening drawers as he went into my closet, I handled my underwear, grateful he didn't inspect it when I shoved it into the bag. He folded and packed four pairs of my darkest jeans. He had given me an obscene budget to buy clothing when I had first Turned. I had used some of it, most on jeans and t-shirts, since I wore those the most and had no access to any of my old clothing.

"Everything in your closet fits, correct?"

"Yeah, everything here will be fine."

"Good. Dark shirts, pack five or six. The outfit you have on now is perfectly acceptable to meet the Alpha in Fairbanks, so no need to change." I grabbed the shirts as he spoke. "As for shoes, I haven't considered needing to fit you for proper boots that would protect your feet if we have to walk or worse, hike. I should have prepared you for a case much sooner. Tennis shoes are the next best option."

I shoved the shirts into the bag and grabbed my only pair of tennis shoes, loading them in last. Without needing to be asked, I grabbed as many pairs of socks as I could and shoved them in while he watched, a small smile forming at my initiative.

"Now, you were loading your work bag. When we leave, we won't be coming back before we go to Alaska. Are you sure you have everything you need?"

"Is there anything you recommend?" He was the expert, not me. There wasn't anything else I could think of. So long as I could get into a device, by force or through a login, I could do most of my job. I'd never used any of my knowledge on someone else's things, either. I had complete control over the electronics in Portland. There was no way it would be the same in Alaska.

"I have some items set aside in my armory for you," he answered. He zipped my bag and took it with him as he walked out. I grabbed my work bag and followed. "I've never taken you into the armory before, have I?"

"I know where it is, but no, you never let me in before. I wouldn't have let a new person into the place I keep the weapons, either, so I wasn't really offended. In fact, I don't really need a weapon, so unless you need something, I'll be fine."

Maybe he could hear my nerves because he chuckled.

"I haven't trained you with anything else, so I'm only giving you a dagger, not only a weapon but a useful tool. Don't worry." He opened the armory as we arrived, his stride unbroken as it opened.

He keeps it unlocked?

Inside wasn't what I expected. In movies, these sorts of rooms were futuristic with lights showcasing the weapons and things that seemed... unnecessary now. They only seemed that way because Alexius had stripped down those images to the most basic and functional room. There was a counter built around the room, weapons hung on the wall, and there were three safes. Bottles and rags were kept in different places. In the center of the room, it looked like there was a kitchen island. On it, a gun had been disassembled and laid out. While I took in the room, Alexius went into the cabinets.

"I was cleaning that and got distracted," he said as I stared at it. He moved the pieces carefully and laid out several things for me. "The dagger should fit well for your hand. I usually use it as a throwing weapon, but it will work for whatever you may need, just..." He frowned. "Don't throw it."

"Okay..." I had no idea what I would use it for, but I sure as hell wouldn't throw a sharp object. He didn't have to worry about that. Thankfully, the dagger was in a sheath, and it looked so simple but was sharp. Until I had to contend with Oscar, I had never considered being in a violent position where I needed a weapon.

"Flashlight. I know we both see well in the dark, but it's useful to keep around. Start packing while I talk."

Placing my work bag on the table, the dagger went in first, then the flashlight.

"A lighter and back-up matches. If both fail, a fire-starting kit. Flint. A compass. Do you know how to use the compass?"

"In theory? The arrow points magnetic north, not true north, but close enough, I think? You use it to get your bearings and move in the direction you need?"

"Well, it's a start," he said, handing it to me.

The three options to start a fire, as well as the

compass, went in next. I almost wanted to talk about how GPS could work much better. Technology was getting really advanced, and most of the time, GPS worked anywhere. I hadn't thought to buy a handheld GPS unit for hikers, though. I'd never needed one. As I thought about getting a few handheld GPS for him, Alexius pushed forward a box of Nitrile gloves.

"Gloves, disposable. This is for handling anything we might want for fingerprints. We won't be able to run them ourselves, but the pack probably has contacts." He pointed to another pair of gloves in supple, flexible leather. "Also for fingerprints, but more appropriate to wear around humans."

"Of course. Can't be running around pretending to be crime scene investigators. People will think it's doctor role play," I mumbled, grabbing those for my bag. Another thought came to me as Alexius gave me a very confused look. "You keep a bag packed and ready to go, don't you?"

"Yes, and after this, you will as well," he answered, but it didn't wipe away his confusion. "What do you mean by doctor role play?" he asked.

I tried to swallow my tongue, only to remember I couldn't choke to death anymore. My face heated. It was worse than the embarrassment of the meeting, where I had kept from being a blushing idiot. Now I was hoping I would just drop dead again.

What is wrong with me?

"Um... it was... uh... a really bad joke."

"Yes, that I understood, but what was the joke?"

"Um..." Opening and closing my mouth, I tried to find a clinical way of explaining, but it was impossible.

Staring at Alexius, how could I explain this to one of the most attractive men I had ever met? One I already had a very strange sexual encounter with. "Role play means pretending to be something you're not to fulfill a fantasy... and some people pretend to be doctors."

"Sounds dangerous. What if someone needs real medical care?"

"It's not used for that intention. It's... something people do in the bedroom if they have a fantasy about... sleeping with a doctor... or some people have like... a nurse fantasy. Where they sleep together... during an examination... and stuff."

I didn't think I could do it, but I had stunned Alexius. His eyes went wide, he stopped breathing, and his body froze. The overall effect made it appear my robotic vampire boss was out of commission after short-circuiting.

As soon as it began, it ended. He broke out in a wide smile and laughed. It was deep, moving his shoulders. As he walked away, his laughter followed him, and I was the one standing there like a robot who couldn't process anything. By the time he came back, he was more collected. He threw things into my bag and closed it, still chuckling as he walked out of the room.

"Let's go. I forgot we need winter gear because it's January in Alaska... Humans. I bet Isaiah does that nonsense." His chuckling turned into deep laughter again.

14

CHAPTER FOURTEEN

"Do you have enough layers?" Alexius asked when I met him back at his study. "I see you brought the spare coat. Good. I checked, and it will be below freezing tonight in Fairbanks and in the negatives at night. We'll be sleeping during the day, and it won't go above freezing for the rest of the month. It will be cold, even for us."

"Do we get frostbite?"

"We can, but we can heal very quickly."

"Then I'll be fine," I promised, thanking my lucky stars I had thought to buy winter clothing. My entire life in Maine, I had needed it, so it had been second nature to replace it. "What are we waiting on?" Laying my spare coat over my bags, I tried to stretch in the jacket, but it was new and stiff. I'd had no reason to wear it since I'd purchased it. I was so much stronger as a vampire, but that didn't lessen the sensation of the stiffness, only making it easier to deal with.

"You look uncomfortable. Something wrong?"

"The jacket is just new, and they're stiff when they're

new," I explained, shrugging. "I had a really nice, worn-in coat... I never got back."

"I see. Your things were packed up by Isaiah and his nest when I brought you here. We had to make sure everything relating to vampires was destroyed."

"I know. I just haven't got any of it back yet, so I'm in a new coat. It's fine." I knew the reason I didn't have any of my own things, which didn't bother me, at least most of the time. Remaking my computers had been something I just had to accept, and it was fun to build computers.

He nodded slowly.

"Have you told Rupert we're leaving?" I asked, trying to fill the silence.

"I have. I told him about the meeting before we went, and while I was getting bags for you, I told him we were going on a case. He'll support us from here if we need anything. That reminds me... he wanted me to tell you to be safe and to listen to me."

"I don't need the reminder, but tell him thank you."

"Tell him yourself. You know how to get ahold of him," Alexius countered.

I did know, but I never used it. It felt too odd being the girl in the basement talking to the people who lived on the upper floors of the bunker-like mansion. It wasn't as if I could ask them to bring me anything or just give me company. And it was the intercom system, meaning Alexius would hear everything. I hadn't asked Rupert for his email. Who wants to email the person who lived in the same house? Last, cellphones barely worked in the basement, so there was no texting or calling even though I had his number.

Cellphones. Shit.

"Do you have your cellphone?" I asked. "In case we get separated?"

"I have the new one you got me," he said, pulling it from his pocket. "Though I'm still carrying my old one as well. Just in case. You were right about these new ones being easier to break."

"Oh, good. I have mine, too." I nodded. "I know you don't plan on letting me do anything by myself, but better safe than sorry, right?"

"I'll also need to call Rupert if we need him or Isaiah," he reminded me. "We're not disappearing like I had to when I went to Portland. This will be watched by many who will want regular updates."

Well... now I feel a bit stupid.

"Good point."

I waited in silence for whatever we were supposed to do next. Alexius put his phone away and surprised me by playing with my coat, zipping it all the way up, and pulling the collar closer to my neck. I stepped back, wondering what had gotten into him. His hands hung frozen in the air as I fixed the zipper and pushed my collar back into a comfortable place. I didn't need to be so bundled.

"I'll be fine," I repeated. "I'm used to the cold."

"Stop being weird, Alexius," Isaiah said as he walked in.

I looked over my shoulder to see him as he stared at his phone. He closed us into the study, not looking at either of us, his phone apparently the most riveting thing he had ever seen. A moment later, only a soft hiss of pain telling me what was happening, Isaiah opened the door to his office.

"Come on. Corissa and Maria should have another door ready for you," Isaiah ordered, walking into the weird Tribunal place. We followed after Alexius gave one more look at the bags we had. I counted, and I felt certain I had whatever I needed.

The nerves hit me again as Isaiah led us out of his office and down a long hall. Maria met us at the door and led us to Corissa and someone else waiting. I heard the loud beating heart of the stranger and Corissa, but this stranger didn't set me on edge the way the werewolves had. Corissa still had that feral air, the wildness of her entire being.

"The door will lead you to the home of Kavik, the Alpha of the pack. He's expecting you." Corissa nodded at the person beside her.

I tried to figure out who, or rather *what*, the person was as they reached for the door. It swung open to reveal a man on the other side.

"Welcome to Alaska," the man called. "Well, once you come through."

Alexius nodded to our rulers, then at Corissa and the person holding the door. He grabbed my elbow and forced me to walk. When I was a foot from the mysterious person, my fangs dropped in my mouth, and I instinctively took a deep inhale. Whoever and whatever he was, he smelled *good*.

Alexius' hand grew a little tighter, and my feet kept moving. He made me walk through the door.

"The Tribunal has a handful of witches and sidhe in

their employ who can open a door anywhere in the world but only with the permission of the Tribunal," Alexius explained as the door closed. "I believe it takes permission from at least two of them, and they must be separate species. That was a sidhe. I was expecting a witch. Forgive me. I would have warned you while we waited if I had known only one of them was available."

"I wouldn't have." I knew what a sidhe was, thanks to Isaiah's political lessons, but he hadn't told me about the damnably good way they smelled. The fae were actually more diverse than just a single name. It was a catch-all term for anything that came from their world. The sidhe were the most prevalent and looked mostly human. They were also the ruling species of the fae.

"Your eyes are red, and your fangs are down. Sidhe are exceptionally tempting for our kind. You didn't lunge, so no one will take offense."

He didn't release my elbow. My mouth was still watering at the smell I could remember so clearly as if it was still in my nose. I resisted the urge to reach out and open the door to see if he would be there.

Someone cleared their throat. Looking up, I saw the man who had welcomed us to Alaska.

"Alpha Kavik," he greeted. "When they told me I was going to get the best of the vampire hunters, I was excited. Then they explained he was bringing a young vampire who might have... some control issues. Now I understand. It's not too late to send her back. While I couldn't argue with Corissa or Callahan, I'm not sure I'm comfortable with a young vampire after recent events."

"She will be fine. She works for me, and her presence

is not up for negotiation," Alexius said. He extended his free hand and shook with the Alpha. "How far away is the family's home? I'm wondering if we could go tonight."

"It's a three-hour trip in the dead of winter. We could certainly make it work, but the timing would be difficult. We're in the dark part of the year, but we still have sunrise and sunset, around ten-thirty in the morning and three-thirty in the afternoon. Plus, my pack and I would need to prepare for winter travel, which takes time. I can round them up, but it would cut into how long we'd be out there. You might end up trapped at the house for the day."

"Then we'll save it for tomorrow evening to give your pack time to prepare. You knew the victims, correct?"

"I did. My granddaughter married into the family and later had my great-granddaughter."

Oh, no. That must have been horrible to find.

Hearing that was enough to knock the memory of the sidhe's scent out of my nose.

"My condolences. Is there anywhere you would recommend we start? Have you done anything to the scene?" Alexius let go of my elbow and folded his hands in front of him.

"We had to remove the bodies, and they're being held at the morgue. They're secure. They've been cleaned of blood, but we haven't started the embalming process. You can look over them. As for the rest... we didn't clean up anything. I wanted a professional to see it and try to find anything my pack and I may have missed. Corissa and Callahan promised they would get a vampire trained to handle these situations."

"They did," Alexius said. "What lodging is available?"

"There are hotels. We're in Alaska, but it's civilization," the Alpha answered, then growled softly, frustrated. "You must want to put your things down. I'm sorry. Pick any one you like. I'll give you a ride and help you get checked in. My inner circle is technically off tonight. I wanted to meet you both alone."

"Dangerous," Alexius commented as Kavik started walking.

We followed, me still absorbing every word of the conversation. Alexius wasn't threatened by anyone, and I realized just how impressive that was now that I had seen the type of people he was around regularly. Even more important, this was all relevant to the reason we were here. I needed to know all of it.

"Isn't the inner circle supposed to meet foreigners with the Alpha to act as both the guard and the attack force?"

"Yes, but I didn't think I would get trouble from whoever Corissa and Callahan sent here. They know you're here, so if you act, well... everyone will know who killed me tonight." Kavik was walking fast. I didn't struggle to keep up, but I had to move pretty fast. When I was a human, I would have stumbled trying to walk as quickly as he could. We went down a hall and turned into a living room or den. Five werewolves were sitting on the couches there, two pretending to read books, one watching something on his phone. Two others glared at us, one baring his teeth with a snarl when I made eye contact with him.

"None of you will be safe if you threaten her," Alexius

whispered. It sent shivers down my spine, a dark warning that made me scared to look in his direction or move. Kavik stopped walking with a snarl, but not at Alexius or me. The wolf who bared his teeth dropped his head, and Kavik kept walking as though nothing had happened. A large hand touched my lower back and convinced me to move again.

We went into a garage, and Kavik grabbed keys from the wall.

"Everly, pick a hotel for us. Book one room for the next week. We'll extend the reservation if we have to."

That got no reaction from the Alpha, and I got in the SUV he unlocked. Alexius sat in the back beside me.

"While we drive, can you tell me what you know about the days leading up to the attack?" Alexius leaned back and stretched out, his arm going over the back of the seat and over me as well. I hurriedly searched local hotels and tried to find one I thought Alexius might like. Kavik opened the garage door and turned on the engine but didn't start driving.

"We were in regular contact with them. I would exchange emails with my girls every few days, and we had just finalized the plans for some trading three days before heading out that way. They had some furs we were hoping to get our hands on, mostly for my wife, while we have... everything they could need. Normally, our trades were purposefully weighted to help them more than us. We could afford it." The Alpha sighed. "So, really, we were just preparing for the trip. I sent her an email saying we were on our way when we rolled out. I wasn't expecting a response, so I thought nothing of it when I didn't get one. What we found when we arrived..."

"I know it's quite cold here, which could change your idea, but how long do you think they had been dead? You had been in contact with them only three days beforehand, so that gives us a range to work with, but your keen nose could prove invaluable."

"I was..." Kavik shook his head. "You'll have to ask my second when I introduce you. I didn't stay long, and he's the one who moved the bodies and looked over the house. I'm sorry. I must appear weak for not investigating an attack on my pack myself."

"Of course not," I said, looking up from my phone as his words hit me *hard*. There was a sorrowful pain, a sense of failure, which I knew all too well. "You lost family. It's only right that people around you should be there to help you find a moment to... grieve. It had to have been hard. It came out of nowhere and..."

"You talk like you know the feeling," Kavik said, suddenly putting us in reverse, hitting the gas hard enough to make me rock.

"I do," I answered.

"Sure," Kavik said, his disbelief clear.

"Did you pick a hotel?" Alexius asked, ignoring the Alpha. He leaned in and looked at my phone. "That's a good choice."

"I need your card," I said, holding out a hand. He pulled out his wallet without a word and handed it to me. I opened it to find a dozen credit cards. "Which one?"

"Doesn't matter."

I grabbed the one in the front, assuming it was the

one he used the most. The name on it was Alexander Jefferson.

"Oh, not that one," Alexius said quickly, taking it from me and putting it back. He grabbed another, read it quickly, then let me have it. This one read Alex Smith.

"Okay, then..." I shook my head as I punched in the numbers. While I did that, Alexius told Kavik the hotel where we'd be staying.

"Will they allow us to check in tonight?"

"Every hotel in the city knows who I am. They'll check you in tonight," Kavik answered.

He drove fast even though there was some deep snow. I grabbed my seatbelt, wondering if we were going to slide off the road. Alexius gently touched my shoulder.

"If we get into an accident, he is more likely to die than we are," he whispered. "He's also probably been on these roads in these winters for a long time. It's okay."

"She worried about my driving? It's fine. I know these roads, and we have gotten little snow this year. Record lows."

"Yeah, I just... drive more cautiously," I explained.

"She hasn't had the reminder that her status as a vampire makes her sturdier than she was as a human," Alexius added. "Humans, clearly, must be careful. They're fragile."

"Ah... yeah, that's always a shocker for everyone. New werewolves are the same. Run them over with a snowmobile once because they couldn't be bothered to pay attention, and they figure it out pretty quick."

I swallowed.

"As we settle in, could your second meet us at the

morgue? Seeing the bodies tonight will be good. It could give me a clear indication of how many vampires were part of this attack."

"Sure. While you get stuff handled, I'll call him. He's on standby."

"One of your werewolves in your home?"

"The one playing on his phone," Kavik answered, nodding. "They're all too loyal to stay away from the house when I'm meeting visitors."

"You just had a vampire attack, and vampires were coming. They were smart," Alexius said. "Not that they could have helped you if I was your enemy."

15

CHAPTER FIFTEEN

A *lexius...*
I didn't know what to say and didn't think Alpha Kavik knew what to say either. We settled into a heavy silence and eventually reached the hotel. Kavik parked as close to the door as he could get without hitting the building. Alexius motioned for me to stay as the werewolf got out. They went inside together as I watched them from the window. There was no one around once they went inside, the night eerie and bright, thanks to the snow. I could have stared at it for hours. My eyes could see it as clearly as I had once during the day, but that only accentuated the eerie effect. Maybe it was the glow of the moon that seemed as bright as the sun, but it was all washed in a blue glow.

I waited until Alexius came back to unbuckle my seatbelt.

"There are humans in the building. You'll stay at my side and leave them be, okay?" He opened the door and let me slide out. The first thing I did was take a deep breath of the air—outside air—a pleasure I had missed. I stared at the sky for a long time.

"Everly."

"Of course. I'll stay with you. I'm not going to run off. No humans."

"Good."

I followed him in, one bag over my shoulder and carrying the other. He walked quickly, but I caught him looking back at me as we approached the building. It was bitterly cold, but it didn't feel below zero. Hearing a door open and close, I looked back to see Kavik following us.

"Better not breathe. They'll think you're stiff if they see you, but it'll keep their scent from you."

"It won't be as bad as it was with the sidhe, right?" I didn't want to hurt anyone. I couldn't bear the thought, but when I remembered that smell...

"Don't breathe," he ordered. "And keep your eyes down. We can't have people seeing they're red. They were green on the drive, but—" he looked down at me "—they're red now. Don't think about the sidhe."

I closed them for a moment, sighing heavily, then took one more breath of the crisp night air, its chill filling my lungs. I didn't want to go inside—I wanted to stare at the stars, feel the wind on my cheeks, and the cold bite of winter—but I knew better than to ask. Following him inside, we walked through the lobby, past Kavik talking to the man at the front desk. I didn't listen, intent on following Alexius. I had booked us a room on the first floor, thinking it would be the easiest to light secure.

"Good job," he said, nodding my way as he threw his bags on the bed. "Let's get this out of the way." He opened one of his bags and pulled out a bag. "I only brought a handful of these, and they'll have to be used quickly because there's no proper refrigeration here. Eventually, I'll need to let you feed on a human but will make sure you don't drain them. Use your fangs, try to feed cleanly."

In the madhouse the night was turning out to be, I hadn't even thought about my feeding. I had thought about eating the sidhe, but not about how I was going to feed regularly without killing someone. Taking the blood bag, I sank my fangs in while Alexius did something else. I didn't focus on him, but I could hear him rustling about while I drained the bag.

"It was nearly midnight in Savannah," he mumbled to himself. "Four-hour time difference... it's only eight. That gives us plenty of time to look over the bodies, ask about the victims, and possibly begin researching the local area for anything out of the ordinary."

While he talked to himself about our plans, I thought about what I was really doing in Alaska. Less than an hour ago, I had been under lock and key in Savannah, told I was too dangerous for humans, too dangerous to leave the basement. Now, I was in a hotel room, feeding from a bag, and later expected to feed from humans. Under his watchful eye, sure, but it was still a living human at risk. Isaiah said it was stupid, and it felt like a wild one-eighty to me. I wasn't going to turn down the chance to leave the house, but I had expected the same sort of feeding schedule.

Though that doesn't make sense anymore. Of course, he can't carry an unlimited supply of blood around for me.

Worse, I realized how much I really didn't know what

I was doing. It was a sinking reality that I wasn't like Alexius. I didn't threaten werewolf Alphas without blinking an eye, and I certainly wasn't unconcerned about the vampires we had to find, something Alexius seemed rather clinical about.

I finished the bag and felt that awful pressure of having eaten way too much. I had fed right before the meeting, only two hours ago based on Alexius' telling of the time.

"I mean, if it's only eight... we could have gone to the house, right? Three-hour drive there and back is six hours." I tried to do the mental math. It seemed like a lot of time. We would have been there at two a.m., and we would have needed to get back by nine for safety. That gave us seven entire hours. Licking my lips, I grew more confident in my assessment, but he still had his back to me. Everything smelled like blood to me, as if it saturated the room, but I knew it was only because I held the nearly dry bag.

"Better to let the werewolves prepare for the trip than rush them. Night travel in this environment is asking for trouble if one isn't prepared. Even if we can survive a car accident, that doesn't mean we should risk one. Kavik driving around the city is much safer than driving out of civilization where an accident could put us at risk for the vampires who might still be around."

"Do you think they are? Do you think they would have stuck around after what they did?"

"Depends. Better to be safe, considering neither of us knows the region." He turned around, his eyes coming to my face. His nostrils flared as he reached into his coat and pulled out a handkerchief as he walked toward me. "Here."

I wiped my face, but I must not have done it well enough. He took it back and ran it over my chin, his touch fleeting.

"Practice will help," he murmured before backing away from me.

"You haven't let me feed like that before," I reminded him. "Hard to practice when I never have the chance."

"Feeding like that calls on your instincts; it's the natural way. You'll do it more while we're here, out of necessity. I'll let you decide how you want to feed at home."

"Why the sudden trust in me?" I asked boldly.

"I've trusted you since I met you," he countered. I stared at him until he sighed. "I'm not a fool. I could see you weren't happy with the current living situation, and this is a good break from it."

I was surprised enough by that answer that my mouth opened. He continued, refusing to break our stare.

"You've quickly improved your control, even if it hasn't been as fast as I had guessed. Clearly, there are boundaries, but we must expand them, or you'll never develop the control you need for everyday life. We would have had to do this in the next few months, or Isaiah would have accused me of keeping you as a hostage. I'd rather it be with strangers than with Rupert or Shania." I knew of Shania, but I hadn't spoken to her yet. She was the housekeeper.

"You wanted to work for me when you Turned. I need an assistant and someone who has different skills from mine. When I offered you the job, I didn't intend to bring you on cases, but as a vampire, you can survive much more than you once could. Then there's Isaiah deciding he would watch over you." Alexius shook his head. "I knew he would."

"Would he really have kept me against my will?" I asked, crossing my arms.

"Possibly, but he would have had to convince more than just you and me he was allowed to and that it was in your best interest. Vampires have autonomy when they aren't in a nest. You are a free person, Everly. If you wanted, you could demand to leave my residence, and I would let you. The restrictions only work because you want them, even if they don't make you happy with your life."

"I don't want to hurt anyone." It seemed simple to me. "You wouldn't really let me leave if you thought I was going to kill the first human I saw."

"You wouldn't just walk out the front door at that moment, no. You and I would have a long discussion about the life you wanted, and I would reach out to contacts to make it happen for you in a safe way." Alexius sat down on the edge of the bed. "I brought you on this case for all of those reasons. I feel a sense of responsibility for you. I made you a vampire, an impulse I don't regret, but it has made me responsible for your happiness, safety, training, and education. You know that."

"I do. I guess this just happened really fast. We both know I'm not ready to hunt and kill vampires."

"I never expect you to be ready to kill vampires. Not

the way I do," he said with a small smile. "You don't seem to have that inclination."

"I would if I had to," I countered. "Sure, that's not my part of this dynamic, but... I've done none of this. I didn't even know what to pack. I grabbed a lot of stuff because I didn't know what I'd end up doing here. I bet you don't even know what I'm doing here. I barely had the chance to think about what I could do and don't know what your plan is for situations like this."

"I don't know *how* you can be useful, not with any level of specificity. I do know you *will* be. Help in any way you can think." Alexius stood and fixed his coat. "Speak up when you have an idea or an opinion. There's no wrong direction to take this early in an investigation. As for my plan, when it comes to these situations, we're trying to find all the pieces we can to recreate the scene. Under the current circumstances, you and I will attempt to discover the timeline leading to the murders, know all the people involved, human and vampire alike, then deduce the reasoning behind why these people, why now, and what will come next. Whatever you might think of to help us speed up that process is useful."

I nodded, thinking for a moment.

"Then I'm going to need all the electronics the victims owned," I said, formulating my plan of how I could help. "Cellphones, laptops, other computers or digital devices. If they could use the internet or make a call from it, I need it. There might be a connection, there might not, but it's good to check."

"We'll tell Alpha Kavik when it feels right. It might not be good to make that demand before we show him we can help, but possibly after seeing the bodies. He might have them collected tonight or have them ready for you when we return from the crime scene tomorrow." Alexius walked to the door and leaned on it. "Are you ready to see the bodies? He'll be waiting on us."

"Is there any way we could go around him for their devices?" I asked. "I mean... movies and television shows always point out this really easy way to keep information from people by destroying or wiping the devices. Even I've done it to keep a few vampires safe when Edwin was looking for people who were helping Lauren go against him. Maybe thinking he might do that is paranoid of me, but it's a risk."

"Paranoid?" Alexius shook his head. "No, not at all. Insightful. If there's sensitive pack information, he will make sure it never enters your hands. It's something I've dealt with for centuries. Diaries, personal letters, records. Everyone wants to keep their secrets. Regretfully, the politicians wouldn't appreciate if we went around the Alpha, so not this time. You'll have to make do with what he's willing to give us."

"Do you care about the politicians?" I crossed my arms as I closed the distance between us. I gave him a surprised look, though it was a little mocking because I had seen his behavior with the 'politicians.' "Because it didn't seem like you did."

"No, not much, but I forced their hands to come here, and I try not to create enemies among the other supernatural species." He put his hands in his pockets as I stared him down. "I have too many of those among our kind. I don't need any more."

"That makes sense, and uh..." I considered dragging my feet, searching for another conversation we could have but realized I just needed to get this next part over with. I went to grab my work backpack, threw it over my shoulder, and met him back at the door.

"Let's go. I don't think I'll need anything else."

He was out the door faster than any normal human. Catching up, I walked by his side and leaned in.

"How do you move so fast?" I asked softly, unable to resist. It was crazy, faster than other vampires, and I knew we could be faster than humans. He became a blur, and I didn't understand how.

"Practice," he answered. "You can, too. We'll work on it when we're done here. Or you can practice on your own. Maybe you can work it out."

"That's not helpful."

"We're in public," he reminded me.

We found Kavik at the front door, leaning on the wall, hands in his pockets. The human who had been at the front desk was gone, which made me wonder if Kavik had sent him away.

"Took you two long enough," Kavik said. "My second, Janek, will meet us there. They'll open the door for him or me, then leave. We'll call them to lock back up before we go. That should keep any unfortunate incidents from happening."

"Thank you," Alexius said, never missing a step when I stumbled, not sure if we were going to stop and talk to the Alpha for a moment. Alexius walked straight outside, me trailing behind him and Kavik bringing up the rear.

CHAPTER SIXTEEN

W hen we arrived at the morgue, I tried to push aside my nerves. I had seen dead bodies before —I had seen *these* dead bodies before—but seeing pictures and videos of the dead was a different experience than seeing the real body. I had only seen two dead bodies, their life gone. I had watched one die right in front of my eyes. The other I had been completely unprepared for.

Kavik didn't say anything as he got out and went inside. I unbuckled my seatbelt, but Alexius didn't move, so I didn't.

"Your heart is racing," he murmured in the darkness.

That didn't surprise me. I had just fed and could feel it. It was my heart. I didn't need it pointed out to me.

"Videos are easy," I said, hoping he understood. "Pictures are easier." I shrugged. "I'll be fine, though."

"You will be. I didn't want to rush you inside without checking how you're feeling. Kavik could smell your emotions, so he probably has a clearer idea of what you're thinking right now than I do. I need to know. I'm not trying to pry, but I don't want to be unsafe. If you aren't ready, this isn't a good idea."

"I don't know what to tell to you. I'm nervous about seeing dead bodies laid out on metal tables. A lot makes me nervous. Speaking up in front of groups of people, for example, or meeting new people. Even asking questions makes me nervous most of the time. I get nervous. Sometimes, I get so nervous, my heart races without blood. We're here. If I thought I couldn't do it, I would have said something."

"If it's *only* nerves."

"It's only nerves. Let's go so I can get past them," I said, wanting to get out of the car.

"There will be some new smells. The cleaning supplies and the bodies will all have scents you won't like; no vampire does. Let me know if you need air," he continued, but I saw him reaching for the door.

"Got it."

He got out first, and I waited until he was on my side of the SUV before I opened my door. He waited for me to get out, and we walked in together. Not taking much time to look at our surroundings or the building itself, I stared at the entrance, trying to mentally prepare myself.

It'll get easier. I signed up to help him with these cases, to stop out-of-control vampires or evil ones from killing people. This is the job, and I wanted it.

We found Kavik in the hall, and he remained silent as we went past the front desk through some official-looking doors, down a hall to a metal door. It swung open and revealed another werewolf. Like all the others tonight, he had a feral energy. He looked at Alexius first, clearly sizing him up, then looked at me.

"I got the first three out for you," the werewolf said before pushing the door open farther and moving. Kavik grabbed the door and growled.

"Introduce yourself," he ordered. The other werewolf came back and glared at us.

"Janek, second of the Fairbanks Pack. I'll say it now. I can't believe the Tribunal sent bloodsuckers to deal with bloodsuckers. I don't like you being here. I came up to Fairbanks to get away from the other supernaturals. Can't trust a single one of you. For all I know, you had something to do with this, and you're a threat to the pack. I'll be watching you, do you understand?"

"I understand..." Alexius took a step closer. "Understand this... if vampires wanted to destroy your pack, they wouldn't get *me* to do it. I have no reason to waste my time on an insignificant pack in a part of the world I don't care about. But *if* I wanted to destroy your pack, I wouldn't need to attack your humans. I wouldn't need to sneak around. I would just do it."

Janek's eyes turned from a dark brown to an unreal green as he snarled. Kavik sighed heavily as if he had seen this before or expected it. Alexius never moved or said anything.

"We're here to help," I said quickly. "We were told about what happened, and this is what Alexius does. He's... uh, like the vampire version of a cop. He tracks down these types and makes them stop. It's how I met him." I reached out for the back of Alexius' coat, hoping I could make him step back, but it didn't appear he or

Janek even heard me. Grabbing on, I lightly tugged. "Alexius, he's just trying to protect his people. There's no reason we need to throw around threats. We're all on the same team right now."

Alexius, much to my surprise, stepped back.

"She's right, of course," he said, putting his hands in his pockets. "We need to move along. If you want to know why this happened to your people, we need to see the bodies."

Janek looked at his Alpha. Kavik didn't move, didn't break the stare, zero reaction from him as the tense moment continued for nearly a minute. Janek was the one who broke their eye contact.

"My girls are *dead,* and your attitude is going to interfere with their ability to help when they might be the only ones who can," Kavik said softly, leaning toward the other werewolf. "You're lucky the little redhead got him to stand down because I'm in the mood to let him tear your balls off."

I couldn't stop my jaw from dropping.

"I'm sorry, sir," Janek said softly, and like that, the entire mood shifted. Janek moved from the doorway, and Kavik held the door open for us.

I could smell something off about the room as we walked in. It wasn't the cleaning supplies Alexius had mentioned, which I could recognize. Things like bleach were always a strong smell, and that wasn't any different now. There was something else, though, and he had been right. I didn't like it.

But it's not that bad. I can ignore it.

I studied the room, having only seen similar ones in

movies or crime shows. Three tables were in the center of the room, and each of them held a covered body. On one wall, a long set of metal cabinets with a countertop that had two incredibly oversized sinks on each end. There were things in the room I couldn't name, much less their purpose. On the back wall was a set of metal drawers going to the ceiling, and I recognized what they were— the drawers where bodies were kept.

Alexius went to the first table as Janek grabbed something from the counter. I followed Alexius tentatively while the werewolf met him at the table. Staying a few feet back, I couldn't miss that Kavik was hovering only a few steps from me.

"These are the reports about these three bodies. We haven't permitted a full autopsy on any of the bodies, but they got preliminary examinations, recording noticeable injuries and trauma."

"Thank you." Alexius took them, then pulled down the first sheet.

The strange, now offensive smell grew worse, and I couldn't resist an annoyed hiss as it assaulted my nose and made me turn away.

"That's the smell of the dead," Alexius said, clearly telling me.

I gagged. I couldn't even begin to describe it, but I knew it was awful, even if I had nothing to compare it to. Everything in my body wanted to get away from it.

"She going to be okay?" Kavik asked loudly.

"When she remembers that she doesn't need to breathe," Alexius answered, and I wondered if he was laughing at me.

I stopped breathing, and the relief was nearly instantaneous.

"You sure?" Kavik took a step closer to me and seemed genuinely concerned.

"Yeah," I answered, trying to use as little air as possible.

He stared at me as if he was about to pat my back or worse, rush to get a bag for me to puke in. To show him I was okay, I walked away, stopping at the side of the table beside Alexius. I glared up at him, knowing he could have told me more in the SUV but figured he didn't need to.

"You didn't warn me it would be that bad." It was a little more of my air, but it needed to be said.

"I've never gagged, so I didn't think your reaction would be so strong. My apologies."

"I'll be ready for it next time."

"Let's get to work," he said, holding out a pair of gloves that seemed to come out of nowhere. I put them on and watched him put on a set as well. "Male, fifty-two. Clearly physically fit. Calloused hands tell me he used them. Some of the scars make me think he was a mechanic."

I looked down at the body.

Like a switch had been flipped, I was in work mode.

The body. It. Detached.

Just like it had been in the nest.

"He lived on a homestead, right? He would have worked on the machinery they owned," I said, looking at the hand close to me.

"Yup. He did all the repairs on their tractor and other

farming equipment. He could fix anything. He was married to my granddaughter, Caro—"

"No names," I said quickly, looking back at Kavik. "Just for now, no names."

Kavik nodded as though he understood. Turning back to the body, I wondered if I should have felt proud about being right. Instead, I kept looking for something that told me more about the victim, something I had never done before. Alexius had completely uncovered the body, the sheet on the floor, so I made a pointed effort to keep my eyes in places that wouldn't embarrass me. While I looked, I didn't touch. Alexius, on the other hand, pulled the jaw open.

"Healthy teeth, none missing," he said softly.

"Does that matter?" Janek asked, tenser than Kavik.

"Not all humans are..." Alexius closed his mouth and straightened. "A healthy human is healthier to feed on. A human who is chronically ill with something like cancer could make a vampire sick for a few days, even a week, if the human is on heavy medication. Drugs can be passed to us through the blood as well."

I had heard that speech before. I finally reached out and touched the body, turning the head to the side. One thing I noticed was the weird way the head moved, with no resistance at all.

I found a bite.

"Alexius."

"His neck was broken," Alexius said, turning back to me and the body. From his angle, I knew he couldn't see the bite. It was positioned far back on the neck, which didn't seem like a natural place for a vampire to bite. I had never seen someone aim there in all the killings I had been forced to watch and erase.

"Yeah, and I bet I know how," I said, mimicking how another vampire would hold the man's jaw, then tilted the head further to expose the location the vampire had decided to feed from. I knew the hold, had seen it in action and been held in it. Now that I was a vampire, I saw the practicality, how it gave control over a person, kept their mouth shut with enough force, and showed the best place to feed from.

It made my stomach turn to think about how I was now the same as the murderer of this family and understood on some instinctual level.

Alexius nodded, touching the bite wound. He said nothing as he looked at the report in his other hand.

"He only had one bite wound, that one," he finally explained, stepping back from the body. "There are a couple theories. There's a chance the vampire stopped feeding and killed him, satisfied. No reason to break the neck, though. The man would have died from blood loss—"

"He died from the broken neck," Janek said quickly. "He was bled out the least of the victims. That's why I brought him out first. He was the only one who didn't die of blood loss."

"Good call," Alexius praised the werewolf. "It's always the one who is different that tells us the most about the story. The other theory, which is now more likely, is that this vampire was trying to feed and could have accidentally killed him by doing exactly what you're showing, Everly. The blood would have told the vampire they had spoiled their own meal. We can't feed from the dead, which is why they give off such an offensive smell. That's why we try to keep preserved blood under proper conditions, exactly as a hospital would store it."

"Is that common?" Seemed like a terrible lack of control that couldn't be common. I had never met a vampire who was that out of control. Even Oscar hadn't done that to me, and he was the only one I could see capable of that. He even had the opportunity.

"No." Alexius frowned and looked at me. "On the other hand, an exceptionally young vampire…"

I looked at the man, then at my hands.

"Someone with no practice or control would find it really easy to make this mistake, wouldn't they?"

"Yes," Alexius answered. "Let's move on to the next body. It's only a theory."

CHAPTER SEVENTEEN

A s we slowly made our way down the line, it grew easier. Alexius was respectful of the dead. He didn't comment about random things that didn't help or make judgments about who they were except for possible occupations, or in one case, a possible illness. The grandmother of the family had been diabetic. He explained to me and the werewolves why little things were important. He noted the relative health of the different victims. He was clinical and professional. Everything he did was methodical and slow as he went over every inch of the bodies, always respectful of them and those watching us.

I didn't think I could respect Alexius more.

"This victim was torn in multiple locations," he said, pointing out the three bites I could also see. The one closest to me was a vicious bite on the thigh, not the neat puncture wounds most associated with a vampire bite. This vampire hadn't just gotten to the femoral artery;

they had torn it out. There would have been no way to save this human once it happened.

Looking up, I saw the bite on the arm, which wasn't as bad, probably thanks to its location. The last was the neck.

"It looks like animals did this," I said, catching the anger in my words. I was angry; I just hadn't expected it to leak out. "This victim and all the others except the first."

"This is what happens when a new vampire isn't given time to control their initial urges," Alexius said, sighing. "This is what happens when instinct is the only thing that rules, and someone isn't eased into controlling the bloodlust."

"So you've seen this before," Kavik said, stepping closer. For the first time since we began, he touched the body, running his fingers down the cheek. For only a second, I allowed myself to really think about Kavik's relation to the victims. I knew he was immortal and ageless, which let me get over the age and appearance discrepancy. The first victim had been his grandson-in-law, age fifty-two. The victim we were looking at now was fifty.

This is his granddaughter.

The pain hit, and I had to turn away for a second. This poor man was looking at his grandchild on a metal slab, torn apart as though wild animals had found her.

"Yes, but not such a..." Alexius trailed off, and I looked over my shoulder to see him gesturing around the room. "A new vampire, recently turned, does exhibit this level of viciousness. However, it's often focused on one victim. The new vampire will feed, normally killing the victim, but not be hungry enough to continue on to another victim unless they killed the first like the first victim we saw. Single, new vampires are easy to hunt down, very predictable. This is all pointing at a group, which is a much different problem."

"Feeding frenzies," I elaborated, turning back to them, glad Alexius could maintain his professionalism. I couldn't look at her body lying there, Kavik still standing beside her. "Vampires can ramp up each other and cause more devastation in groups once they lose control together." I directed that to Janek, who was now standing beside his Alpha. Now, the second of the pack was on his best behavior, and I bet it was because he saw we were clearly trying.

"Exactly," Alexius confirmed. "A group of young vampires, probably younger than Everly, is bad news for all of us. When I saw the pictures, I figured this would be three or four, and I still believe that applies. Four, to be exact. Like humans, we have our own bites, and from just these victims, there appeared to be four different bite patterns."

"There's still..." Kavik sighed.

"Your great-granddaughter," I said, turning to the last covered body. "Alexius..."

"Why don't you both step out and let Everly and I do this one alone?" Alexius asked, and I wondered how he became so gentle so quickly. "We won't do anything differently, but it might be easier on both of you. I have the report and will tell you what I find when we come out."

"Alpha?"

"Thank you," Kavik whispered. "She was so young, not even twenty-one... That would have been this summer." Kavik walked away briskly, his head down. Janek nodded at us, then followed his Alpha out. The door closed softly, the click echoing in the room as Alexius moved to the last body.

"Female. Twenty years old," Alexius said, pulling the sheet back. "From the report, she sustained the most injuries of the group."

I looked down and tried to find that place of detachment again, but it was lost, and I wouldn't get it back looking at the young woman.

"Broken arm, broken collarbone, broken neck. One bite wound, though it's better aimed than the one her father had," Alexius continued. Each injury made me angrier. How could anyone do this to someone? "Broken ankle. Severe bruising, pre and post-mortem most likely."

"She's too young for this to have been personal, right?" I asked.

"Never assume that with supernaturals. It might not have been personal to her, but it could have been aimed at Kavik since she is the youngest member of his family, the one with a bright future ahead of her. Still personal."

Leaning down to see how some of the bruising wrapped around her wrist, I gently turned her hand over and saw the bruising made a handprint and quickly checked the other side.

"Someone held her wrists," I said, stomach in knots with sickness and fury. "We didn't see that on the others."

"Good catch." He looked away from the bite to inspect one of her wrists. "There's something odd about the bite. Come see," he said, waving me over. I moved fast, knowing the sooner we got done with this, the sooner we could leave. All the bodies had been washed off, leaving only the wounds but none of the blood. It made the bite so easy to see, and Alexius was right. Something was weird.

"Is that a cut in the middle?" I asked, leaning in closer. "Why?"

"I haven't the faintest idea, but it leads me to think it happened somehow, then…" He gestured at her, then the others. "It set off all this. No one else had an injury that seemed like it happened before the attack."

"How old do you think these vampires might be? I wouldn't do this over a little cut, right?" Standing with the dead and the horrible understanding that I could have done this… I needed his confidence in me.

"A couple of weeks after their Turn, maybe even younger. You would have when you first Turned, but not now. You've trained yourself to stop breathing and moving when you smell blood. It's only step one, but it's enough. Add in that you have me, and I will always hold that line for you if your control slips."

"If I didn't have control, would I be a monster like them? It seems as if they mindlessly killed these people. Random violence with no care in the world… no care for them. At the nest, it was more… calculated when vampires killed. Oscar had the control to wait for the right moment. Claire led her victims away and cleaned up. They were… serial killers versus this, which looks like..." I didn't even know how to keep putting my thoughts into words.

"None of you are monsters," he countered. "We're long past the days of vampires being mindless killers. No, young vampires now can keep the veneer of being human... for a short time. They'll smile, laugh, act completely human, but in the back of their mind, they're controlled by the need for blood. The problem lies with the ability for the smallest thing to set them off and get a human killed. A small cut or even a particularly strong heartbeat can start it. Many young vampires make one kill and feel incredibly guilty."

I was kept in the basement until now so I could get past this point. I knew it was for safety, but...

"Now we need to find the vampires, right?" I asked.

"Ideally, I need to figure out how they came here and if they're outsiders or locals. I don't think we're going to learn much else here."

Nodding, I moved away from the body. Dawn wasn't for hours, but I was exhausted. My night had started so simply, and now, I was staring at dead bodies, talking about murders and how young vampires worked, even though I was one.

"Come," Alexius said, suddenly beside me, offering me an arm. Taking it, there was something comforting, but I resisted the urge to lean on him. He led me out of the autopsy room, the werewolves remaining quiet as he made sure the door was closed.

"Anything?" Janek asked.

"I'll tell you what I can put together now. Some of this, you heard inside. Four vampires, all young enough to have been Turned this month. This is the first incident we've heard of, which means they could have been Turned within the week or even more recently. With them so young, we'll also need to keep an eye out for an older, more controlled vampire. Someone had to Turn them and let them loose without proper control. More than likely, because of the age of these vampires based on their behavior, they could have been locals. It's difficult to move young vampires without taking care of their feeding needs or drawing attention because of the risk." Alexius looked down at me, and there was an expectant silence after he finished.

"I'm hoping to get the electronic devices from the family," I started, catching on. "Maybe we can find out if the victims and the vampires were connected." I stumbled over my words as I tried to think about what Alexius had just said. "Which is even more likely if they were from Fairbanks or the local area. They probably would have known each other as humans if they were aware of each other."

"I…" Kavik frowned, and his eyes shifted from dark brown to a lighter shade. The sensation that made me aware he was a werewolf grew stronger. "I can see why you would think they might have known the vampires. Strangers didn't go out to the homestead. They would have been treated as intruders."

"Alpha, should I call the house and have someone collect everything for her?"

"Yes," Kavik said, nodding in Janek's direction. Janek pulled out his phone and started typing on it. "We can have the pack ask around the city if there's anyone who might have left town if that would interest either of you."

"That would be more than welcome," Alexius agreed.

I listened as I thought about everything Alexius said about young vampires, how this area was so isolated, and even that Corissa had mentioned Kavik was worried vampires were attacking the pack. There were so many possibilities at play, and I wanted to say something, give him one of the best scenarios I could. One that made me feel less evil for just existing.

"We found some small evidence that could point to the attack being more an accidental loss of control rather than an attack. It's just one of the possibilities, but it's one worth looking at because of how little control vampires have in their early days."

"It's plausible," Alexius agreed. "We can't rule anything out yet, of course."

"Or an older vampire came into my city, Turned some innocent humans, then set them loose on my family," Kavik said stiffly, a growl coming out on the word family.

"It could have been both..." I said, trailing off as Kavik looked at me.

"We need those devices for Everly," Alexius said, his hold on my arm growing tighter. "While she works on that, I shall coordinate with you and see if we can find out who might have gone missing or left town."

"Their stuff will be at the hotel in thirty minutes," Janek said, looking up from his phone.

"Janek will drive behind us. You'll be given the SUV we've used this evening for any travel," Kavik explained and started walking. "It's free for the entire pack to use, and if there's any way our pack can help you find out the truth, we will do it. You've already told us a lot this evening, and I need justice for my girls."

Alexius replied, but I stopped listening, thinking about what I would need to do when we got back to the hotel. I didn't know what sort of devices we'd be getting or if we'd get passwords for any of them. I thought about it until we were halfway back to the hotel.

"Does the pack keep the logins for their things? Has anyone been able to log into them so far?"

"For security purposes, I have my granddaughter's and great-granddaughter's logins, and I can get into their phones and computers," Kavik confirmed. "All of it will be given to you. I don't have the information for the others. They weren't my family, but they knew to report to me if they received any threats. Security, even out here with no neighbors, is taken seriously."

"Thank you," I said.

When we got to the hotel, two werewolves waited and handed me a large duffle bag. I heard everything rattling inside and hoped none of the screens were cracked. It wasn't impossible to get around, just needlessly annoying. Kavik gave Alexius the keys, and they exchanged cell phone numbers.

When we got back to the room, I emptied the bag, tired but knowing there was still so much work to do. I was moving slower than normal

"Get some rest," Alexius ordered. "Lie down, watch television, anything. Don't work for a moment."

"I can get started on this, and maybe we'll know more,

sooner rather than later," I said, huffing. "People are dead, and we need to find out why."

"They'll still be dead in an hour. It's almost midnight. We just spent over three hours looking at dead bodies. Take a short break," he said, grabbing the cellphone from my hand and putting it away from me on the table. "One hour. You'll feel better for it, believe me."

18
───────

CHAPTER EIGHTEEN

Stepping back from the table, I checked the time and sighed. I wanted to figure out everything, wanted to know why this had happened, but he was right. I had been awake for nearly twelve hours now, and the morgue had been a dreadful experience. I was so tired. Sitting on the edge of the bed, I tried to will myself to relax.

"Is it possible for us to nap?" I asked.

"I'm certain it is, but I've never found it easy." Sitting on the other bed, he put his feet up, then kicked his shoes off. "I don't recommend trying right now."

"Yeah, I would probably have nightmares about what happened to them. I don't think I will ever be able to forget tonight. I've never done anything like that."

"You did well, and you said the right things to Kavik. He's a reasonable Alpha. Not all of them are, and under these circumstances, others certainly would have been more aggressive."

"Is that normal? Them being aggressive?"

"It varies for each Alpha. Alpha werewolves are in charge of a community. Over the centuries, I've realized there's some level of magic to it, not that they confirm or deny that. They closely guard the secrets of how their structuring works and what it truly means. Every Alpha is different, just like every man in power could be. Some take the power of being an Alpha to subjugate the pack, an army of slaves to do their bidding. Others are fatherly, patient and frustrated at the same time but normally would never hurt their own werewolves unless pushed that far. Most live somewhere in the middle of the two extremes, much like a Master or Mistress of a nest, except werewolves are more prone to violence over politics."

"Kavik must lean to the fatherly side of things," I said, looking at the television I had yet to turn on. I considered reaching for the remote, but I couldn't be bothered. My mind was restless, going in circles with the facts we knew, but my body didn't want to cooperate.

"You did well tonight," Alexius repeated. "You should know that."

"Thanks. I was just following your lead. Tonight was a few steps outside of my comfort zone, but this is the job, right?"

"You'll get more comfortable. You're already doing better than I believe Isaiah would have expected. I don't think he sees you as someone who can do this job."

"And you do?" I chuckled. "Behind a computer, sure, but inspecting dead bodies? You really think I can do this regularly like you do?"

"I think you have a need to stop people like this, and

that will push you until there's nothing you can't do. Isaiah hasn't recognized that in you, not yet. I have, and I'm seeing it again now."

I nodded.

He's so confident in me.

Ten minutes later, I got up, unable to sit in silence any longer with nothing to do. Everything was repeating in my head, over and over. The face of each person, the photos of them in their home and on those cold metal tables, every injury we could find, the sad Alpha as he touched his granddaughter's cheek.

I couldn't sit still. There was no way.

Alexius hissed softly, but I ignored him as I sat at the table and opened my laptop.

"One hour, Everly. Just take one hour to clear your mind. You have to take care of yourself, too. We're immortal, but that doesn't mean we're immune to the effects of exhaustion and stress," he said, and I heard the bed creak. I logged into my computer, pointedly ignoring him as his footsteps let me know he was coming closer. When he was over my shoulder, I grabbed my laptop screen before he could close it.

"I need to work. I need to, okay?" I held tightly as he tried harder to close it. "You can't expect me to see those... poor people and think I'm going to take a break. I can't... I can't stop thinking about them. I can't stop thinking about how this might have happened and what I can do to help. So, I'm going to work. You don't need to coddle me."

"I am not *coddling* you," he snarled.

It sent chills down my spine as his accent appeared. Normally, he sounded like a very well-educated American, but now, his Greek accent was back. He let my laptop go, and I was frozen as he leaned down. I could see our reflections on the black screen, how he hovered over my shoulder.

"When someone is tired, they make mistakes. You are tired. *I* am tired, which is why I am letting the werewolves take point to find more information for us."

"I can do this," I said. "Let me."

"Why did I think you would have the sense to take care of yourself?" he asked, straightening. "Fine. Push yourself to the point of falling asleep on your keyboard."

"Oh, screw you," I snapped, looking back at him. "You dragged me to Alaska four hours ago to solve murders, and now you want to accuse me of not taking care of myself? Why am I not surprised you are suddenly an overbearing asshole? We haven't even been here for a *night!*"

His wordless growl was the only response I got as he stalked into the bathroom.

What the fuck?

I went to work. Kavik had been good enough to give me the logins he knew, so I started with his great-granddaughter's phone. I picked it for two reasons—a combination of her injuries and her age. The injuries made it clear she was the one who had been targeted, if that was part of this. If she hadn't been the target, then she had been cruelly unlucky. Her age made her the most likely to use her phone frequently, so it would have a higher chance of relevant information. I saw it all the time with vampires. The younger the vampire, the more they liked to use technology, and with humans, it wasn't too much of a stereotype to say young people were always using their phones. At twenty-seven, I was one of those young people, except I traded the phone for a computer.

On autopilot, I reached for my keyboard to login in when I saw the date and time on the screen.

January eighteenth, five minutes past midnight.

I dropped my hands, staring at it until it clicked another minute.

Do birthdays matter as a vampire? Or is this a case of no one caring anymore? Is my new birthday the day I became a vampire?

I logged in, resolved to get to work. I didn't have the time or emotional energy to consider that I was twenty-eight today, that this was my first birthday without any of my family or my old friends. I didn't even know what Kas was up to these days and had no idea what Travis or Kaleb were doing. I didn't even know my brother's job.

The life I had known was behind me, and nothing made that clearer than this birthday. It had snuck up on me, and nothing made it remotely similar to any of my previous.

This is more important.

Grabbing the cellphone, I logged in, then connected it to the laptop, copying her pictures, contacts, and videos. Once that was done, I disconnected the devices and logged into the first of several social media apps. I looked through each one, typing notes on a document to track what I was seeing—who commented, who she messaged and what they talked about. She was going to college, but she planned on using what she learned in school to help her family. She posted about school, beaming in pride as she completed courses and got great grades. She had some really supportive friends, but I knew public comments and what people really felt could be completely different.

In her private messages, I found her more private conversations—her secrets. She was waffling about asking to join the pack, wondering if that was the future she wanted or if she wanted to stay human. She only shared that with a handful of her friends, three names I had seen repeatedly on her public profile, always commenting with support and calling her their bestie. One was against her becoming a werewolf and had called the pack and her great-grandfather some incredibly harsh things. I had a feeling most werewolves didn't like to be called mangy mutts or rabid dogs. They probably didn't like hearing someone thought they should be shot like wolves, nuisances that needed to be exterminated. Glaring at the screen, I took screenshots of those messages and got the young woman's name.

I was so focused on the work, I didn't hear the bathroom door open but caught the smell—aftershave, shampoo, and the wave of steamed air. I hadn't heard the shower going but knew I would have caught it if I had been paying attention.

"Anything interesting so far?" Alexius asked. "Or is it too early to ask?"

Looking over my shoulder, about to answer his question, every word I had hoped to say died. He was only wearing pants, rubbing a towel over his head with one hand as he walked to his bed. In his other hand, he had the button-up and undershirt he'd been wearing. The only reason I saw him hold those was their proximity to the part of him I was staring at.

"Everly?" He looked up, and I tried not to be a pervert, trying to meet his gaze instead of staring at his bronze abs.

"Too soon," I said quickly, shaking my head as I turned back to my computer in the hope I could clear my daze. "There's some stuff here the pack might want to see, but nothing concrete yet. I'm still on the first phone, the great-granddaughter's. Her name was Elizabeth." I knew her name, thanks to my access to her accounts. "She was in college, had some close friends she told everything to. She had been thinking about becoming a werewolf, but I'm still digging. There might be nothing, and this could have been random, but anything could be useful, right?"

"Yes, we're still very early in the case."

It felt as if his tantrum about me working was nothing. Glancing at him, trying to assess him before getting back to work, I watched as he shook out his undershirt and pulled it on. I nearly asked why he was putting on worn clothes after a shower, then remembered we only had clothing for a few days. He probably didn't want to change into something new without needing to.

"What are you planning to do with the rest of the night?" I asked as he methodically buttoned his shirt.

"Normally, I would go directly to the scene, but the circumstances here are unusual. It's too cold and too far for us to go tonight without the pack. I'll call around to see if anyone has information about a vampire traveling to Alaska."

"Do you think... if the young vampires were locals, that means an older vampire came here and Turned them, yeah? What if the older vampire also sent you the postcard?" I was only theorizing, but his hands stopped with only two more buttons to do. "And if that's what happened, shouldn't we think about why they wanted you here on this case?"

"Yes, that's..." He finished buttoning his shirt. "That postcard changes everything."

"If we were in a movie, this would be a trap. I didn't think about that earlier."

"I did, but it doesn't matter. I have a job to do, and we can't allow young vampires to kill indiscriminately. I'm sure Isaiah is mulling over the possibility as we speak, and we'll dive further into the mystery once the immediate issue is resolved. Someone who wants to get my attention, intending to kill me?" Alexius smiled in my direction, one of the fullest I had ever seen from him. "If they're that foolish, they don't know who they're playing games with. I won't let you come to any harm. You'll be safe with me."

Nodding, I turned back to work, accepting his words. Truthfully, it wasn't about whether I trusted him to keep me safe. I wanted to prove I could do this, wanted to help him solve this case, and that someone was possibly planning on killing him wasn't enough to put me off. I needed to see this through. After seeing those people, their lives ended way too soon for no reason and probably in the most terrifying moments of their life, I *had* to see this through.

So, I accepted his confidence because to deny it meant I wasn't brave enough.

I wouldn't be able to live with myself if I tried to back out now.

19

CHAPTER NINETEEN

ALEXIUS

Alexius watched Everly return to her work and knew he'd said the wrong thing. If he was working alone on this case, he wouldn't have considered the postcard meaningful yet. It was interesting but a mystery he would be fine to solve slowly. First, he needed to stop the vampires who had killed a family of humans and hopefully do it before they killed again. Then he would dive into who Turned them and why he was sent the damn postcard.

This is why I wanted to hire her. She's a fresh perspective with the ability to find information I would have to work much harder for if I could even get it.

She wasn't as confident as he was. He didn't think anyone would be smart enough or powerful enough to kill him, not using this sort of ploy to draw him out. Was that arrogant? Alexius knew he was arrogant when it came to his power and expertise in these situations, although he was much less confident in his ability to work with others.

He was trying to be careful with her, and he'd made a misstep, not once, but twice. He had tried to coddle her when they had returned to the hotel. He'd seen how hard it had been for her to look at the bodies. Anyone in their right mind would have found it troubling. The backpedaling he had to do had pissed him off because he hadn't wanted her to see him trying to coddle her, so he disappeared to take a shower to clear his head. Her wanting to work was a good thing, and he should have commended her for the level of dedication and drive she had on her first case, even after the exhausting review of the victims. His need for her to rest hadn't been one of the lies he'd told her.

He'd wanted her to rest because he hadn't liked how tired she had looked. He'd *hated* how tired she'd looked, but that was his problem, not hers. It was the same problem he had with Isaiah and Corbin around. Something made him want to bundle her up and protect her from everything.

Maybe because I failed to do so once before.

Now, with her back turned to him, he'd made his second misstep and knew it also probably had to do with how things had gone with Jacob's nest and Edwin. He knew it had to be something she was thinking about.

"I'm serious, Everly. You'll be safe this time." He sat across from her as she typed, the sound of her fingers on the keyboard a fast series of clicks in different tones. He wondered, just for a moment, if she realized she was typing fast as he could move. There was a lot she did without realizing it. "I will keep you safe."

"I didn't say you wouldn't." Her fingers stopped as she looked over her laptop at him.

"I know our experiences together have ended poorly. If someone is trying to kill me, I will make sure you are safe. Your safety is more important than my own. You didn't ask for this, not truly, and if you want to back out because you feel unsafe, let me know. I can arrange travel to send you to Isaiah."

"No. I'm not leaving now. Don't start talking like that. I have a job to do. I'm helpful. I want to do this."

Alexius wondered if he'd misread her. There was something frantic and stern as though she was *telling* him she wasn't leaving and was willing to argue about it. He'd heard it from her before.

"You aren't concerned about being in danger?" he asked, frowning. He'd been certain she didn't trust his ability to keep her safe and couldn't blame her. He'd been minutes too late that night. She could have continued a normal human life if it wasn't for his tardiness.

"Sure I am." She leaned back in her chair. "But you know what? Edwin and Claire couldn't scare me enough to stop me from going against them. Some postcard and the theory someone might be trying to catch you in a trap will not stop me now." She pointed at the laptop. "This girl had a life ahead of her. Elizabeth had a life, she had friends, and she had a family who loved her. She was smart, she had plans, and fuck whoever started this. They're going to pay for it. Kavik had to look at his granddaughter on a metal table. He couldn't bear to see his great-granddaughter."

Alexius remained silent as she gave him the fiery look

he'd seen before. He'd heard her give a speech like this on the phone when he'd snapped at her the first time they had spoken. This was the Everly who had drawn him in and made him interested—too interested. He wanted every single one of those fiery looks and could listen to her impassioned speeches for hours.

"I had to bury my mom and keep going every day while her murderers tormented me and killed around me. Fuck that. I'm going to help you hunt down every single vampire who steps out of line and watch them burn. In fact, the only thing I regret about Portland is I didn't get to see Edwin die."

He let her finish her speech, not daring to interrupt, and waited for her to settle down. He realized he should have trusted his first impression of her, trusted the strength she kept hidden under her insecurities. She could be a mouse, and he wasn't the only person who saw that. Isaiah had seen it; Maria had as well. The werewolves had probably thought she was just his quiet assistant, no threat to anyone. Out of everyone, only Isaiah had seen what he could, and even he only had the smallest peek.

This redheaded mouse was actually a dragon in disguise with fire in her blood. He knew she needed to be reminded of it and was willing to give that reminder.

Sometimes.

She certainly doesn't need a reminder right now.

"I misinterpreted this," he admitted. "I'm not going to send you to Isaiah if you don't want to go."

"Good, because I wouldn't leave even if you tried. Beyond the fact that I can and want to help here, I definitely *don't* want to spend my birthday with Isaiah," she snapped. Her hair fell into her face as she went back to looking at the phone. "Would rather stare at dead bodies all night than do whatever he could think of. He seems like the type capable of hosting a coming-out ball to marry me off as an eligible woman. He could probably have it organized to begin at sunset without breaking a sweat."

"January eighteenth," he said, closing his eyes.

"You know my birthday?" Her surprise made him feel terrible.

"Yes." He rubbed his face. "Forgive me for not realizing it was coming up."

"I didn't say anything," she said with a shrug. "It's not a big deal."

"If you say so." But it had been to him, and he'd lost track of time *again*. He spent the first days of every new year preparing his calendar. He wrote down all the birthdays of those who worked for him and tried to make the day special for them. It had started centuries before when one of the humans he had been raising asked why other children got gifts every year. He'd forgotten what a birthday was at that point. He had never celebrated his own, and the vampires he knew had stopped celebrating theirs long before. He'd promised he would never forget again. Sometimes, time would slip away from him, but he always made up for it.

Everly was a vampire now, not one of his human staff, but he'd wanted to give her something normal when much of her life wasn't anymore.

"Do vampires even celebrate birthdays?"

"Depends on the vampire. I don't. I don't know what it is. Isaiah sometimes celebrates milestones. At two thousand years old, he threw a very large, incredibly excessive party."

"All right. I don't know if I want to celebrate mine. Clearly, it didn't come at a good time. I'm going to keep working now. You said you were going to call some people, didn't you?" She went back to looking down at her laptop and the phone she was reading.

Alexius knew a dismissal when he saw one, and he didn't know what to think about that. He wasn't dismissed by anyone.

He smiled when she started typing at speeds that caused her fingers to blur.

Pulling out his phone, he called the first person he could think of. There were two nests in the Pacific Northwest, and he was lucky to have both their numbers. There had once been three, but the Master of Seattle had gotten himself and his entire nest obliterated by a few supernaturals.

He'd deserved it.

"Noah of the Vancouver Nest speaking. May I ask who is calling?" The man was confident, clear, and professional. He'd called Vancouver first since it was the closest vampire nest, and hopefully, their network of information reached as far as he was hoping. Their Mistress was more likely to know something than the Master of Portland in Oregon.

"Alexius, the Hunter, calling for Lorraine."

"Yes, sir," the vampire said, his professionalism and

confidence shaken. The waver in his words and his higher pitch gave it away.

Alexius waited as Everly's nonstop typing continued in the background.

"Alexius, is there something I can help you with?" Lorraine was short with him even though she tried to sound welcoming. He knew the difference between Lorraine in a good mood and Lorraine in a bad one, though. His call, or possibly something else, had put her in a bad mood.

"I'm calling to see if you've heard any rumors about vampires heading in or out of Alaska. Don't worry, I'm not in your city or even remotely close to it."

"No, I haven't heard of any vampires in Alaska, not anything out of the ordinary. Sometimes, we need to use Anchorage for refuels when we travel. Where in Alaska?"

"Too far north for this to be normal movement and hours away from Anchorage."

"No, and I keep an eye on when other nests use Anchorage. Everyone who has stopped there to refuel has left with their plane in the last six months."

"Before that?" He'd go back years if he had to. A vampire with control could hide for a long time with no one realizing they were there.

"I handle it when someone stays in Anchorage," she said with a hiss. "It's not my city, but it's my vulnerability to deal with. I don't let the Russians leave people there."

"And you're positive you haven't heard of anyone else? Even a whisper or a suspicion."

"Positive. Now, is that all?"

"Why the mood? Is there something I can help with there?"

"No. The mood is because you're calling," she snapped.

It took him a little too long to remember why Lorraine no longer liked him. It had been over thirty years, but sometimes, that wasn't enough time to move on from what he had done.

His job, but sometimes, people took that personally.

"I'll let you go," he said. "Thank you for answering my questions."

She hung up on him.

"Wow," Everly mumbled. "What did you do to her?"

"We had sex," he answered without thinking. "Then I killed her sire."

"You used sex to get information out of her, didn't you?"

He didn't like what her tone implied.

"She seduced me because she had known her sire had lost his mind. I don't use to sex to get information, and no vampire would fall for it if I tried," he retorted. He thoroughly enjoyed sex, but it was for pleasure, *never* work. "Isaiah's children are much better at those tactics. She had convinced me to sleep with her, and I went along with it. She's a beautiful woman, and I had the time. I didn't ask her for information. It was still early in the case, and we didn't talk about it in bed. When I discovered the one I was hunting was actually her sire, I realized I had been played. She continued the act up to the point when I killed him. It's been... tense between us since, and truthfully, it was my mistake to fall for it. It was a moment of weakness. I had never fallen for it before, and I won't fall for it again."

"So, she hates you because she couldn't convince you, her 'lover,' not to kill her sire and holds a grudge. Could she have been lying to you? Maybe she sent the postcard."

"She wouldn't risk it, or she would have done it years ago," he said, shaking his head. He liked the way Everly thought, though. Not the part where she had assumed the worst of him, but the intellect to put some of the pieces together and ask questions. So many didn't have that.

"Have you found anything from..." He waved at her work, all the electronics he had no patience to learn about. There were just too many of them.

"No, not yet."

He nodded and went to another call, trying the Master in Portland, Oregon. After that, he attempted Calgary. He reached out to Maria and got the numbers for Tokyo and farther. Anyone who might have their eye on Alaska, he tried to call.

It was nearly three in the morning when his phone rang, and he saw Kavik's number.

"What do you need?" Alexius asked.

"We don't think this is an attack on the pack anymore," Kavik said softly. "I just got a call from a lone wolf who lives down in Beaver Creek, just across the border in the Yukon. A small town with a year-round population of about a hundred people. He knows everyone."

"What happened?"

"He went to have dinner with a friend last night, who said his neighbors didn't come by like they normally did. A bit out of the ordinary, but I don't know the specifics. He went to check it out for his friend after dinner, just curious. Accidents happen, and everyone has to be attentive, you know. He found them. A younger couple, bitten in multiple places, bled dry. Home covered in blood and everything is a mess. He took pictures and sent them, asking me for support with the problem. From the pictures, it looks a lot like what we have here, and I told him as much."

Everly's head snapped up when Alexius growled in frustration. This was already escalating, and it wasn't escalating in the way he normally saw. Typically, new vampires with no support stayed in their local area. If they were traveling, he and Everly had to move as well.

"Everly, find out the travel time—"

"It's five and a half hours in good weather," Kavik answered.

"We'll make it there tonight if you'll let us keep the vehicle." Alexius didn't have a problem with driving in the snow, even if he had to do it quickly. So long as there wasn't an active snowstorm, he would make it.

"Take it. I'll tell him to be prepared for you. He'll get you into shelter once you arrive. I'll give my guy a call at the border. Normally, they don't look too closely at supernaturals, especially this far north. With my word that you're only passing through to help the pack, they'll look at your details and ignore that you're driving one of my vehicles."

"Everly, collect our things," Alexius ordered. She

jumped up as he continued talking to the Alpha. "Has he disturbed the bodies?"

"No. He wanted someone to come out and see them. Clearly, he's right. We just don't see these sorts of attacks up here."

"Of course. We'll swing by for printouts of the pictures, so we can compare them to your humans."

"I'll be waiting."

Alexius hung up and shoved the phone into his pocket. Everly already had both of her bags and was packing away the things the pack had given her. He grabbed his bags and waited only moments at the door for her, then they raced out of the hotel and threw their things into the SUV.

"Alexius, do you think we'll catch them before they kill again?"

"No," he answered honestly. "Unless we figure out what direction they're moving and why."

"I'll keep working on it while you drive. There has to be something we're missing."

He knew there was. He just didn't know what it could be.

20

CHAPTER TWENTY

I had never known a longer night. Adrenaline was still pumping through me as we sped out of Fairbanks. The stop at Alpha Kavik's house had taken only a few minutes. I had exchanged emails with him, and Alexius had grabbed the pictures. Not much was said, but there was one thing I wanted to ask.

"Why did you ask him not to send werewolves?" I asked, staring at the dark road ahead of us.

"Because I haven't met all of his werewolves yet. I don't want to stumble on them and get someone hurt. They could think we're the ones who committed the attacks, for example. Plus, they could contaminate the scene. They didn't have a choice, but at least we saw the bodies. We can compare the new victims to what we've already seen, and we have pictures of both scenes. Both will help us verify this is the same group."

"Makes sense. Okay, what do you want me to do? I can keep looking into our first victims. Maybe they have the secret we need. Kavik can look for missing people who left town in Fairbanks. That's still the plan, right?" I didn't look at him, my eyes staying on the dark road ahead of us. He was driving fast as Kavik had done.

"Kavik is also going to reach out to contacts around the state to see if there have been other attacks. His pack is fully supporting us," Alexius confirmed. "If we can confirm the attack on his family was the first, that makes it all the more likely this originated in Fairbanks."

"I'm going to..." I turned, trying to reach for stuff in the backseat. "Damn it."

Alexius reached out and undid my seat belt. "Go," he said.

Taking the cue, I tentatively climbed into the backseat. I hadn't been moving as fast as I could have through the devices from Elizabeth and her family. I was still on her phone and hadn't even touched her email yet. Once I was in the back seat, that was where I started. I didn't even think to put my seatbelt back on as I searched the bags and grabbed what I needed.

"I'm going to lose service soon, so let's hope I can get something useful before that," I said, mostly to myself. "Maybe my phone will still work well enough for a Wi-Fi hotspot." I started setting that up, seeing how my bars were already dropping.

"Anything you can discover could potentially help."

"Our cellphone bill might be pretty high at the end of the month."

"Money is not a concern."

I had a feeling it wasn't. I got to work, recording everything I could think of from Elizabeth's phone. If she blocked someone on social media, I put the name into my notes and copied the messages she had exchanged with them. I had a lot done on her phone before we flew out of the hotel, before we even spent a night there, but since I didn't know what I was looking for, I was looking at everything.

"She had a terrible ex-boyfriend," I commented, seeing the mean stuff the guy named Jaxson said to her after she ended things. She eventually blocked him, and based on the last messages between them, that had only been a few weeks ago, right in the middle of the holidays. The breakup was so bad, she canceled a trip she was planning because he was also going.

Alexius said nothing, and I kept going. Eventually, I felt satisfied I had gone through all of Elizabeth's phone, so I went to her mother's, Kavik's granddaughter. She didn't have nearly as much on hers, mainly emails upon emails. While they lived on a homestead, as others called it, she had a regular job and traveled for work as an Alaskan Wildlife Trooper when it was needed. I knew I was looking at sensitive information as I went through her emails. There had been threats against her for doing her job, but none of them seemed to be pointed at her supernatural connection. No one hated or liked her because her grandfather was a werewolf or mentioned it at all. I told Alexius everything, even what I didn't see, like her relation to Kavik.

"That's a good thing. Her work isn't, but Kavik is probably already handling that angle. It's not my job."

"How much of this is his job?"

"He needs to find an appropriate cause of death for the family, make sure all evidence of the supernatural is destroyed, then report it. He needs to continue being a distraught man who just lost his family, which will remove suspicion from anyone. Few, if anyone, would accuse him of killing his granddaughter or great-granddaughter, though. He seemed very attached to them."

"How would you do it?"

"I would put the bodies back in the house and burn it down, all the way to ash. There are plenty of ways to stage arson without anyone catching on, and it's a rural location, which makes it unlikely anyone would happen on the fire before it's finished destroying the evidence."

It was a terrible thing to destroy their bodies, but I also knew my previous nest had done something similar for most of the bodies. My mother got a burial because of her position and Edwin's plans to keep control of the nest. Edwin had known cremation without a funeral would have made people suspicious when she had always wanted to be buried next to my father.

Hearing a noise, I looked at my laptop, hitting save on my document and hoping it worked as my screen went black.

"Damn it," I hissed as I stared at the dead laptop. "I should have put it on the charger at the hotel. It would have lasted longer. Shit, did I even bring my charger?" Frantically, I searched my bag and sagged with relief when I found it. "I wasn't paying attention to the battery. Stupid mistake."

"Why don't you come back up here?" Alexius asked. "You can read through the other things, but I'm beginning to think it's unlikely we'll find anything from that family. We could... talk about other things."

Climbing back into the front, I checked the time on the dash. I hadn't been paying attention to my battery or what time it was as I had worked. It was already nearly seven in the morning, yet the world was still dark.

"It's been a long night," I said as I put my seatbelt on in the front seat, mostly because I didn't want to get launched out of the window if we ended up hitting anything.

"It has," he agreed. "This will be one of the longest nights of my life, and I'm certain yours as well. That's why I believe we should take our minds off it for a moment. I normally don't work on the road, and I've never had... company before."

"How long is this night going to be? Close to eighteen hours of darkness? More?"

"I think you're close. The time zone change awarded us extra, very needed time, but it's tiring. Try to sleep if you feel the need, and I'll wake you when we arrive. I'm not going as fast as I would like, thanks to this snow, but I am matching the speed limit. We should be there around eight-thirty, which gives us two hours before sunrise. We won't have time to do anything for the case, but it will give us time to shelter properly.

"What if we don't make it?"

"I'll teach you how to survive as we are. In one of my bags is a blackout kit. The worry would be making sure humans or other supernaturals won't breach the car and let light in. Or we could camp in the woods off the road, but then we'll need to worry about staying warm. There are options. None of them are perfect, but we have them."

"You don't have a tent," I pointed out.

"We wouldn't use a tent. I would park one to two hours before sunrise, and we would bury ourselves."

Oh, hell no.

"Drive faster, please," I ordered, grabbing the bar above my window.

"Don't like that idea?"

"Not at all."

"Good, I hate it, too, but I can't push this thing to move any faster. It's not as secure on the snow as I hoped, and I can't risk us slipping on a turn. We'll be fine unless I hit something." He pointed to our right, and I turned in time to see the moose standing there before we whipped by it. "Let's hope nothing jumps into the road."

With that, I knew I needed to distract myself from the slowly ticking time. I debated continuing to read through the stuff in the back but decided this was a good chance to talk to Alexius. If there was any time to ask deeply personal questions to get to know someone, a long night drive was a good one, and he was the one who wanted to talk.

"Can I ask you about... you?" I treaded lightly. "I feel as if I don't know you as well as I should even though we've lived together for over two months."

"Of course. All you ever had to do was ask."

"I'll start simple. Where did you come from? Greece like Jacob, right?"

"Some say Macedonia, some say Greece, but really, I predate all of them. I was a human who lived somewhere on the coast of the Mediterranean, but I don't remember the name of the culture or the language. I've never gone looking, either. It doesn't matter to me because I have no memory of it."

"You don't remember where you came from?" That wasn't the simple answer I had expected.

"I don't remember any of my human life. I don't know exactly how old I am. Jacob and Isaiah used to debate it at length. By the time they became vampires, I was already quite old and powerful compared to everyone we met. Probably a thousand years older than Jacob, if not more. Clearly, there are others out there, and I just hadn't met them, but all have a similar problem. We don't remember. We had to pick up language and culture later, our own lost to us."

I couldn't believe it. I hadn't known exactly how old Jacob had been, and he never acted as though he was over two thousand years old. When Alexius had told me two thousand six hundred, I had thought Alexius was a similar age, maybe a few centuries older. I had looked up his name and found it had a Greek and Roman version. Pieces were falling into place, and I had been *certain* Alexius had been Greek, too. He even had a pretty typical Greek accent when he was angry.

"Was it because of how much time passed?" I asked, curious and sad. I couldn't imagine forgetting my human life and the people in it. It hurt to think about one day not knowing my own life and where I came from.

"No. Many of us who are so much older than everyone else... we're almost a different type of vampire. That's not the right way to say it. You heard Isaiah and me speak about how younger vampires, those Turned now, have more control, correct?"

"Yeah. How it took Isaiah a century before he felt comfortable feeding off humans by himself while it might only take me three years."

"Yes. Well... I was..." Alexius frowned.

"You don't have to tell me if you prefer to keep it private."

"You should know," he grumbled. "It's more about my disappointment in myself and who I was that makes me hesitate. I don't want to keep secrets from you, and many people already know this. It's common knowledge and often referenced." He ran a hand over his jaw. "Vampires my age... we remember nothing from our beginning years as vampires except survival. None of us remember our human lives at all. I don't remember what I did during those years except try to blend in and find my next meal. I had no friends, no allies, no life. It was me and the next human I was going to kill."

I was certain the surprise I felt was on my face, and he saw it.

"In those times, there was no one to teach vampires. We had no laws or culture. We didn't even know what we were. Then I Turned Jacob, and as a vampire, he didn't want to kill. He showed me we didn't have to. My son changed me. Thanks to him, I understood I could have a life with people in it, so long as I kept control over my bloodlust. Having a life was a new experience because I didn't remember having one before."

"Did you pick up the Greek accent to blend in before you met Jacob? It seems like the most natural for you."

"It is the first language I remember learning and could be considered my native tongue. You assume I'm Greek because I taught myself in the effort to get to know Jacob. Perhaps you need the full story... Yes, that's what you need. I might as well start at the beginning. Jacob was to me as you were to Oscar."

"Oh my God," flew out of my mouth before I could stop it.

And Jacob survived... No, he didn't. He ended up as a vampire.

"I caught the scent of his blood on the wind and had never felt anything like it before. I was drawn to hunt it, that perfect smell. Vital and something I hadn't had in so long. Jacob's blood... made me think of sunlight. I tracked it to a home and looked inside to find a boy, no more than five, crying over a skinned knee. I was able to stop myself because I was fascinated by why this prey made me so interested, and it nearly drove me mad. I'm certain his age had something to do with it," Alexius continued in a soft whisper. His eyes seemed endless as he stared at the road ahead. "Children had never been my prey."

I heard the pained guilt eating him alive even though he hadn't killed Jacob that day. I didn't think I could get him to stop this story now. It sounded like something he needed to say, either for me to hear or just to put it into the world.

"For years, I watched Jacob grow up. I was never far away. He nearly drowned when he was ten, and I saved him. To me, he was mine. I just didn't understand how yet. I didn't want him to die, and so long as he wasn't bleeding, I didn't feel an urge to attack him. I learned

Greek, picking it up and testing it out on the humans I hunted. I frequently hunted because I knew I was less dangerous to him when I had recently fed. I learned to dress and bathe so I could... I don't know. He did those things, so I did those things."

"Jacob and I met when he was on the cusp of manhood, going to live on his own and find his own way. I followed him, and he caught me, finally forcing a confrontation. He admitted he had seen me growing up and remembered me dragging him out of that lake. He had imagined I was his missing father, always watching over him and wanted to know the truth."

And you had actually wanted to kill him. At least in the beginning.

Like a lot of things in my life, I didn't know which of two feelings to pick. Was I disgusted? Or was there something incredibly powerful about holding back for so long? Oscar couldn't. Oscar had gone off the deep end, but Alexius had stopped himself.

Then he stalked Jacob his entire life.

"We became friends and lived together. I tried to tell him about things I could remember, and he knew I wasn't human. I told him how I had found him, why I had stayed close by, all about what I was, and how I had to live. However, in the end, he taught me more than I taught him." Alexius took a deep breath. "He was thirty-three, and we had lived together for over fifteen years, by his account, when he accidentally cut himself with a knife while making dinner. I had just woken up, and I was hungry."

"Oh, no." I could read the writing on the wall.

"It was a risk we knew we had to live with every day, and finally, one accidental slip and the life we knew was over," Alexius said, nodding. "I drained him, and... destroyed the first and only good thing in my life. I fed him my blood, a mad hope, instinct telling me it was the only way to bring him back. It worked." Alexius broke into a strange laugh, startling me. "He took it rather well. The Turn brought on the connection of the bloodline. Jacob looked at me and said, 'You are my father now, as I have always hoped you were.' You would have thought he was happy about it." He stopped for a minute, and it was as though he shook himself out of the memories. He was back in the present, his dark eyes no longer endless pools. "I'm sorry. That was probably too much. I would understand if it changes the way you see me."

I needed to process, needed to think. I looked out my window, trying to see Alexius as that man—the one who had nearly killed a child.

But he didn't. He only wanted to. He stopped himself, and I know the sort of help vampires need when they find someone like that. Alexius had stopped himself on his own when he didn't have laws to follow or people to help him. That's admirable. In fact, he decided to go in another direction, even if it was creepy.

I thought about the picture in the study. Seeing them, they weren't father and son by appearance, but it was the look in their eyes, their expressions.

This isn't mine to judge.

Alexius didn't cut into the silence, afraid of my judgment and waiting for it stoically.

"That's a lot," I finally said, feeling lame it wasn't

something profound. "I didn't think you and Jacob had such a..."

"I know. What I did was heinous. I have always believed so. It's not a vampire thing to do. Other supernatural species find it quite normal, but I have always found it... distasteful."

Oh, that's right. He's the master of self-loathing.

"I was going to say complicated beginning, but maybe you were two souls who *needed* to find each other." As I spoke, the picture became clearer. "You fought against all your instincts for nearly twenty years when you had never done so before. He never thought you were dangerous enough to escape or tell anyone about you. He pushed you into finding your humanity, and you gave him the protection and love of a father he had been missing his entire life."

"I killed him and made him into a monster like me. Not very fatherly."

"You know, I knew him most of my life, and never once could I describe Jacob as an unhappy man," I retorted. "Maybe he was just fine with how things turned out. That is possible, you know."

Alexius slowed the SUV and turned to me, stunned, as if I had just given him a great piece of knowledge.

"What?"

"Nothing," Alexius said, looking back at the road and putting his foot on the gas.

21

CHAPTER TWENTY-ONE

I didn't pry. He'd just revealed a lot about himself and whatever revelation he had was clearly something he wanted to think about—or just not share. Either way, it didn't bother me. I felt as if I knew him better now. The self-loathing I finally understood, able to see where it probably had come from, and his dedication to Jacob made so much sense. He'd been dedicated to Jacob since the first time he saw his son. I spent my time thinking about him, about Jacob, and how my life ended up here, in this car on this dark drive. About what we were doing here and what we had been working toward at home.

Thinking about everything kept me from focusing on the intense burn growing in my throat.

"We'll be there in ten minutes," Alexius said eventually, and I yawned. We had just crossed the U.S.-Canadian border, so I figured we were close but hadn't realized we were that close.

"That's great," I said, sitting up. My words sounded dry. I tried to clear my throat, but it didn't work. The large meal I'd had hours before was finally not enough. "I'll need to get everything on chargers before we have to rest."

"I thought you were asleep. I wasn't expecting a reply."

"Oh, no. Just lost in thought."

He reached down and pulled out his wallet. I frowned as he searched through it and finally held something out.

I took the penny and chuckled.

"Really?"

"We only have ten more minutes. This will be my last chance to ask what you're thinking until we find another moment alone. I don't know what it will be, but I'm curious about what you're thinking. So, a penny for your thoughts."

"I don't know. I always figured my thoughts were worth at least a dollar. Inflation and all that."

"If we follow inflation, your thoughts would be worth roughly thirty-three cents, but I don't have the change. I'm amazed I had a penny. I could give you the quarter."

"I'll put it on your tab. You owe me thirty-two cents." That made him chuckle, and I smiled to myself. "I don't know. I was thinking about..." I wondered if there was really any way to describe it. "Everything."

"I know the sensation."

Yeah, I bet you think about everything all the time.

We fell back into silence as we passed a sign for Beaver Creek.

"Kavik told the werewolf we would head directly to his home," Alexius explained as he turned down a few roads. "I didn't consider this as part of the drive time, but it could be another ten minutes."

"And on some rough roads," I pointed out just as we hit a hard bump that nearly sent my head into the ceiling.

"That as well."

I saw him first, the werewolf. Looking out my window, I saw a man running in the trees just off the torn-up road. He made eye contact with me in the night and sped up.

"He's out there." I looked at Alexius' speed, fifteen miles an hour. "He was just running alongside us in the trees. As a human." Part of me didn't want to believe what I had just seen. Something about it was unreal, almost magical.

"Werewolves and their cousins, the werecats, are physically fit. He will probably beat us to his home. He knows the land and could probably keep up this speed for miles, even in human form. Werecats can jump up to fifteen feet if you push them to it. It normally takes something important to get either of the moon-cursed species to use their more inhuman abilities in human form. It's one way they keep control of themselves. He is probably more relaxed, living out here. There probably aren't many who don't know what he is."

"So, not weird?" I asked, wanting to get past his explanation to the answer I needed.

"Not weird," he confirmed.

"The moon cursed..." I leaned my head on the window. "Do you think they got it better or worse than us?"

"I think we're different types of unfortunate. They are man merged with beast, twisted by magic, an echo of both, but no longer either. They are forced to leave their human bodies under the full moon, which is when they are most dangerous, with less control over their animalistic urges." Alexius sighed. "We are humans condemned to stay in the darkness and feed on our own kind for eternity. You'll have to make your own decision about which you would rather be."

"Are there other supernaturals that start as humans?"

"Yes, but not as widespread as us or the moon cursed. Werewolves are one of the largest supernatural populations in the world. Others have very small populations or unique cases of magic transforming a human into something else. I've only encountered a handful in my life since many supernaturals are still very insular."

"There's so much... I grew up with vampires, but there's a lot I don't know about... being one or any sort of supernatural."

"You have all the time to learn," he reminded me. Turning down a dirt road brought into view a cabin with a man standing on the porch, his hands at his sides. Alexius parked in front of the cabin beside a pickup truck and got out. This time, I didn't wait on him. Knowing we were coming, I believed this werewolf wouldn't keep humans around.

"Welcome to Beaver Creek. Thank you for coming out here," the werewolf greeted, hopping down the stairs, light on his feet. I heard his heartbeat pounding in my ears, but I wasn't hungry enough to get past the feral air around him. "Alpha Kavik said you were there looking at the deaths in Fairbanks. A shame he lost his girls. I hope you catch these blood... these assholes."

"You can call them bloodsuckers. It wouldn't be the first time someone said it tonight," I said, smiling at him as he came closer. This werewolf seemed much more friendly than any I had met. He extended a hand toward me as he came closer. My fangs dropped, and the burn intensified, but I didn't want to bite him, thanks to the sense of wildness around him.

Then Alexius was in the way, pushing between us so hard, he knocked the werewolf's hand into the side of the SUV with enough force to make it bounce off. I was left speechless as Alexius snarled in the silence.

"Okay." The werewolf pulled his hand back, shaking it out in surprise. "I didn't realize how serious Kavik was. He said you were protective. I was just saying hello. No harm intended. I'm Henry." He extended the hand again, but this time, not to me.

"I'm Alexius, and this is Everly." He gave a simple gesture toward me but didn't let the werewolf look at me for long before forcing the werewolf to focus on him again. He shoved his hand forward, making it clear he wanted all of Henry's attention.

I was amazed they shook hands. Henry didn't seem all that bothered by the behavior, but I realized I needed to talk to Alexius about this. Henry hadn't been threatening me. He seemed like a pretty nice guy, even under the circumstances.

"Do you need help taking anything inside?"

"No," Alexius answered, still stiff. I elbowed him

when he came to my side, then looked at Henry with a smile.

Clearly, having to smooth out his rough edges is going to give me a lot of practice in diplomacy and talking to people.

"No, but I would love to know if you have electricity. I need to charge my work laptop. It has all my notes and died on the drive here."

"Of course! I have solar panels." He grimaced and looked up. "Not that they get enough time in the sun over the winter, but that's what the generator is for. I get gas from town in the winter when the solar dies, and I need heat or power."

"We'll pay for a few tanks of gas for you," Alexius said. Henry seemed okay with that, so we grabbed our bags and followed him inside. The cabin was very much that—a cabin. Everything was wood, and I had a feeling there was no insulation. It was built out of logs, maybe even trees cut down from the area. The furniture was sanded and stained, with threadbare cushions. The table by the kitchen looked hand-carved, and the stove in the kitchen looked like it was wood burning.

We stopped in the living room, and Henry pointed at a door to my right.

"I have a basement that doesn't get any sun this time of year that I use for my winter stockpile. Cleared some space and moved a mattress down there for you for safety, and it doesn't stink. It's just cold down there, so I threw blankets and pillows down, too. I'll be out of the house for the day, asking around town about who's passed through." There was something so earnest about him.

"Did you know the couple?" I asked, hoping it

sounded gentle but still had the hoarseness that had started in the car.

"Not as well as I would have liked," Henry answered, sighing. "They were actually new to the area, but they had both grown up in places like this. I can tell you they were friendly, and if they heard someone needed to crash for the night or a warm meal, they would have opened their doors. I wish I knew more for you, but it's been..." He checked his watch. "Six hours since I told Kavik, and everyone is asleep."

"You got some rest, right?"

"I did. Thank you for asking. Slept a good five hours. You two won't be able to come up until around five-thirty, so I might take the chance for another nap before you get up. I want to be helpful tonight, and Kavik told me you two don't do clean-up. Once you're done with the house and the victims, I'm going to handle it."

"Have you done it before?" Alexius' words were a bit more professional than mine, not feeling nearly as nice as I was.

"Yeah, I have," Henry said, turning away. "I know what to do."

"We can assist if you need it. While I don't normally do clean-up if there are other supernaturals, this is a specific situation. You don't have the support of a pack to do it."

"I can handle it." Henry turned back toward us, his face blank. "I did clean-up for decades before I moved out here."

"I see. Then I shall leave you to it when we're done tonight."

"Have a good rest, you two. Everly, you'll find a wall outlet by the bottom of the stairs. There's a power strip on the table you can plug in if you need it. I'll get gas for the generator while I'm out."

"Here." Alexius pulled out his wallet again, and this time, he went for the bills. I didn't know Alexius carried cash and certainly not the bills he pulled out. "This should cover it."

"Yeah, it will," Henry mumbled as he accepted the money.

I went into the basement first and threw my clothing bag toward the lonely mattress on the floor. As Alexius passed me, I was already plugging in the power strip. I set up everything I needed to charge, then pulled off my heavy coat. Throwing it on the table beside everything else, I got to business.

"The sun comes up in a couple of hours, right? What do you want to do until then?"

"Read," he answered, sighing. "But I forgot a book. Often, I'll buy something new at whatever airport I'm passing through, but we didn't use the airports."

I never pitied a man so much.

"Give me your phone," I ordered. "Let me show you the world of eBooks."

"I know what an eBook is." He narrowed his eyes at me over his shoulder. "I don't like them."

"Oh, well then." I lifted my hands. "Never mind. We can talk about how rude you were to Henry. He was just trying to shake my hand. I was in control."

He dropped one of his bags and opened the other, pulling out a blood bag, throwing it before I knew what was happening. I caught it, immediately sinking my fangs into it as hunger hit me. I snarled as he walked closer to me, clutching my meal against me to keep it out of his reach.

"You did well with Henry. He probably doesn't seem like a good meal," Alexius said as he stopped only a couple of feet from me. "But you're very hungry, and I wasn't going to take the risk of you putting a hand on him, feeling his pulse and how strong and healthy it would be. That could have brought your hunger to the surface. Plus, I didn't want him putting a hand on you because I hadn't judged his character."

I heard everything, and most of it sank in. The entire time I drank, Alexius' eyes stayed on mine. Slowly, his eyes lightened from black-brown to blood red. I didn't stop until my stomach felt like it couldn't fit another drop and felt blood pour over my hands. Alexius was there, grabbing one of my wrists. He took the bag and let me go as he finished it.

I was trying to think as he was muttering something to himself in a language I didn't know.

"Sorry. I knew I was hungry, but I thought I was fine. I thought I could handle it."

"Your control hasn't magically gotten better over a single night. Just be watchful. If you're hungry enough to be hoarse, you need to feed."

"You didn't say anything in the car."

I knew my throat was burning and should have said something.

"I didn't think there was enough time to feed you and let you clean up before seeing the werewolf, but we had to get here and make sure we would be secure for the sunrise. You need to clean up before seeing other supernaturals. To do otherwise, especially in these sorts of situations, is distasteful and could provoke a fight we don't want." He shoved away the empty blood bag and grabbed his handkerchief for me again. He didn't need to clean himself off, so I wasn't surprised when he brought it back to me.

"I got it," I said, snatching it from him. I wiped my face down and caught some on my neck.

"Change your shirt before you go to sleep. We'll have to burn that one, but I can at least seal it before the wolf thinks something happened," he said, nodding downward.

"Damn it," I snapped. "Do you have another one of these? I have it all over my arms and... I just don't think this will be enough."

"I have an easier way, and it won't go to waste." He reached for my elbow and made me lift my arm. I watched in utter fascination as he leaned in and licked up my arm, some of the blood rolling to his tongue on it's own. His eyes were still blood red as he stepped in closer, and I stepped back. I kept trying until my back hit the wall. He finished with the blood on my arm and hand, then moved to the other, pulling the handkerchief out of it. He growled when I tried to pull away, and I tried to think about the last time *he* had fed. He was right; if I just wiped this off, it could go to waste.

The practicality didn't make me any less aroused.

The logic certainly didn't stop my gasp as he found

more blood on my neck and his hands spread out on the wall on either side of me.

He knows I'm attracted to him. I mean, we've been over this. He knows. He barely touches me until it's necessary. This is just... practical. That's all.

Then it was over. He backed off, his eyes still blood red, and I could still feel every line he'd licked over my skin.

"I'm..." He ran a hand over his face as he took several steps back. "I'm sorry. Apparently, I am also hungrier than I realized. I didn't know this sort of long night would have this effect on me."

"It's fine," I croaked. "Just, uh... give a girl a warning next time."

Alexius nodded, turning his back to me.

"You can change now," he said, his voice low. "Claim as much space on the mattress and whatever blankets and pillows you want. I will be fine with whatever is left."

I pulled off the blouse I had picked for the meeting, which felt like a lifetime ago, then pulled on a t-shirt probably more comfortable to sleep in, anyway.

Eventually, I settled on the mattress, claiming two of the blankets and a pillow for myself. I curled into a ball, trying to secure myself to stay warm because Henry had been right. The basement was cold. Alexius didn't lie down as the sun came up. He was leaning on a wall as sunrise forced me into some much-needed sleep.

22

CHAPTER TWENTY-TWO

My eyes opened to the dark basement. Replaying the night before, it took me several seconds to register how I had gotten there. My muscles were stiff and sore, everything yelling at me to not move as I pushed off the blankets and sat up.

"Alexius?" I called out.

"I'm here."

He was close enough that I was startled into falling over onto my side again. He wasn't just close. He was filling up the space I had left on the mattress, but he wasn't curled around me or anything. He was staring at the ceiling, no blanket over him, his arms behind his head. He had all the same clothing on, even his socks.

"Oh."

"Are you ready to get to the next victims?"

I knew he wasn't asking if I could leave right away. He was asking about my mental state, if I could handle seeing more dead bodies, more blood everywhere.

"Yeah, let me get up and stretch. You know, for weeks,

I thought vampires couldn't get sore, but..." I pushed myself to stand up, having to kick the blankets out of the way before I tripped. "Now I know different. I mean, I learned last night after you had me do all those squats and crunches, but now..." I put my hands on my lower back, leaning back and hoping I would stretch enough to stop hurting.

"Through years of testing, I found the best mattresses on the market. I'm glad you like the one in your suite, and it's been suitable," he said, sitting up. "And you've had no physical activity to work your muscles. While you slept, I was thinking about how long the night had been for you. While the workout wasn't much for me, it was for you. Then there was the meeting and coming to Alaska for a case. We've driven several hours, seen dead bodies. I'm not surprised you're sore." He stood and looked down at the mattress, even kicking it once as if he was disgusted. "Especially considering that is *not* a quality mattress."

"Did you sleep?"

"I did and woke up moments before you did, actually." He started patting his pockets. "I need to check if anyone called, and you need to feed... cleanly. I'll finish the bag if you can't. Find a blood bag while..." He growled, patting around harder. "I find my phone."

Finding his phone with the blood bags, I held it out to him as I counted how many bags were left. Only two and we were about to split one of them.

I held it away from my body, trying to get my fangs into it without spilling any, and drank as Alexius got someone on the phone.

"Rupert, it's good to hear you," he said, sounding

more relieved than I had ever heard him. "It's been a long trip already. Has anything unusual happened? No? That's good."

I felt full only a third of the way through the blood bag and gave Alexius a desperate look. He nodded once I made eye contact with him.

"I'm going to give you to Everly, so I can feed."

The switch was fast. I pulled my fangs out, then he grabbed the bag and was drinking as I fumbled with the phone in my now empty hands.

"Hi, Rupert!" I said, so glad to hear from someone I remotely knew.

"Hello, Everly," he greeted, sounding happy to hear me as well. "How's the trip going for you?"

"What's Alexius told you?"

"I haven't gotten an update since you got there. You can tell me anything you like. The lines are secure."

I talked as Alexius finished feeding but didn't give the phone back to him, telling Rupert about the long night, the new deaths, the werewolves, and about how I missed breathing the fresh air. For all the bad going on, the fresh air was a positive.

"I hope he lets you out when you get back. It sounds like you're ready, as long as he keeps an eye on you."

"I just didn't think it would be like this," I admitted, knowing Alexius was listening to every word. Looking over my shoulder, he had his head down.

"He's only done it because he knows you wouldn't live with yourself if you made a mistake. I really hope this trip tests your control enough for him to bring down the barriers a bit."

"Fingers crossed," I said, sighing as Alexius stepped closer again. "Well, I think that's everything, and our Dark Overlord is demanding the phone back."

"Our... Dark Overlord," Rupert said. I smiled when he chuckled, and Alexius bared his teeth. "Oh, yes. He's going to keep that nickname."

"I can hear you," Alexius snarled, his eyes going to the phone.

"Oh, I'm sorry, Dark Overlord. I mean... Dark Lord—"

Alexius grabbed the phone from me.

"I do not need another nickname from you," Alexius snapped, his chest against my back.

"Ah, but you have one now!" I could hear Rupert clearly, thanks to how close Alexius was. "Well, I should let you go. You two are busy, and you're meeting someone. I shouldn't make you late. Have a nice night!"

"Rupert!"

Rupert hung up, and Alexius was left glaring at his phone over my shoulder. Then he turned his eyes on me.

"I dislike nicknames," he growled.

"He seems like he's in a good mood, considering where we are," I pointed out.

Alexius sighed, the glare fading as he put his phone away. Stepping away from me, he grabbed his coat from the table.

"He was trying to keep the mood light because of where we are. He's good at it. You know Rupert can be serious when it's called for, but right now, he knows we're both here and..." Alexius studied me. "He made you laugh. You'll need those laughs before we go to the house."

My stomach dropped.

"Oh, yeah." Rupert had done a great job distracting me for a minute.

"Grab anything you need, and let's go. We don't have much time." He was holding a camera bag as he stopped in front of me.

I followed him upstairs, and we found Henry sitting on the porch.

"I know it probably wasn't comfortable down there, but I hope it was secure enough."

"More than enough," Alexius said, nodding. "Thank you for providing a space for our needs. I hope we're not in the way."

"Better you in the way than no one out here helping," Henry said with a shrug. "Come on. I'll take my truck, and you can follow me."

Alexius drove. We found a small cabin that looked more in this century than Henry's. He waved us to follow him, but from the outside, I could already smell the blood and death inside. I stopped breathing as I collected myself and mentally prepared for what I was going to see. I had looked at the pictures, so I knew what was inside. I shook myself as Alexius waited on me, then went inside before him. For only two people, there was so much carnage in the house just from the front door—bloody handprints on the walls, torn-up cushions, broken furniture.

"Vampires aren't normally this... destructive, from what I know," Henry said as he led us through the living room.

"Don't assume. Vampires are very much capable of this," Alexius replied. We stopped before a small hallway.

"This leads to the bedrooms. There's blood all the way back into the bedrooms, even though one body is in the kitchen, by the sink, and the other is in the garage."

"Anything you think might have been stolen or is missing?" Alexius asked.

"No, but I've only come over here a few times. There could be things missing I didn't think to check."

I looked around, frowning because I knew the same thing Henry did. Vampires normally didn't destroy entire homes when feeding. They could get blood everywhere, but they didn't break furniture. I looked down and saw footprints in the blood with broken glass everywhere. They couldn't be ours because the blood was dry. They went everywhere, with no pattern or trail I could follow. They overlapped in chaos, stomping on pieces of fabric and pictures of the couple and other people. Looking around, the walls had small nails where pictures should hang. There had to have been dozens of them, but only a couple were on the floor. I found others in the living room as though they had been thrown.

Alexius didn't move, but I knew he was taking in the scene. I didn't know what he was thinking, but everything I saw told me one thing. Reaching the broken dining table, I found handprints all over it, along with large smears, even a couple of footprints.

"Alexius, why does it feel like they were... having a party? This feels like youthful destruction. I saw it in college all the time. People would get drunk, break things, and call it having fun. Never something I really understood."

"If it feels youthful, it very well could be the case. People stay relatively close to the same mental age they were when Turned."

"That's fucking disturbing," Henry growled. "The partying. I know you vampires tend to act your... age."

"It is," Alexius agreed softly. I was still staring at the table when Alexius walked up behind me. "Something about this table you find interesting?"

"I think someone had sex on it," I said, crossing my arms. "Which is disgusting."

"I think you're right," he said, patting my shoulder before pointing at the table. "That would be an ass and the hands—"

"I can put the image together; I don't need an explanation." I would have been embarrassed, but that emotion couldn't beat out my anger. "They killed this couple, then threw a party in their house... destroyed their home... had sex in their blood."

"They were riding the death high. If they didn't know about it in Fairbanks, they know now."

"That makes this even worse. They're going to chase that feeling now." I thought back to Portland, to Claire, and how things had happened in the nest. "They're going to escalate. First, it was Kavik's family, which was more people, but they might have been newly Turned. That incident might have been an accident, and the injuries showed a lack of control over their strength. This was their first *hunt*, and they knew if they killed the couple, they would get high. They succeeded." I turned to

Alexius. "They partied, then moved on. There are four young vampires, but only two humans here. There's going to be more next time."

"Yes. There will continue to be more until they've overwhelmed themselves and someone gets away. We need to stop them before it reaches that point." Alexius seemed as if he already knew the conclusion I had to work toward.

"Well, I know how *that* ends," Henry said, sounding more bitter than I expected.

"We don't have to kill survivors every time," Alexius said, turning sharply to the werewolf. "Many times, their memories can be wiped, and we find a reasonable alibi for their disappearance, then put them somewhere they can be found."

"I'm going to see the body in the kitchen," I decided, walking around the table. I found the wife staring at the ceiling. Even from a few feet, I knew she hadn't just been bled out. She had been so thoroughly drained, I wondered if she had any blood left. Her skin was ghostly white, and there were no visible veins. She looked unreal as I knelt beside her. I closed her eyes but knew it wasn't effective. There was a chance they'd reopen, but I couldn't handle her staring at me, not right now.

The bites on here were the same as the many on the family outside of Fairbanks. Not small puncture wounds like I was used to seeing, but arteries torn out, which explained the blood on her clothing and the floor. Behind me, I heard footsteps and doors but ignored them as I looked at the blood on the floor. There were streaks missing.

Did they... lick the floor?

I kept going back to youthfulness. This had been so excessive.

Like a bunch of drunk teens or college students. I mean, it... it just screams delinquents.

Pulling out my phone, I realized I didn't have Kavik's phone number, but I wanted to know if this theory had any weight.

"Alexius, can you call Kavik for me?" I asked loudly. He didn't reply, so I straightened. He and Henry weren't in the room anymore. Heading through the door that had been behind me to a mudroom, the bloody footprints tracked into the house then back out. Alexius and Henry were in the garage, looking over the husband's body.

"Hey, can you call Kavik?"

He pulled out his phone and held it out. It was the new one I had gotten him, and I knew the passcode. I scrolled to Kavik's name, his most recent call with this phone because he had talked to Rupert on the old brick.

"Alpha Kavik. What do you need, Alexius?"

"This is Everly," He hummed as if he was okay with that, so I continued. "I have a theory, and I was hoping you could use it to narrow your search for anyone who has left town in Fairbanks."

"Let's hear it."

"Teens or college students, partiers. They might not have been party animals as humans, but they're embracing it now."

"I'll see what bites I get with that. That bad down in Beaver Creek?"

"You saw the pictures, but yeah... seeing it in person,

it's worse. Have you heard of any attacks besides Fairbanks?"

"None of the other werewolves I know in Alaska have had any vampire incidents, but they're out checking on friends now and have been since my girls and their family were killed. I'll call if they find anything, but I think we're right to assume it started here in Fairbanks. My pack has been asking around the city for anyone who might have left town recently. They should start coming back in the next couple of hours. I just have nothing yet."

"These things can take time," Alexius said, and I repeated that to Kavik.

"Yeah, they do. Good luck on your end."

"Thank you."

I handed Alexius his phone back.

"We need to go through the entire house. I agree with your theory. Young people, not just young vampires, a bad combination of youthful passion, energy, and invincibility." Looking at the body, his head tilted to the side.

"Destruction sometimes makes drunk or high people excited, depending on the person, but these are definitely destructive for the joy of being destructive types. It doesn't feel like a fight happened."

"No, it doesn't. He has no defensive injuries. They had caught him off guard, two of them feeding from him. From the angle,—"Alexius tore open the man's shirt, revealing bruising across the husband's chest "—one grabbed him from behind, locked their arms around him, and held him for the other to strike first. They each took a side of his neck."

"And two fed from her, divide and conquer, and with their first successful and intentional hunt, they celebrated." Alexius might have had his own ideas, but I was convinced.

"You're not going to do any of this, right?" Henry asked, and I knew the question was for me. "Kavik said you're pretty young, and you don't look a day over twenty-five. You did the red-eye thing earlier."

"I was twenty-seven when I was Turned, just over two months ago." I didn't tell him it was my birthday. I tried not to think about it, though it was hard, considering I was spending my birthday in the middle of a house where murders had taken place. "I'm sorry if you saw me hungry this morning. I hadn't had a chance to feed. But no..." I curled my hands into fists as I looked back down at the dead man, furious at the implication, furious at the ones who were so viciously killing these innocent people. *I will never be like them.* "You won't see me doing anything like this."

"She didn't behave like this as a human, so she has no inclination to behave this way now," Alexius commented, still intently looking over the husband's body. "Becoming a vampire changes us, but not so radically as to add new facets to our personality. It can reveal something others missed about a person, and oftentimes, that is surprising to those around the new vampire. It can bring out the best or the worst in us."

"So, you were a goody-two-shoes human, and you'll be one as a vampire?"

"I guess. I certainly don't plan to murder innocent

people and roll around in their blood while I destroy their home." Seemed pretty simple to me.

"Did Kavik have anything?" Alexius stood and brushed invisible dirt off his pants, then fixed his sleeves.

"No, but he's had werewolves asking around all day. He said he should start hearing from them in a couple of hours."

"Then let's comb the house. Maybe someone was sloppy and dropped a hint to their identities or how they became vampires. Henry, I would like to hear if you learned anything in town."

CHAPTER TWENTY-THREE

W e started in the garage since we were already there. I moved away from the body and found the keys to the truck parked inside.

"Was this their only vehicle?" I asked, unlocking it.

"Yeah, as far as I know. Well, they have another shed with a snowmobile, a couple ATVs, and a mountain bike. Pretty standard stuff to get things done around here throughout the year. Nothing was stolen."

I went into the truck, looking for anyone out of the ordinary, and found a gun in the glove box, which didn't seem out of place, considering we were in the Yukon. There had to be wolves, bears, moose, and many other animals out here humans had to protect themselves from.

"Did they run into a lot of wildlife?" I was curious if there might have been another reason for the gun.

"We've all had a bear try to get into our houses, looking for a bite to eat." Henry was behind me by the direction of his voice. "Found his gun, huh? Everyone carries a little protection, just in case. Normally, I don't need it. A lot of the wildlife is pretty skittish, and those that aren't, you should be skittish of them. Doesn't normally get violent unless someone is stupid, and no one in Beaver Creek is stupid, but we carry a gun, just in case."

"All right." I closed the glove compartment. There wasn't the scent of blood anywhere in the truck, so I exited and closed it up, hanging the keys where I'd found them. Henry was actually standing between Alexius and me. Alexius was in the empty space of the garage, looking at the concrete floor.

"There was a second car here," he said as I stopped beside him. "The couple was nice enough to let them use the garage."

"It was open when I got here," Henry added. "I closed it up because his body was here. I turned off all the power, locked everything, so people thought they left town if someone came by to see them."

"So, they met the couple in town..." I looked at Henry, wondering if he was going to tell us what he had learned.

"Oh, yeah, town." Henry pushed his hair out of his face. With his shoulder-length hair, he had a certain rugged mountain man or homeless look. "I couldn't ask too much without people getting curious. They know I'm a werewolf, and when I ask questions, they start thinking it's supernatural. They're right, but I prefer to make sure no one in town feels as if they're in danger. Normally, they're not. Well, there was a group of people who came through but didn't have the money to stay at the inn. A girl working at Buckshot Betty's said they heard them talking about it in the parking lot while she was on break."

"What's... Buckshot Betty's?" *I should have done some research about Beaver Creek on the drive.*

"Oh, the one restaurant in town. Sorry. We have one gas station, one restaurant, the church, and the airstrip."

"Oh, okay. You can keep going. Sorry for the interruption."

"Yeah, well, apparently, these two were there that night. Might make sense if they left, saw them still there, and offered to let them stay the night here. No one could confirm they did that, though."

"And no one got an idea of how old they were or what they looked like?" I sighed when Henry shook his head.

"She overheard, but she didn't pry."

"At least it fits the timeline," Alexius said as he walked around the garage. Nothing looked out of place. Someone kept this garage perfectly organized, down to the last screwdriver. When he was done, he headed to the door back into the house, and I followed him. We passed through the mudroom into the kitchen, where I pointed out the wife's body.

Disturbingly, her eyes were open again.

"I don't know if she fell on her back or was rolled later. They took some large bites out of her throat. I bet most of her blood ended up all over them instead of..." I didn't think I needed to finish. "Then all four of them were covered in blood." There were blood streaks on the walls. "Henry, could you smell them?"

"Everything in this house smells like Leah and

Johnathan. That's the problem with you vampires. I know vampires had to do this, but I can't smell you."

I looked at Alexius for confirmation. I had never heard that before.

"We don't seem to produce scents the way normal creatures do. I believe it's subconscious magic we use, though others think we don't make one at all. I told you we can mask our scents. It's something we do naturally. Hence why every vampire can do it. We are masters of stealth hunting and blending in. We have to be." He walked out of the kitchen. "I know many can't catch our scents with their noses. Werewolves and werecats find it frustrating because they rely so heavily on their sense of smell."

"But you do smell like your most recent victims," Henry said, waving around the home. "Doesn't help me here."

"No, it doesn't," Alexius agreed. "It also doesn't help after a few hours if you were to track them, either. Oftentimes, that scent will dissipate on its own in that amount of time. A smart vampire will know how to keep a human's scent from clinging to them, not that these vampires were smart. They would have reeked of their victims."

"But they got into a car and drove away," I pointed out. "I take it we can't track a car."

"No one here can," Henry said.

"Not without a license plate or a tracking device," Alexius confirmed.

We walked through the kitchen and living room, looking for anything that didn't seem to belong. I turned over papers that had flown everywhere, searched through the stack of mail the couple had left in the entryway. Alexius moved furniture so I could see if anything had gotten underneath. Henry watched us as we looked over the blood-soaked home.

The single bedroom in the back made me ill, but I tried not to think about the bloodstains on the sheets and let Alexius do the bedroom. I went across the hall to the other door, finding the bathroom.

The bathroom looked used. There was blood on the mirrors, but only around the edges. It reminded me of a bad cleaning job, as if someone had tried to wipe it off. The sink had the similar vibe of being half-clean. Someone had gotten blood on it, then ran the water. The shower had a few bloody handprints in suggestive places, but the tub was mostly clean.

"They cleaned off before they left," I decided as I turned to leave. Alexius came out of the bedroom at the same time.

"There's some blood in the closet. It makes me think they stole some clothing, things Henry would have missed," he said, looking over my head. "The bathroom?"

"They cleaned up. Probably changed into new clothes, then headed out."

"Which means we need to keep moving. There's nothing else we can learn here."

"That's it?" Henry asked, standing at the end of the small hall. "There's nothing else?"

Alexius tensed beside me, subtly moving his body between Henry and me. Not enough to block my view of the werewolf, but enough for me to notice. His message was loud and clear. He didn't like Henry's tone.

He's trying to keep me safe, but I don't think Henry is a danger.

"None of them dropped a wallet, personal clothes, a cellphone, or a credit card with a name. There's nothing else here. What we have here only furthers the theory of what sort of vampires we're looking for and how many of them there are. I'm sorry we don't have the answers yet."

"They rolled through my town, killed two people, and there's nothing you have yet to stop them?" Henry shook his head. "What good are the fucking nests if they can't keep all the vampires under control? What good are you if you can't stop them before it gets worse?"

"What good are werewolf packs if they allow lone wolves?" Alexius retorted, which made Henry drop his head. "We're going to head back to your home and collect our things. We'll let Kavik know when we've finished, and he can pass that along to you."

"Drive safe. House is unlocked."

"Thank you."

We walked out together, leaving Henry behind.

"He's going to burn the house down, isn't he?"

"Yes. He can't put it off because it's close to town, and it's a close-knit little community. Someone would know something was wrong sooner rather than later."

We got into the SUV, and I pointed out the obvious as Henry's house came into view after the short drive.

"We don't know where to go next. Kavik hasn't gotten back to us. We have nothing."

"We'll pack up and move out of Beaver Creek so the

locals don't see us and think we might be part of the fire Henry is about to start. Look at the map on your phone. Unless they've gone off the main road, there's only one direction these vampires could be moving. We will stop at every gas station to see if anything out of the ordinary has happened. We'll gain on them because they're going to spend much longer in one place than we will."

When we were back in the basement, I pulled up a map on my phone. He was mostly right, but there was a fork we would reach at midnight.

"Alexius," I said, showing it to him. "What should we do when we reach Haines Junction? We're, what, two days behind them? They're probably already made their choice and are way ahead of us."

"We hope we have as much intel as possible to make our best guess."

We loaded back into the SUV, and he started driving. I went back to my research to pass the time, reading through emails and private messages, taking notes, but it felt as if it didn't matter. He filled the tank at the gas station, and we got lucky. It was closing in twenty minutes. If Alexius had found a reason to stay for even one more hour, we would have been stuck in the city until the next evening, time we couldn't lose. Neither of us spoke as we left Beaver Creek. We had spent less than twelve hours in the little city.

I kept hoping we would hear from Kavik, but as minutes turned to hours, I lost hope. We stopped at small towns as we drove, five small communities as we made our way to Haines Junction. I was frustrated as we slowed down and stopped in Silver City, the last community I saw on the map with a name.

"Why hasn't he called?" I asked, grabbing Alexius' phone from the cupholder. It was the nice new one I gave him. I checked the calls and made sure he could make calls, checking the service and the Wi-Fi. I was still using a hotspot from my phone, which meant his phone could make calls using the Wi-Fi. Kavik should have called.

"We'll lean on my training until he does. Do you really believe he'll be able to find the answers?" Alexius shook his head as I looked up at him. "He's most likely stuck and has nothing to tell us that would be helpful. That's okay."

"It's not okay! We can't chase these vampires around Canada while they kill people, always two days behind them. Kavik needs to hurry up and tell us whatever he's learned. It might give us a chance." I growled, an unusual sound from me. "I'm going to call him back."

"Please don't harass the werewolf Alpha." Alexius was fast as he reached out and grabbed the phone from me. "If you do, he'll take it as a sign you lack confidence in him. That you, a young vampire with little experience, don't trust his age and competence. That you don't trust him to get the job done."

"Do you trust him to get it done? He said a couple of hours, and it's been nearly four since that call. We left Beaver Creek three hours ago."

"No, I don't trust him to get it done, but I won't rub that in. I work on my own and rarely rely on someone else. I always have other ways. The fastest and simplest way to get answers rarely works. Nothing is ever that simple."

"We'll be in Haines Junction in less than an hour after we're done here, and then what?" I shook my head. "We don't know what they look like or what car they're driving. We don't know if anyone will even talk to us."

"Maybe they're here," Alexius countered.

I looked up Silver City and snorted.

"Yeah, they'll be in a ghost town with no registered population."

Alexius got out, and I had little choice but to follow him. We looked over the ruined cabins, left for years. We found abandoned tents, and Alexius found animal tracks.

"Do you smell anything?" he asked me as we walked around one of the tents.

"No. Do I have a better sense of smell than you?"

"I wouldn't say better. You have a more sensitive nose right now. As young as you are, you are hyper aware of the scent. All vampires are attuned and aware of the scent, but you, right now, are the better bloodhound."

"So, my sense of smell will fade? It'll get worse? Is that what you're saying?"

"No. As you mature as a vampire, you'll be less likely to acknowledge or notice old blood or small amounts because you'll subconsciously register it's useless to the hunt. Right now, your mind smells all blood, then you have to process if it's what you need. I can smell it, but it takes active thought for me to focus on trying to find those specific scents. It's tied into your control."

"You know, Isaiah said you've never trained a young

vampire, but you know a lot about them... us. And you Turned Jacob."

"I know a lot about young vampires because they're often the ones I need to kill. Unfortunate, but true. Through that, I learned about how young vampires hunt, their sensitivity, and their lack of control. As for Jacob..." Alexius started back to the car. "I Turned him, but he trained me more than I ever trained him. I told him what I knew about myself. He was the one who did something with it."

"Yeah..." I followed him, hands in my pockets, and got in when he unlocked the SUV. "I still think Kavik needs to hurry and call us."

"It would certainly expedite everything, but we make do. There will be times when no one is trying to get information for us. I've encountered hunts where I had to hike through mountains with no way to call others for information. We will catch these vampires."

"We better," I mumbled as he turned on the engine and started driving again. As we continued toward Haines Junction and the crossroads where we had to choose which direction to take, I tried to think of anything that could help us decide.

24

CHAPTER TWENTY-FOUR
ALEXIUS

They arrived in Haines Junction after midnight, and Alexius was grateful to see real civilization again. Beaver Creek had been such a quaint little place, he barely had the chance to look, but too small and quaint for him. Alexius didn't like places where everyone knew everyone. Too much gossip where things that needed to be secret were suddenly front-page news.

"Haines Junction, population just over six hundred," Everly started. Alexius was damn grateful to have her around. He normally had to stop and look up these sorts of things on his own before going into a new town, so he was prepared. She expedited the research. "There are a few motels and inns, a twenty-four-hour gas station, a convention center, and a Yukon University campus. Oh, there's more. Let me zoom in... a campground, a visitor's center, and even more. It's a town on a major road. They probably get many people passing through and using it to refuel or stop for the night. Our group probably stopped here to refuel if they had any money."

"They stole clothing. Henry didn't notice anything else missing, but he wasn't close to them. It's not beyond belief they could have stolen credit cards or cash." It was easy to get money to keep going if someone was willing to kill and steal.

"That's what I was thinking."

Alexius pulled into the gas station, and she kept talking as he got out and started filling the tank. He left the door open, wanting to hear what else she had to say. With a town this size and the facilities it had, there had to be more.

"We have two options. We keep following the traditional Alaska Highway, which is currently Yukon Highway 1, or we head south on Haines Highway, Highway 3."

"What do you mean by the traditional Alaska Highway?" He'd never heard of it, but then, he hadn't visited this region in a few centuries. The longer he spent in the cold north, the more he remembered about the few times he had been needed to be here.

Those had been dangerous nights.

"Well, apparently, there's a route of connected highways people call the Alaska Highway. It's got a few official names, but it's a highway route constructed during World War II to connect Alaska to the rest of the U.S. If we follow it, we'll get on the British Columbia Highway 97, which officially ends in Dawson Creek, British Columbia." She shrugged. "I'm just reading what I see on the internet. Apparently, this is a route people like to take for trips."

"I see…" He could work with that. Traditional routes

called to people. It was historical. It meant something. It might not apply to his current quarry, but it was worth considering in their predicament. "Stay in the car. I'm going to pay for the gas and ask if anyone has seen four young people pass through."

"But—"

"Stay in the car unless there's an emergency," he ordered, then closed the door. He heard her hiss as he turned around and walked away. There were people inside the gas station, and he would not test her control when she was in a bad mood, thanks to Kavik.

That damn wolf. I know better than to rely on others for intel, but he's upset her. She was relying on him because she's not as hardened as I am.

When he went inside, a bell rang over the door. The attendant behind the counter smiled, putting on an act he had played thousands of times.

"Good morning," he greeted, leaning on the counter. The attendant smiled, but Alexius could tell the man was tired. Tired was fine, but he needed focus.

"I was hoping you could help me with something. My girlfriend and I are lost and trying to track down one of her family members." He rolled his eyes. "Younger siblings. I'm glad I don't have them."

Alexius felt only a tinge of guilt calling Everly that without her permission, but he needed an excuse to have a shy woman in his car who wasn't too threatening or unusual. He needed them to be human for a minute, and this late at night, a man in a relationship would do all the talking in a new place if the woman didn't feel comfortable. He was leaning on roles he had seen play out countless times.

At least we're appropriately aged. I've been told that with the right smile, I don't look much older than thirty. She looks younger than she is, but that's something she could correct for people.

"Yeah, they can be trouble," the attendant agreed as he put his hands on the counter, spreading them out like a bartender would. Alexius wondered if he had that job at one point. "Brother or sister?"

Alexius went on gut instinct, pulling together everything they knew so far to make a human snapshot of the group.

"Younger sister... would be with a group of friends... a bunch of wild kids with no care about who'll get hurt from their road trip. We know she's been abusing drugs and want to catch up with her before her *friends* help her OD. Or worse, get into a car accident out here. She's an adult, so calling in a missing person's report isn't really helpful. We're from Fairbanks, so we've already put a lot of time on the road. We know they passed through Beaver Creek, and we didn't see any sign of them camping out on the side of the road."

"But now you've gotten here and don't know what direction they went in?" The attendant sighed. "That's terrible."

"If you've seen a pack of twenty-somethings, I would love to know. There are four of them." Alexius tried to add some pleading to his words. The bell over the door rang again, and he turned to see Everly.

Damn it.

He reached out and tried to make it clear he wanted her hand. She tentatively took it, her expression full of guilt.

"I couldn't just sit in the car anymore," she explained.

"I was asking if he's seen your sister and her friends," Alexius told her. She nodded.

"Yeah, she's in trouble. I'm convinced of it," Everly muttered. Her grip on his hand tightened. "I can't believe she would run off with them."

"She's been doing drugs, and they supply her. Her ability to make rational decisions isn't exactly trustworthy," he said, trying to keep his own frustration out of it. Part of that had been for her. He'd asked her to stay in the car, and she hadn't. "I thought you were going to stay in the car."

"My sister could be hurt right now. I couldn't just stay in the car anymore," she snapped. "Plus, I need to stretch my legs sometimes, too."

"Hey, I can try to help you guys out. I can't *show* you the cameras, but I own this place with my family, so I can look at the cameras and see if I can point you in the right direction. We're looking for a group of four people, younger, yeah?"

"That's right," Alexius agreed. "They wouldn't have driven through in the day. They're night owls, all of them, and no one wants to score at noon, you know?"

"Oh, yeah. I'll call my brother. He was the one on the last few nights, so he might remember something."

"Thank you so much!" Everly smiled, then pressed her face against Alexius as the attendant smiled, then walked into the back. Alexius stiffened as she pressed against him, their fingers tangled together.

"We'll wait here," Alexius promised, moving to pull her into his chest, her back to the attendant. He couldn't miss how her arms wrapped around him *under* his coat.

I shouldn't have picked this cover.

He was paying for his mistake. He was physically attracted to her, but that was easy to ignore. She had emerald-green eyes he had liked when she had been human. Her body was taking on curves since she had Turned, and he enjoyed a little bit of curve. He was physically attracted to many people and had never had an issue with his control.

When he'd seen the blood on her chin in Fairbanks, he'd been a little aroused, and it had made him uncomfortable because of their living situation. Seeing her feed in Henry's basement had been more than he had been prepared for. There had been a feral look in her eyes and too much blood. He'd crossed a line, and part of it had been his hunger. That hadn't been a lie.

It wasn't only my hunger.

There was something about her that tugged on primal instincts he'd never indulged.

For weeks, I haven't had a single reaction to her feeding. Why now? Is it the way she's feeding? Drinking from a cup isn't natural, but driving her fangs into...

He had to stop that thought as he realized that was *exactly* the problem. She looked different when she fed that way, and that difference turned a simple physical attraction into something fiercer. Add in the long nights requiring more feeding, and he hadn't been ready for how much he would enjoy the sight and the behavior it would elicit.

I will be next time. I can't make her uncomfortable. I didn't save her to have sex with her. I won't degrade her or dishonor myself by making her think that's something I want or would require of her. She is here because of my choices. She lives under my roof and trusts me to teach her. I have all the power here, and I won't abuse it. I won't do it.

Alexius couldn't move away from her the way he wanted to if he intended on respecting her the way she deserved, but now he had the clarity to behave appropriately. He liked her, but not only in a sexual way. He wanted to see her flourish and see the fire burn. Not only for her, though he found her charming and interesting, but for himself. She was the perfect addition to his household.

My response to her feeding was completely natural, and I'm not a man who reacts purely on impulse anymore. I just need to remember it happens and ensure it doesn't overcome me. Jacob would be ashamed if he saw me in that basement with her. Completely ashamed.

So, he held her carefully, keeping up the act but trying not to push it further than it had to go. He was stiff, but if he let his mind wander, he'd give her a terrible impression.

It took too damn long for the attendant to come back.

"I have good news. My brother remembers a group of rowdy college-aged kids passing through the night before last. They bought nothing, only filled up their tank, then took off, but they were loud enough, he watched to make sure they moved on without a problem. We don't get many travelers at night this time of year, and if there is, they're looking for a place to sleep, not a party. He said they were in a blue SUV, something newer by the shape of it, but it was late. He said it looked like one of them was even wearing colored contacts in the brightest red he had ever seen. Seemed brighter in the light, but he didn't know if it was the lights playing tricks on him."

"Oh, I know who he's probably talking about. Which way did they head?" he asked, aiming for earnest as Everly tried to pull back. She stopped before he had to stop her.

"They kept on the Yukon 1," he answered. "Not back toward the border. You're on the right track. That was two nights ago. I hope you catch up to her and stop this foolishness."

"We do, too," Everly said, and Alexius heard the barely restrained fury in her words.

Keeping an arm around her as they walked out, he escorted her to her car door, opening it. She got in, and he saw her red eyes. He didn't want to address them yet, closing her door, then heading to the driver's side.

Time to figure out why she left the car.

He couldn't bring himself to ask until they were out of town. The entire time they sat in silence, and the only reason he finally spoke up was so he could cut her off.

"Look—"

"Why did you get out of the car?" he growled.

"I thought I could help," she said, leaning toward her window. "You're really intimidating, and I didn't want them to call the cops the moment we left because some threatening guy was asking about a bunch of kids and stalking them. But when I got closer, I realized—"

"That I'm smarter than threatening *humans*?" He shook his head. "I know how to act with them and dozens of stories I could tell them to make them sympathetic to helping me. I gave him a cover story about us and why we were looking for them, and with you not there, I didn't need to worry about us matching details. Also, your control is not good enough."

"My control was fine," she hissed.

"Your eyes are red," he snapped in return.

"That doesn't mean I was going to attack him, and I figured it out on my own. That's why I kept holding you when he came back, so he couldn't see them. I'm not a complete idiot, Alexius."

"I didn't say you were, but this wasn't your best decision. You could have jeopardized everything."

"You can't say I wasn't helpful. A desperate sister looking for a loved one who is in with the wrong crowd? I thought I nailed it and only added credence to your story. What kind of sister doesn't come in to ask about her druggie sibling who ran off? I made him think of us as a good couple, desperate to stop a young family member from imploding and made your story look more real." She crossed her arms.

"I heard the story as I got closer. I was listening really closely because once I got out of the car, I was committed. I knew I had to jump in without a problem. No, I've never done anything like that. I followed your lead, but I'm not sorry. So many people are *dead*, more people are going to *die*, and Kavik won't fucking call us back. I need to help. I need to do something. Anything."

He didn't like her choice, but he couldn't find it in him to keep arguing. He'd wanted her to work for him, and now she did. He was grateful this happened here and not in a more dangerous place, like a crowded city. It taught him more about her.

She's driven and doesn't like to feel useless. I need to be mindful of both those things and keep her busy, so she doesn't lose her sense again.

She was sulking, so he gave her the praise she had rightfully earned instead of trying to find the energy to continue the argument.

"Well, one thing has been nearly verified. I think we can assume your belief these are young humans who have been recently Turned is correct. You got that right."

"You would have figured it out on your own," she said, and he didn't like how she seemed down.

"Actually, I wouldn't have cared. I would have wandered and waited for them to kill again, then used that to give me the next location. They would have messed up. This group wouldn't have the skill to keep from making a mistake after more than a couple of hunts."

"I don't buy that. You would have seen what they did to that house and thought the same thing I did."

"No, I would have thought they got high from the kills and had violent sex, which can happen at *any* age. In fact, that's what I thought until you connected it to the idea of rowdy young people. How did you put it together?"

"It wasn't organized chaos like... a fight would be. You

know, you get into a fight, and things get knocked off the wall or tables, but they stay in their... relative position. A picture gets knocked off the wall, and it falls to the floor beneath where it had been, but that house... was just chaos. They took pictures off the wall and threw them ten feet away, hitting another wall. There were some behind the couch even though there was nowhere to hang them up there. It was stuff like that."

"I see," he murmured. He had never looked that closely before. Part of him regretted not seeing the first attack site because Everly might have seen more if she had been there, even if he got what he needed from the pictures. "I don't look at patterns in the destruction. To me, it was just destruction, and I had seen it before, several times, all with different causes. Good job." He felt better as her head came up.

"Thanks."

25

CHAPTER TWENTY-FIVE

An hour and a half later, we drove into the next town, Whitehorse, the largest place we'd seen since Fairbanks.

"Do you think we'll find anything here?" I asked after I read off the twenty-five-thousand population.

"No, but we need to decide where to go next."

Sighing as he parked at a gas station, I zoomed in on the map. We had just done this in Haines Junction, but Whitehorse was too big for us to make a guess they stopped at a gas station. This time, we had to make the blind choice. I looked up and down both sides of the map and started looking up local news, hoping there was a clue, while Alexius tried calling someone.

"Alexius, it's good to hear from you," Isaiah said. "How's the hunt?"

"It's more traveling than I'm used to." His conversation with Isaiah was a distraction, and I listened in instead of looking for intel like I was supposed to. "They're in a car, hitting places as they get hungry. The kills in Fairbanks were the first, then in a small town the next night over five hours away. We've confirmed they were all in their early twenties when they Turned, and they can't be more than a week into their new life, or there would be more bodies."

"Traveling..." Isaiah sounded bothered by that. "Newbies don't do that."

"A group of new ones might," Alexius countered. "Something is keeping them moving. Maybe it's to find a good hunting ground or the idea they might get caught by humans. They clearly don't know the way things are done. Have you heard from Kavik tonight?"

"No. Actually, I'm glad you called. Corissa told me he dropped off the grid and hasn't told her anything in several hours. It's not like one of the Alphas to ignore her or Callahan, especially in something like this. It has to be connected."

That made me put my phone down, and Alexius realized I was listening. He hit the speaker and continued speaking.

"It does. We've been waiting for him to get back to us. He was supposed to be looking for any missing persons in Fairbanks or anyone who left town and give us names if he could find them."

I frowned, something bothering me. Why would Kavik disappear? It was weird, but I was stuck on the *why*. Why now? What would make him disappear instead of helping us?

"I even gave him a relative age to look for," I added.

"Everly is the one who realized they had to be humans in their late teens or earlier twenties."

"Eighteen to twenty-three or four," I said, looking away. I was still confident in that, then it hit me.

"Good job," Isaiah praised like I was a puppy, but I didn't care. I was climbing into the back seat as Alexius tried to say something. I accidentally knocked the phone from his hand.

"Everly, what are you doing?" he demanded as I sat down, yanking my laptop out of my bag.

"I had an idea," I said, pushing my hair from my face. "It might fit everything."

"Oh, I would love to hear this," Isaiah said, and I wasn't sure if he was serious. That might have been because the phone was under the seat.

"Talk," Alexius ordered as he reached down for it.

"Elizabeth broke up with her boyfriend, Jaxon, over the holidays. Elizabeth was Kavik's great-granddaughter and one of the victims in Fairbanks. Well, not in Fairbanks. They lived nearly three hours out of the city or something like that. She was only in the city when she had classes. Not many people went out there, or that was the impression I got from Kavik."

"Agreed."

"Okay, so she canceled this trip she was planning over the summer because Jaxson was going to be on it." I hunted in my notes and saw some of the planned stops. They were going to get a hotel in Whitehorse on the first night. It was a ten-and-a-half-hour drive without stops, reasonable for a long road trip. I didn't do long road trips, but that seemed realistic for a long road trip, and they were planning on going in the summer when the sun was up more than not.

I tried to find more information about the trip on Elizabeth's phone and found a conversation from weeks back between Elizabeth and Alpha Kavik. They were going over the itinerary and who would be on the trip.

"She was going with four people, all about her age. Jaxson, Stacy, Calvin, and Amanda. Stacy tried to convince her not to cancel. I didn't know she was going on the trip when I read that. Amanda and Calvin are dating, so that might be the couple."

"Two of the vampires had sex at the second killing," Alexius told Isaiah.

"Ah, blood and sex. Typical." Isaiah seemed completely unsurprised.

"If it's Jaxson and these other three, they would bother Elizabeth," I said, staring at Alexius. "And her injuries have always made us think it had to be personal. You wondered if it was an attack on Kavik, but to me? I really thought it was her, and based on what Jaxson said to her, I could see him resorting to violence." His eyes closed as I explained as though he was envisioning exactly what I was saying. "She had to block him on everything because he wouldn't leave her alone." In my gut, I knew I was right.

"That's not your entire theory," Alexius said, his eyes opening and revealing blood red.

"Jaxson killed Elizabeth with his friends, who Kavik would know are also missing. They hit the road, probably thinking no one has any idea they're vampires. It's Alaska. Animal attacks happen all the time, right? Humans only know about a few supernaturals unless we're part of the whole charade. Werewolves, witches, and fae are the publicly known supernaturals. Vampires are particularly secret, more guarded about privacy and secrecy than most other species even need to be." I took a deep breath. I didn't need it, but this was a lot of talking at once for me. It let me collect my thoughts for a second to get to the next part.

"Kavik was looking into people in a certain age group who left town. If Kavik knows how bad the break-up was and how badly Elizabeth was hurt compared to everyone else..."

"Oh, shit," Isaiah snapped.

"He would have the same theory. I bet he thinks Jaxson went on the trip with his buddies to get the hell out of town and never go back. He probably disappeared so he could kill them himself."

"You have a copy of the itinerary they were planning?" Alexius asked softly.

"Yeah. They weren't planning a stop in Beaver Creek except to get gas, but they made the stop... and got the money they needed from the couple and ended up stopping in Haines Junction instead, smart enough to get away from the murders." I climbed back into the front seat with my laptop and her phone.

"This only leaves the mystery of who Turned these kids and let them free to terrorize everyone," Isaiah pointed out thoughtfully. "It doesn't sound like they were good candidates to be vampires. We don't Turn them that young anymore."

"We'll discover that once we eliminate the greater threat," Alexius growled.

"What's the timeline?" Isaiah asked, sounding so serious.

"We're two nights behind them, but we know how long they can travel every night. They won't be able to resist feeding every night, either, which will take them much longer than it will us. They'll want to indulge like they did with their last kill, which will continue to slow them down. They had to have spent at least a few hours in Beaver Creek."

"I was about to check the local news to see if anyone had been found mysteriously murdered by animals before I heard Isaiah on the phone," I said, going back to my phone. I had three devices in my lap, but juggling between them didn't bother me. "Also, we're staying on the Alaska Highway all the way to Dawson City. After that, they would head to Edmonton, Calgary, cut back to Vancouver, down into Washington State, Seattle, Portland, and farther. They wanted to see the west coast, San Francisco, L.A., all that. Then they would have turned around and headed back, but... I don't see that happening now."

They're headed for my brother. I mean, they wouldn't know who he is, but they're headed that way.

"There could be a hundred dead by the time they make it to Vancouver," Isaiah said softly. "Four out-of-control and completely unaware new vampires. This is a disaster."

"We'll catch them before they reach Edmonton. There's a werewolf pack in Calgary I would rather not deal with. I don't need two fucking packs on this,"

Alexius snarled. He put the phone in the cupholder without hanging up.

"I know you will," Isaiah murmured. "My mind is just running over the possibilities."

I grabbed the handle on the door as Alexius slammed the gas and flew out of the parking lot in reverse.

"Stop doing that. We'll take care of this," Alexius snapped. "You get Corissa to stop Kavik from making this any bigger than it needs to be. I don't want his fucking pack trying to kill Everly or me on accident because he's out of his fucking mind with grief and can't tell them who we are." I had never heard Alexius use language that vulgar. An occasional curse word here and there, but this was fully pissed off. "They might be ramped up and willing to kill any vampire they meet. We'll just end up as unfortunate victims."

"Well, if someone wanted you dead, that's... uh..." I trailed off as his blood-red eyes flicked in my direction.

A good way to do it.

"Is that a theory behind the mysterious postcard? I'll just say... clearly, whoever sent it must have Turned these children. They wanted you chasing them and dealing with the problem yourself, Alexius. Everly might be right. Someone might have dragged you into this to get you killed by werewolves. I know it's unlikely to work for them in the end, but it's possible."

"They could get Everly killed," he snarled.

"Well, who took her to Alaska?" Isaiah retorted.

"I did," I hissed at the phone. He wasn't going to blame Alexius for me being involved. I wouldn't let him. I wanted to be here, and Alexius hated himself enough for things I couldn't change, but I wasn't going to be another reason for him to do so. I wouldn't be that for anyone. "I get to make those choices in my own life."

"Orphans... all that free will. This is why most of us die young," Isaiah muttered.

"Would rather die young than live without a conscience," I retorted.

"Yes, I do believe you've tried the dying young thing once before. How did that go for you?" Isaiah countered. "She has a bigger bite now, Alexius. I don't know what you've found to feed her in the north, but... stop." This time, I knew Isaiah was amused.

"She's full of fire," Alexius whispered.

"I can tell. Good to see her stop trying to be a mouse and proving to have the mind for the job. In fact, she's perfect for you. She thinks differently."

"I told her something similar," he replied as he sped us out of Whitehorse.

"Well, I know my role in this. I need to let Maria know everything. I'll tell her and the werewolves what the current theory is. Good work, Everly. I look forward to seeing you both when you report that you've killed these vampires. Don't get killed in the process." He hung up.

At that moment, I felt the second-guessing coming, and my eyes went wide as horror spread through me.

"Oh God, what if I'm wrong?" I asked, turning to Alexius.

26

CHAPTER TWENTY-SIX

"Then we adjust," he answered as if it wasn't that big a deal.

"But if I'm wrong, more people could die, and I'll... look like an idiot, reading too much into things."

Alexius shook his head, and it felt so dismissive.

This is serious. If I'm wrong...

"Yeah, it's easy for you to shake your head. You won't be the one who—"

"I get theories wrong all the time," he said, sighing. "Isaiah was wrong about Jacob's cause of death. He never blamed me for having to adjust my plans because my idea of the situation was wrong. I wasn't mad at him for getting things wrong with Jacob... mostly. We get things wrong because we don't have all the facts, not because we're... idiots, as you want to call yourself. When you live long enough, you get comfortable with being wrong sometimes. It has happened and will happen again. We can only make decisions based on the information we have. This is what we have, and without you, we wouldn't have it."

"You would have—"

"I would have asked the pack to look through their devices, but they wouldn't have told me anything. Kavik would have figured it out on his own, and I would be blind because clearly, he's not keen to tell us anything now. I would have been in the dark to the movements of the Alpha of a werewolf pack, which is not a good place to be. Now, we can reasonably and safely assume he's following the same trail we are, and we're ahead of him. But he'll catch up when we have to sleep, and he'll have an entire pack to rotate while driving."

"He's not dead, is he?" It was a question I should have asked sooner.

"We'd know if he was dead," Alexius replied. "Off the grid and dead are two different things for werewolves. Dead would be easier to confirm. His pack would shout it from the rooftops even if he ordered them to silence. His orders mean nothing when he's dead. Janek would be the new Alpha, and he would have immediately declared his loyalty to Callahan."

"So not dead, just missing. Silent and refusing to get in touch with anyone." I checked the time. It was nearly three in the morning. We had another six safe hours of driving, if that. I knew we were moving south, so the mornings would be a little earlier.

"You were going to check the local news," Alexius reminded me.

Luckily, most news was digital now, and I found exactly what I thought we would.

"A family of four was killed in Whitehorse. Unknown animal or brutal murder. The police don't know what to say about it," I told him, shaking my head. "The news broke... yesterday morning, and police believed they had died around midnight." I tried to think about the timeline of the deaths to judge if we were gaining on the vampires. "That puts it..."

"Just over twenty-four hours ago. We're only one day behind them, then."

"It doesn't take that long to get from Beaver Creek to Whitehorse. Why did they stop so soon? Do we want to go back and look at the scene? Isn't this a huge security risk for us?"

"They're not trying to make time. They're trying to feed and party every night, but they know they can't stay in town when they do it," Alexius reminded me. "The humans will never find the murderers. They'll never connect it to other murders because they don't know about them. Some will whisper about an old legend in fear, but no one will find anything."

"And?" I knew there was a way this could go wrong.

"I will call Isaiah back, and he will send someone to destroy anything left behind on official records, don't worry. People will know something happened, but there won't be any evidence. They'll even assume it's supernatural, but that's not my problem. They can't prove anything happened if it doesn't exist. No one likes when humans get their hands on our victims, but we've dealt with it before. It'll become a local horror mystery."

"Are there legends up here that could be... similar?"

"I haven't thought about it in a long time, but our

driving has made me think about it tonight. Yes. In fact, feral vampires once lived this far north and further. They would wake in winter, feed on villages and hunters, native and foreign, then return to a deep hibernation in the summer. In the summer, they only fed if someone stumbled on them."

"What happened?"

"I was asked, along with other vampires who do the same job, to clean it up. They were animals. They were like me before I met Jacob... worse. I could go into a city without turning heads. They could not. They lived as creatures of winter, and a few didn't even look human anymore. They had so adapted to the life that the shadow magics you've seen done temporarily were permanently active for them. We eradicated the vampires we found—without mercy. We captured a couple to show Isaiah and Maria. It happened about four hundred years ago." Alexius shook his head. "But those aren't around anymore. Only whispers and legends among the locals. There are other local supernaturals to consider as well. Someone could well blame this on a wendigo. Those are real and oddly similar to us... in our own way."

"Don't say it," I groaned in disgust.

"We're also cannibals," he finished. "They blamed most of the vampire-related deaths on the wendigos. They might have believed those vampires were also wendigos, so we have the advantage of potential folklore on our side."

"We're not..."

"It's a bit... Actually, it's considered obscene and taboo

to call vampires cannibals," he admitted. "Isaiah, Maria, and many other vampires like to believe we might have come from humans, but we're not human anymore. Or maybe it's different since we're capable of rational thought and don't have to kill our victims and consume their flesh."

"I think... I'll go with Isaiah on this one," I mumbled. "Let's, uh, decide where we should stop next. If they only went from Beaver Creek to Whitehorse in a day, then... I mean, that's not very far."

"What is the next town with a hotel? These vampires wouldn't risk protecting themselves from the sun without proper shelter. My guess is they left Beaver Creek, filled up their gas tank in Haines Junction, then made their way into Whitehorse. They slept the day, then hunted before leaving. They'll probably do the same tonight, establishing a pattern, a safe way to have their fun."

"What if we're in the same hotel?" I asked softly.

"Perfect," he snarled with a smile.

I looked, but everything was pretty bare until Watson Lake, nearly five hours from Whitehorse. Alexius hit the gas, accelerating as I explained.

"It's about the distance they want to drive," he explained. "They would have reached the city last night and found a place to stay."

"Which means they would be hunting and heading out... right now," I said, looking at the clock. "Or moving on."

He nodded.

"Wait..." I kept looking at the map. "There's a ton of

small settlements along the drive. What if... I mean, they want to escalate, right? A town of six people, alone... they could do anything. That's why we checked the small towns coming down from Beaver Creek to Haines Junction, right?"

"That's exactly why, but they've been staying close to populated areas. They're not afraid to expose themselves or their kills. Give me names," he ordered. "We'll make the stops. We'll make them fast, five to ten minutes each unless we find something. If out of sight from the main road, we'll pass it. That seems like too much work for them."

I gave him each name and watched our approach on the GPS each time. We searched quickly, trying to find the scent of blood or evidence someone else was around or had just left.

Coming up on the last of the small names on the map, it was nearly eight in the morning, and I was edgy. We were just under two hours from Watson Lake, but we only had about two hours until sunrise. We were pressed for time. I had already booked our room, but I didn't know if it was going to be enough.

I was feeling a little on edge.

That's probably an understatement.

"The sun—"

"We'll make it." He kept his eyes on the road, and I kept mine on him, wondering why he wasn't stressed about the time. "I'll look around this one, then we'll leave. If everything is closed up, then we'll move on and hope we didn't miss something."

"Okay, but then we need to head to the hotel in

Watson Creek. We're going to need to drive fast." This had been my idea, and I was regretting it.

"I can handle that. Plus, you need to feed. You should now, so you're safe for humans." We rounded the corner as I jumped into the back seat. It had been a long night, and I'd forgotten that our supply was nearly done. He was already out of the SUV before I could say something. I drank it, finishing the bag because I hadn't eaten since sunrise, over twelve hours before. Climbing back into the front seat, I could see him knocking on windows and checking the doors. I lost sight of him as he went behind a building but was back in view in under a minute.

He got back into the vehicle, shaking his head.

"Nothing here. Their hours show they're closed much of the night, so our vampires would have seen no lights and figured there was no one to hunt, even if the motel had people staying."

"Well, that's good," I said as he hit the gas, kicking up gravel, and we drove toward Watson Creek. "Oh, I drank the last blood bag."

"Then tonight, we'll have to set aside an hour for you to feed. That's not a problem." He gave me a short look, then went back to focusing on the road. "You're scared you're going to kill someone the way they are, aren't you?"

"Just a bit, but I don't want to, so I'm going to do everything I can to stop myself from... being like them. I know you'll stop me if there's a chance I don't succeed on my own."

We arrived in Watson Creek, going faster than the speed limit, and Alexius quickly found the hotel I picked out.

"Stay here. I'm going to make this as quick as I can." He jumped out and ran inside, leaving me wondering if we were going to beat the clock or have to hide in the shadow inside. I knew we wouldn't burn just because the sun came up, but in all my time as vampire, I hadn't raced the clock. He would be able to stay awake, but I wouldn't. The moment sunrise happened, I would drop wherever I stood or sat. People were going to think I fainted and needed a visit to the hospital.

Or Alexius drugged me. That's a possibility.

He was back only two minutes later, and we grabbed our bags, heading inside. I heard the beep of the SUV being locked as the automatic door closed behind us. Once we were secure in the room, I relaxed as Alexius started making sure the windows were fully closed.

"I'm so glad hotels are making early check-in easier to schedule," I mumbled as he light-proofed the room. I was staying out of his way because I had a feeling we didn't have time for a lesson, not a safe one. He was using duct tape to make sure the curtains wouldn't budge.

"Agreed. I used to have to do some convincing or just avoided establishments altogether."

"I'm not surprised. You would camp in the woods if you could, wouldn't you?"

He finished his duct-taping and turned on me, shaking his head.

"Absolutely not. Like you, I am not all that fond of the dirt. I certainly don't want to bury myself alive. No, I would break into homes and sleep in their basements or attics. I would look for someplace with no one home. They were easy enough to find." He continued to shake his head as he put away the duct tape, muttering again in a language I didn't understand.

I checked my phone as Alexius came over. He made me stand up, then pulled the blankets off the bed and dumped my pillows onto the floor as I stood there with my mouth open.

"Sleep behind the bed, between it and the wall. Here." He pointed to the tiny walkway on that side of my bed. "I'm going to sleep between the two beds. If any light breaches the room, you'll be in a safe location. Remember, if something happens, like the window is broken or someone breaks in, you will wake up. Your instincts will recognize the threat. The first thing you have to do in that situation is check what sort of light you're going to if you move. Don't sit up immediately, or you could risk burns."

"Oh, okay..." I wasn't prepared for a sudden survival lesson. "Um, you didn't do this at the first hotel."

"I was going to, but we didn't stay. I didn't want to clutter the floors yet, either."

I looked down at my phone and finally pointed out the one problem we would have when we woke up.

"It takes fifteen hours to get from Fairbanks to here. Kavik could pass us before we wake up." I sighed. "Why aren't we letting him kill these vampires? I mean, I know it's your... our job, but..."

"He will not care who Turned them, and that's the root of the problem. He's enraged. He'll see them and think of his humans, then tear them limb from limb. If Kavik wants his to be a successful hunt, he'll have taken time to prepare for it. That's means we have extra hours. Get some sleep, Everly."

I did, but the entire time I waited for the sun to come up, I wondered who died tonight. I wanted to know just how many people would not see the sunrise just like me.

Except I knew I'd get up again, and they wouldn't.

27

CHAPTER TWENTY-SEVEN

A lexius and I moved fast when we woke up. I searched for local news while he was grabbing our things. He had three of our four bags, and I was nearly touching my phone's screen with my nose while carrying the last bag as we walked out. I ignored the burn in my throat, not as bad as it typically was when I woke up, and I had a feeling it was thanks to the short days. He kept a hand on my lower back as we walked through the halls and the lobby, which had so many people in it. I heard at least ten heartbeats, able to pick between them. Some were accelerated but were calm and steady. One felt weak, and I turned with curiosity to see an elderly man talking to a younger man. The elderly man had a weak heartbeat while the younger man had a strong one, strong enough to make me stare as my fangs slowly descended. Alexius' fingers curled, and he had a handful of my shirt. It was the only reminder I needed, and I went out the door with him, and we got into the SUV.

"Good job," he said as he locked the doors of the SUV

around us. "We'll feed on a stop, somewhere less populated. Any news?"

I looked back at my phone and nodded, holding it up.

"Alexius, it was here. Bodies were found at four a.m. by a coworker of the husband and father there to pick him up..." I trailed off. "Same size family, though. They might not have found what they wanted. There's also evidence of a break-in. Like they forced their way in and committed the attack. Police don't want to confirm it was people, but I think they assume it was a sick home invasion." Which was ten times worse than an animal attack.

"A different hunting pattern than they used in Beaver Creek. It's probably what they did in Whitehorse as well. The trap of needing help probably didn't work a second time, so they took matters into their own hands. They targeted a home with people, and it cut a step."

I looked over the map, trying to find where their next place to attack would be. If we drove fast enough tonight, we could catch them. Punching in town names, I tried to see what would be populated enough, and there were a lot of options.

"There are three towns coming up with roughly a hundred people in them. The next biggest town is Fort Nelson, with over three thousand."

"How far is Fort Nelson?"

"Six hours, almost exactly, and it doesn't look as though there are many hotels before that. I don't think they're going to find any RVs at the one RV park, either."

Alexius stopped and put gas in the car as I kept checking, just to make sure. I tried to do the math in my head. Sunset was at 5:15 in Watson Lake. We needed six hours to get to Fort Nelson, which put us there at eleven.

"Do you know what this dead zone really means?" he asked as he got back in. "It's unlikely we'll be able to find a safe place for you to feed."

"Could Isaiah find a way to get blood to us?" I asked, looking up.

"I could have asked him, but doors to anywhere take his coworkers, which could leave me in someone's debt. Corissa might agree because I am doing this case as equal trade..." I watched him think. With Alexius, I was beginning to tell when his wheels were turning. In reality, they always were. "Text him with *my* phone, not that other one. He'll find a way. Tell him where we're headed, and we might be able to schedule a drop-off. Six hours is plenty of time for him to plan."

Finding Isaiah's name, I texted, quickly explained the problem, my fingers fumbling over the fact Alexius was using an old phone that didn't have a screen keyboard. I had to fix errors more than I got it right.

I should make him upgrade completely to a better phone.

Isaiah called back almost immediately.

"Look, I can do it, but you two are idiots," Isaiah said. "Tell Alexius that. Tell him he didn't think this through, and I'm going to make sure he remembers this. Forever. I fucking knew he didn't think this through, but you were both so damn insistent. *Free will* and all that."

I side-eyed Alexius, who was rolling his eyes but said nothing.

"I think he heard you."

"Good. Now, I'll ask Corissa about agreeing to get a

door open with me. Alexius, if she doesn't do it for free, you're going to owe her the favor."

This time, Alexius nodded.

"He's okay with that," I told the irate ruler.

"You'll need to secure a location. Rent a *motel* room right now and give me the room number. We're going to need the ability to get off the property as quickly as possible."

Grabbing my phone with my free hand, I got busy finding a motel.

"Now, I can bring preserved blood, a two-day supply at most. It'll be a bit stale, but you'll survive. Do you think you can catch these vampires in the next town... Fort Nelson?"

"If they're there, I bet we can find them," I confirmed, with Alexius nodding again. "He thinks so, too."

"Good. I'll bring a few of my people to help and tell Corissa this is a great chance for her to come and try to head off Kavik with her own werewolves. She agrees with your theory. A human family member is one of the very few things she's positive will make an Alpha go dark instead of report to her. Together, we can search the whole damn place. They won't get out."

"See you then. Everly will send you the motel information," Alexius said, reaching out and taking the phone from me. "And I might not have thought this through, but you can admit she's been incredibly useful on this case." He held the phone between us.

"Yeah, she has. I said that during the last phone call. But—"

With a small smile, Alexius hung up on Isaiah.

"I wanted you to hear that," he explained as he dropped the phone in the cupholder. "Call the motel you pick and tell them you need a confirmed room number before we check in, and we'll be arriving just before midnight. We'd prefer something on the first floor. We don't want anyone to hear too many footsteps."

I secured all the information I needed and sent it to Isaiah with my phone this time, not wanting to fight with Alexius' old phone. When he confirmed receiving the information, the ruler said nothing about how Alexius had hung up on him.

"He just doesn't seem like much of a ruler," I pointed out again. That impression hadn't changed at all.

"You haven't seen him play games. He's more relaxed than a lot of the other members because he's confident in himself and his bloodline. He's secure in his power, but he doesn't act so relaxed with others. I've seen him judge other situations, ones where he's made tough decisions. He sees it all and makes the best decisions for vampires that he can, his resolve in his decision never breaking once he's made it. He and Maria often butt heads over who is truly better for the vampires and the goal of the Tribunal."

"Who do you think is?"

"I'm friends with Isaiah, but I rarely judge them that way. In fact, it's better that we have two different viewpoints of the ones in charge. Sometimes, and I've said this to Isaiah, I agree with Maria, and I'll explain why to him, but truly, Everly, I am not a man for politics. Certainly not politics at the level Isaiah is involved in. Neither was Jacob. We had wildly different personalities and different reasons for staying out of them, but we had that much in common."

Since we had another long drive, I continued the conversation. These long drives were slow, but at least they offered me this opportunity. I decided on the softball question first.

"Why did Jacob stay out of them?"

"His heart was too good. He didn't want to deceive and lie to people to get what he wanted. He wanted to lead by example, to be a force of change with his actions and not schemes. His heart was too good for all of us."

"Why do you stay out of them?"

Alexius sighed, but no answer came immediately. I waited in the dark, wondering what sort of answer I was going to get. With him, it could have been anything.

"I stay out of them for selfish reasons. A mix of distaste and laziness bred from the knowledge I could kill most of them."

"Most?" It took effort for me to get that out.

"There are a few who would... concern me. The werecat is older than me. The current King and Queen of the sidhe would be fights I could lose if I wasn't properly prepared, but that's not the point. The point is, I just don't care. I found my role, and everyone leaves me alone. I decided what I wanted for my immortality centuries ago, and politics didn't factor in. Situations like this one annoy me. Too many people on the case, hovering around and watching us. I don't enjoy camping, but those hunts bring me some level of... peace. Serenity. Me and the target. It's simple."

I probably wasn't the only person who had heard that

explanation before, which meant I could be the only person who saw the parallels between it and his time before Jacob.

He refocused the drive. That's all. He took his old hunting tendencies before he met Jacob and turned them into his job. That's probably one way he stays in control of his bloodlust, by feeding that *need.*

"I don't ruin that?"

"No, but we're on a politically charged case. Perhaps if you were stomping around the woods somewhere, but I'm certain I would get used to it. Getting used to it is worth someone covering my weaknesses, though. You have a softer way of talking to people I can't manage with other supernaturals. They would know it's false if I tried, but you... you might have confidence issues, but you know how to be kind. You're more empathetic than I am. Any other personal questions?"

"Figured me out?"

"Clearly, but I would tell you if I had a problem with answering them." His smile was there, and I realized the funniest thing.

We could be friends, and that would be... well, kind of amazing, actually.

"Why did you start this job? You said you just did this because you didn't want to see things go back to the old times, with out-of-control vampires everywhere. But really, was there an inciting incident?"

"Oh." Alexius sighed. "Jacob had just started his first nest. We had begun learning the secrets around vampire units living together and seeing it involved a blood exchange... I decided against it. I could have been in his nest, but he found his place, and I didn't truly feel like it was my place. I had known and lived around vampires for some time, but the idea of being in a structured community wasn't a life I wanted, not even with Jacob. He understood. I considered finding Isaiah, but he was forming his own nest with his first offspring. He was also making waves. A naturally charismatic leader, Isaiah. He was talking to others forming nests about how they could govern everyone and such. Agreements were made... and some vampires disagreed and went against it in bloody fashion."

"So, you started killing them," I said, pulling my feet onto the seat to rest my head on my knees.

"No, not immediately. Isaiah and others went after them. Many died. It's a bloody piece of history for our kind." Alexius curled his hands on the steering wheel, and I was entranced, desperate to know how this story ended. "Jacob sent me a letter detailing how he was trying to help new vampires. These dissenters were Turning humans and leaving them to cause devastation. It frustrated me to see my son so lost about how to stop the killing. Eventually, they tried to turn me against Isaiah and the others who wanted these new rules. I told them no, and they tried to kill me, thinking that if I wouldn't join them, I was a threat to be eliminated. The second time I told them no, they didn't have a choice but to listen, and I made sure they wouldn't cause any more trouble, for me or for anyone else."

"Ahh..." *I knew there was some inciting incident. There had to be.*

"I saw a way I could be part of this new community,

and I took it. To protect it for Jacob and for Isaiah... and to protect it for me. Without them, without their ideas of what the future could be, I would have reverted to a beast, eventually. I didn't want that. I decided to become the sword. The world my son and Isaiah wanted to build... I would defend the world they built because I and many others needed it to be this way. I was an effective and powerful predator who had little to do in the new world, but I could do that. I still do. My job is one that will never be done. I'm okay with that, and it's grown over the years as humans have advanced, and we've discovered pockets of vampires like the ones we found here in the north. I became the antithesis of Jacob, killing ones he wished he could save, but I was also his greatest supporter. And I could be there for him. When my son met vampires he couldn't save, he had his father to help him, to do the hard task, so he didn't have to stain his own soul after trying so hard to help them."

I didn't know how to reply, but I didn't need to. A moment later, Alexius continued.

"For roughly nine hundred years, I did this job alone. When the Tribunal formed in the thirteenth century, Maria and Isaiah reached out to other vampires, powerful warriors, and asked them if they would help enforce the new Laws. They didn't ask me because they didn't need to. If a vampire did something that jeopardized us, I would deal with them whether or not they asked me." He flicked a look at me. "You're the first vampire I know of, aside from me, who hasn't needed to be asked by Isaiah or Maria. The others are also paid handsomely as part of their agreement to do the job. I take... donations if they force them on me, and sometimes I bill them for minor expenses to annoy them, but I don't require a paycheck. There is no price I would take for doing this job."

"Then we have something in common," I pointed out.

His serious expression fell away, and he revealed that smile again.

"We do," he agreed.

"We don't need money, fame, or anything else. We just know this has to be done." I couldn't begin to describe how saying those words really made me feel. I knew why this was important. I was part of it now.

"We do," he repeated, and his smile grew a little more.

There was one thing I could identify by saying the words.

They felt right.

"We're going to catch these assholes," I declared boldly.

His smile had fangs, top and bottom, and his eyes flashed blood red.

"We will."

28

CHAPTER TWENTY-EIGHT

W e reached Fort Nelson earlier than planned, and my throat was burning like someone had shoved a lit torch into it. At eleven, I picked up Alexius' phone and texted Isaiah, letting him know. His response was fast, only telling us to stay put. He couldn't rush anyone to move sooner than midnight, no matter how pressing it was.

"But we're here," I muttered, knowing how terribly hoarse I sounded. "Why can't he get here faster?"

"He's dealing within the rules established by their organization," Alexius explained. "It probably has to do with his attempting to organize a large group to travel through the Tribunal's domain. There must be some sort of security check he needs to have done before he can come, which cannot be rushed."

"It's ridiculous. We're only asking for something a few minutes early. Thirty minutes at most."

"I agree it's frustrating, but the Tribunal has strict rules to keep them from betraying each other. This is one of the reasons I dislike such politically charged situations. There's red tape everywhere. We don't have to deal with it, but our allies do."

"What are our options?"

"I can take you hunting now—"

"No!" When Alexius gave me a surprised look, I tried to explain. "I don't... I don't trust myself with a human right now. I don't want to get out of the car right now. I don't want to see them, hear them, or be near them."

"It's good you can think clearly enough to recognize that and tell me how you feel. I'll make sure you don't go near any humans." Alexius stopped at a red light. "Then we have two other options."

"What are they?" I asked once the light turned green. "Give me something to think about. Something other than..."

"We'll begin a preliminary look around the city," Alexius said as he passed the light and took the first right into a gas station. "Or we could check into the motel early so you can hide. How do you feel?"

"What's the preliminary look around?" I wanted so badly to keep being useful. I had to make sure this wasn't something too important to skip because of me.

"We would just drive around, maybe spot their vehicle, maybe see a home with lights on. Could be anything, and it would help us point others in the right direction once they're here. We wouldn't be as effective as the people Isaiah will send into the city with us later, though. With more people looking, it would be more thorough. The chance you and I find four vampires in a city with over three thousand is... unlikely by ourselves, not with a tight schedule and the condition you're in." He stopped at the pump and started getting out. Before he did, he looked back at me. "I recommend the motel."

"Yeah, I like the motel idea." I was hungry. I needed to feed. There was no reason to take more risks than necessary. Getting into the motel would be tricky enough. I couldn't stop breathing, as though my nose was hunting for the scent of blood. I could hear the smallest sounds in the car, from the squeak of Alexius shifting his weight to the way the fabric of his pants rubbed against the seat. The world became too loud as Alexius opened his door, and I tried to hear everything and block it out at the same time. The world smelled like gasoline, which overwhelmed my sense of smell. He quickly shut and locked the door, the clicks echoing in my ears. It took everything I had not to unlock and open my door to try finding something to eat. I didn't look toward the building, where I knew humans would be.

My stomach growled from being too empty for too long. My heart squeezed as it looked for something to pump through my system. My throat burned, desperate for blood to pour down and quench the thirst.

I hated every one of those sensations. My body was demanding something I couldn't give it.

When Alexius got back into the car, he drove straight to our motel. When we arrived, he didn't get out immediately, picking up his phone. He texted faster than me on his old model, and I heard the punching noises, insistent and demanding.

"Isaiah, damn it. You have this power, and you can't convince them to move a little faster?" he snarled. "Everly, do not look up and out of the vehicle. Keep your head down and your hands in your lap. Do not get out without me, okay?"

"Okay," I promised, my voice nearly failing me. "Is this normal?"

"Yes, and I'm sorry I pushed you so long without feeding. We should have hunted in Watson Lake."

"It was... too early," I reminded him. "Can't hunt at six p.m., right? Too early. Too many people are awake and around."

"Yes, it would have been too early," he agreed, sighing. "Could have stopped."

"We made a plan. I'll... I'll be okay. Get the room." I didn't want to walk through the lobby. I knew it would be a disaster. Even thinking about hearing a steady pulse made my fangs ache.

"Stay." He left, closing the door again.

But it didn't stop a breeze from flooding the car and making me inhale deeply, all my instincts telling me I needed to hunt. I could smell the cold night air, the scents of the world beyond the SUV carried by it. Trees, snow, the crispness of wild air. This was a fairly developed town, but there was still something wild about it. No pollutants like gasoline, just beautifully perfect air.

My mouth watered, and my throat burned. My hands shook as I held them firmly in my lap. I closed my eyes, not even wanting to look at them.

I tried to focus on the case. Jaxson. That son of a bitch was out there with his friends, killing people, draining them...

The burn grew to an inferno, blazing more painfully than I'd ever felt before.

No, not that. Can't think about that.

Something buzzed in the car, and I raced to check it, wondering if it was Isaiah saying they would come sooner than midnight. I breathed only the smallest sigh of relief to see my hands were normal, with no vicious claws waiting to be used.

The text, though, wasn't to Alexius' old phone, the thing I wanted to throw in the trash. It was to his new one, the one I had picked out just for him, and he refused to make the full switch. I saw the name Kavik but didn't have time to read the text as I heard footsteps.

Looking up, I saw Alexius walking toward the car. Undoing my seatbelt with one hand, I unlocked my door with the other. I needed to get inside. I had to. I had to hide and wait for blood. He would see the text and figure out what Kavik wanted.

I grabbed my door handle, and he was suddenly there. Alexius made sure I couldn't open the door. I pushed harder and gave him a confused look through the dark windows.

"I'm driving us to our room," he explained through the window. "That will shorten the walk you have to make."

That made me let go of the door, and I hit the lock again, pulling away as if it was on fire.

Walking around, he opened his door and got in with a strong wind, carrying more than the crisp night air. The exact scent I wanted was there, a faint bit, but I caught it.

It had to have been carried a long way to get to me, but it didn't matter how far it was.

I was going to find it, and it was going to be *mine*.

Fresh blood.

I lunged for my door, able to get it open before Alexius knew what was happening, before *I* even understood what was happening. My body was telling me I was moving, but all I could think about was the scent of blood on the wind. I didn't stumble or lose a step as I jumped out of the car and started running toward it.

"Everly!" Alexius roared, sounding distant. He might as well have been on a distant mountaintop, too far for me to care that he was saying my name.

I ran, unable to tell my legs to stop, not *wanting* to tell them to stop. Something else took over, and my vision grew sharper and tunneled at the same time. I forgot where I was, only seeing obstacles I had to get over or around.

I was several properties away when I realized I was being chased, and something told me to run faster. I needed to feed, and the other predator couldn't take this from me. I wasn't going to starve, not tonight. This was my hunt, and no one was going to keep me from it. Somewhere to the north, prey had bled and exposed a weakness. It was strong and healthy, and I needed it.

Someone shouted as I entered a neighborhood. I wove through the buildings, jumping over fences, knowing I needed to shake this other predator, this competitor. Scaling a house, I jumped to the next roof, and my feet were silent when I landed. I did this for several rooftops, then dropped between two and took off into the trees again, letting them give me cover once again.

As I raced through across backyards, through trees, always heading into the wind, I only looked back once and hissed in satisfaction. The other vampire wasn't on my heels anymore.

Now it was just me and the blood.

Passing a last row of houses from what I could see, I entered the thick woods behind it after jumping the last fence in my way. I couldn't stop or slow as the scent of blood continued to grow thicker in the air. I could hear the heartbeat growing louder and more intense with each stride I made.

I heard a second heartbeat, thumping to life and getting stronger and faster with each second.

The scent of blood was thick and heady, too much for me. I snarled as I ran.

Then I saw my prey in the arms of someone else.

Then my prey died, the smell hitting me like a brick wall, a red flag that there was nothing here for me anymore, at least nothing good.

The body was dropped unceremoniously into the snow, and I snarled at the one who killed her. The blood pouring from the body now was worthless... even less than worthless—it was spoiled. It would do me more harm than good.

That was mine!

The other vampire looked up and wiped his mouth, looking surprised by my sudden appearance.

"Oh shit, there's more of us," he said, then grinned, revealing double fangs. Not like Alexius' but paired on his upper jaw. I had never seen fangs like his. "Well, damn, I didn't know. Hey, Stacy! Get over here, look at what just showed up!"

I didn't move as another vampire ran up, going so slow, I wondered if she had been on the hunt.

Not a threat.

"What the fuck?" she said, looking at me. "What's wrong with her hands?"

I looked down and saw my fingernails had become claws and realized I was in the worst place possible.

I tried to get rid of the claws as horror overcame me but wasn't able to.

Oh shit.

"What's your name?"

I looked up and recognized the face of the vampire who had just killed the woman in the snow. I knew his face from pictures online and his character from the messages he'd sent to Elizabeth.

Jaxson.

"Can you talk?" the girl asked.

That one is Stacy.

"Everly," I answered, my voice hoarse. "My name is Everly."

And I shouldn't be here, but I'm going to make sure every single one of you dies tonight.

CHAPTER TWENTY-NINE

ALEXIUS

She's faster than lightning.

That had been his first thought as he'd grabbed his phone and chased after her. He knew she was riding entirely on instinct, and it was pushing her to her limit of speed and agility, telling her she needed to find the meal she had caught on the wind.

He cursed as she went into the neighborhood and knew she must have caught the scent of their killers. This was their preferred hunting ground, people's homes, where their victims would feel safest.

He ran as quickly as he could, and he wasn't a particularly slow vampire for his size. His training saw to that, but she was everything he wasn't—lithe and driven by intense hunger. He realized as they jumped fences in the backyards that he would lose her. There was no way he could close the distance between them.

Everly, please come off the hunt. Do it for me.

She didn't. He scaled a home he had seen her on and

saw her drop between two others much farther down the road.

She's fucking smart. Damn. She's a natural predator and never knew it.

He couldn't help but respect it a little, but that respect was overwhelmed and shadowed by the knowledge Everly was going to do something she regretted. He had to stop her, but he couldn't catch her.

I need another tactic. I'll find the source...

He lifted his head and inhaled deeply, hoping to catch what she had in the wind. It was obvious once he had it but so faint, his mind hadn't even thought to register it. His hunger didn't care about such a distant meal. He had to focus on the smell of blood. He was too old and advanced as a predator to think it was a prospective meal.

She's too young to ignore it. I made this mistake and every other mistake that will happen tonight. This is on me. I should have left her with Isaiah. It would have hurt her, but I should have left her. All I wanted was to give her a purpose, to free her from the basement, and let her do what she wanted from her first night. To help me, to work with me.

I have failed her.

With that guilt and regret, he started jogging, knowing her racing would still beat him if he ran. He needed backup now if he was going to run right into the problem while Everly was out of control.

If I don't have an extra pair of hands... I might have to kill her, too.

The idea of that made him call Isaiah.

"How many times—"

"Everly caught the scent of fresh blood on the wind,"

Alexius started, cutting off Isaiah's irate opening. "Faint. It has to be more than a mile from our location. She took off at top speed while I was getting in the SUV to drive us to our motel room. She's faster and agile. Her instinct is strong, and I believe she's heading directly toward the vampires we've been tracking. There are other possibilities, but none as likely. If she kept at top speed, she's already on the human and feeding. There's just no way I can catch her before that human is dead."

"Oh, fuck."

"Indeed. I need you to hurry and get everyone here. I have two hands, Isaiah. Only two. There are five young vampires and blood in the air. You can imagine how this might end."

"You only need to capture one alive," Isaiah murmured, but it wasn't comforting. They needed to capture one of the four killers from Fairbanks.

"Two hands. If I don't have backup and soon, I might have to make a choice. If Everly is still out of control by the time I track her down with them, I'll need to choose. Get Everly out alive or one of them."

"I know. Let me pass this along. We're due in ten minutes if you think you can hold out."

"Everly might kill someone," he reminded his old friend.

"Every young vampire will kill at least one person. How they feel afterward is what keeps them alive or not."

"I have no doubt she'll regret taking that life for the rest of her life... In fact, she might regret it enough to end her life early. Killing someone would kill her," Alexius snarled. "She's too good, Isaiah. She feels so strongly about this. I offered to take her hunting when we arrived in the city, but she told me no because she didn't trust herself around a human. Over twelve hours without a meal and she resisted the offer of a hunt. I didn't think she would catch the scent of blood over a mile away."

"It had to have been the perfect wind and freshly spilled. It's damn impressive she caught it from that distance."

"Get here," Alexius snarled.

"I can't rush it!" Isaiah roared back. "The truth of the matter is, Corissa and I have pushed the other Tribunal members to get involved. Alexius, with the number of people we're trying to move through the Tribunal domain, all of them had to be woken up. We're moving over thirty people into the domain. It looks like a coup to the others. We had to fucking find everyone, then we had to have talks. We've agreed on midnight. I can't move it up because the others are bringing in security for themselves in case we're lying to them." Isaiah snarled wordlessly at the end, and Alexius knew his friend was furious with him, with the whole damn situation.

Alexius trudged through the snow, following the wind and the growing scent of blood. He stopped the moment he realized the blood, and the person it came from, died.

Oh, no. Everly...

"A human just died."

"You wanted to protect her from me and make her *happy*. You reap what you sow, Alexius. Now you'll have to deal with her personal fallout because she just accidentally joined the monsters she wanted to hunt with you." Isaiah's condemnation rang true, but from Isaiah's curse, Alexius knew there was going to be an immediate backpedal. "I'm sorry. That was harsh and unkind. Alexius, I know you don't have many people in your life, and you just lost Jacob. I know how important a solid relationship with her is to you and know you were just looking out for her best interests in your own way. These are things people disagree about all the time. You had a plan. The plan was working. There's no way you or she could have known she'd pick up the scent from such a distance."

"I'm going to help her," Alexius swore. "I won't let her be destroyed by this."

"If she's your replacement for Jacob, I have no doubt about that. If she's anything like Jacob, this just might strengthen her convictions and push her to do better, but you know her better than anyone else. She's an unknown. I was just piecing her together."

"She's not Jacob's replacement." Alexius repeated those words to himself more often than he wanted to. The things he felt around her weren't what he felt with Jacob, but a thought he had long before came back to him.

A little fire isn't the sun, but it's warm enough.

"It's not the same with her," he continued, needing Isaiah to believe it.

"No, Jacob was your son, and you have made sure she is not yours in any way. That right there makes it very clear this is not the same situation. Get her away from that body. Drag her out of the damn town if you have to.

When we get there, we'll go after them, so you can focus on her. They won't outrun us."

"Thank you."

Alexius almost hung up, but a werewolf's howl filled the night, followed by several more.

"Let me guess... that must be Kavik's pack," Isaiah said, his words dry.

"It must be. I have to find her. They'll kill her if they realize she's killed a human. They won't care she's mine or if she's helped this case. They'll only think she's become like the others."

Hanging up, he started running again.

CHAPTER THIRTY

I heard the howls and turned toward them, not even thinking about the other two vampires as I got caught in my own frantic thoughts. I didn't know the time or how long I had been running from Alexius, trying to track the source of the blood. I hadn't checked the time in the SUV while I had waited for him at the motel.

Which meant I didn't know if those were good werewolves or less-good werewolves. Both groups were hunting the murderers I was with. The difference was, one group was less likely to kill me with them.

"Holy shit," Stacy said, and I heard the crunching of snow. The fear in her made her voice shake. "They found us? Do you think it's the Fairbanks pack? Do you think it's Elizabeth's family?" That fear from her felt so *real*, because I was feeling a little bit of it myself.

"Fucking dogs," Jaxson hissed. "Need to be exterminated. You know what? Stacy, go back to the house. Tell everyone we're killing some fucking werewolves tonight. They walked all over us when we were human. Not anymore. We're fucking immortal now, too. Fuck them. I don't need to follow their fucking rules. We left Fairbanks. They don't have any fucking power here."

I was a little stunned by Jaxson's bold and cruel confidence.

Is he an idiot? Those werewolves are going to tear him apart limb by limb while he screams because he won't die until they decide to tear his head off. Kavik is going to make this brutal.

"Hey, Everly, yeah? You should come with us! We've got blood to spare," Jaxson called out.

I turned around, quickly deciding on my act. I wanted to hit this guy. I wanted him to be torn to shreds, but I had to be careful. There were more of them, and I was alone. I knew Alexius would come for me, but until then, I could be useful. I could make my monumental mistake into something productive. I could watch and listen. I could talk to them and learn all their plans and motivations.

You try so hard to be a mouse.

Isaiah's words, but he was right. I did try. I didn't much feel like one right now, but I still knew how to act like one. It would make me seem harmless, and people weren't careful around harmless little mice who didn't have any power.

"Oh, thank you," I said, taking a step toward him. "I mean, only if you're okay with it. I, uh, was really hungry when I caught her scent and came running. I was going to hunt when I saw her die. I wasn't expecting to see other vampires here."

"You a local?" he asked, waving for me to follow him as he started walking. I jogged to catch up, and we followed Stacy through the trees. They all ran, but it was human slow, and I felt sluggish. I wasn't sure how I had gone so fast earlier, but I knew I could again if I needed to. This just felt... terrible.

"No, I've been traveling. The long nights here are really interesting. I'm from farther south. Georgia, actually. Not born and raised there, but it's home right now. The nights aren't as long there, so it's been really nice to have more time awake." Talking was easy. With no need to breathe, I didn't have a lung capacity problem like I had in high school when they made me run a mile.

"Oh, shit, I didn't even think about that!" Jaxson laughed, and Stacy looked back, a disgusted look on her face. The house came into view, and the backdoor opened with a guy in the door. I caught the smell of the blood inside, but this time, I didn't go running. The scent of death was still too strong from the woman's body behind us. Even then, it still took so much of my will not to go running for the people inside.

I can't kill them. I won't do it. I want to make sure they get out alive. I have to.

But my throat burned like hellfire.

"Hey, how was your little game, Jaxson?" Calvin crossed his arms, glaring down at us. "And who the fuck is this?"

"This is Everly. She's another vampire passing through," Jaxson explained, laughing. "And my game was fun. She wanted to run. I let her." He ended with a satisfied growl, a cruel grin twisting his face. "Stupid bitches always think they can run or fight. Women."

"Everly?" Calvin looked over at me. "You look like a freak, Everly."

"Oh, um…" I looked at my hands and nodded. "Yeah, I do this when I'm really hungry."

I followed Stacy and Jaxson up the stairs. My heart would have raced if I were human or recently fed, but it was eerily still. Without the heartbeat, I found it easier to stay calm and think about what I was saying and how. However, it was also a sign of just how hungry I was, and when the last of the group showed up next to Calvin, her face covered in blood, I had to stop walking to keep from doing anything.

"Well, we have blood," Amanda purred as she wrapped her arms around Calvin and started pulling up his shirt. She looked me in the eye, and I was surprised to see so little of hers. Her pupils were *massive*. Then she pushed a hand down his pants.

"How many have you let her kill?" Jaxson growled, grabbing Calvin's shirt.

"Two, but we got three more. You know how fucking slutty she is when she's high. It's amazing."

"Yeah, well, you two might not have heard it, but there are werewolves howling and they might be from Fairbanks," Stacy snapped. "Amanda, quit being a dirty whore, and let's get ready to bunker down before these assholes come here."

The crack of a slap made me take a step back. It happened fast enough, I didn't see the slap, but Stacy was on the ground, her hand over her face while Jaxson snarled over her.

"Who is in charge here, Stacy?"

"You are," she whispered.

"Who fucked you when no one else wanted you?"

"You did," she answered again, and if I had anything in my stomach, I might have lost it.

"Who's the dirty slut who fucked her best friend's boyfriend?" he asked softly, his smile even more twisted.

"I did."

"Don't fucking forget it," he growled, then stormed inside.

I couldn't move. What sort of person wanted to hang out with this guy? I didn't, and getting over that was proving difficult.

I need to know how this happened. I have to move. I know I do. I have to get them talking. Inside is safer than outside if the werewolves are coming, but...

I don't want to be in the same house as him.

I don't want to be in the same country as him.

The rage and disgust I felt for Jaxson was the only thing that matched the burn in my throat. Then Amanda spat at Stacy and stuck her tongue out. Calvin chuckled, shaking his head as he pushed Amanda inside and shut the door. I was completely forgotten, but my fury was growing with every passing second. I had to refocus it. Now wasn't the time. I was on my own. I reached out to Stacy, leaning down to make sure she wasn't hurt.

"Are you okay?" I asked softly.

"Get away from me, bitch," she hissed, pushing herself

to her feet. "Jaxson is *mine*, do you hear? Eventually, he's going to admit I'm the one who's always with him, the one who will never leave him. He'll apologize for that later and make it up to me like he always does because even if he won't admit it, he knows. So, if you get within ten feet of him or even look at him the wrong way, I'll fucking kill you. Once I deal with Amanda, that sloppy, dumb bitch."

With no idea how to react, I let my hand drop when I saw the disgust she directed at me. I tried to keep my expression neutral, even a little scared, but really, I pitied her. I hurt for her.

"I don't... I only came because I could smell the blood," I promised, stepping back. Another howl filled the night. Instinctively, I knew it wasn't any closer. "I'll stay out here if it makes you feel more comfortable."

"I would prefer if you disappeared. We don't need another dirty slut in the group," she hissed, then went inside, leaving me on the porch.

You know what, Stacy? Right now, me too. Disappearing sounds like a great idea.

I turned back to the trees and tried to focus on not moving. If I could stay outside, the werewolves might think I was helping them, just listening while I waited for backup. I was backing up on my idea of inside being safer. There were people in there, and I didn't want to see them, but remembering them made me focus on their intense, fearful heartbeats.

I could just fucking run. That's what I should do. I don't have blood on me. I don't smell like any of the victims...

No. No, I'm going to help *these people. I'm not going to kill them. Their hearts are going to still be beating tomorrow morning.*

The door opened, and I was startled to see Jaxson.

"So what are you doing?" he asked, coming to my side as the door swung shut. I tried to keep from recoiling as he smiled down at me. He was tall, nearly six feet to my five and a half, on a good day. He was muscled, clearly either in a sport or did manual labor. There was no way he had his kind of body without doing something.

I was revolted by it.

"I was thinking about the werewolves," I admitted. "You should have cleaned off before walking back here. If you don't smell like the human you feed from, werewolves can't smell you."

I shouldn't have given him that advice, but it would keep him busy. He didn't try to kill me when I ran up on him, so this seemed like a fair trade to keep from pissing him off.

And it might get him talking.

"Really?"

"Really. We don't produce a smell they can track. The only thing they can track is…" I waved at the blood on the snow, marking his trail. "But the snow tracks would help them even if they didn't have the blood, so…" I shrugged. "Normally, werewolves don't care about vampires hunting. They have their needs, and we have ours. They should leave us alone."

"They fucking better," Jaxson said, snorted as he crossed his arms. "You seem like you know a lot. Do they even know about vampires?"

"Of course, they know about us. We're one of the

many supernatural species in the world. There's a government and laws. The whole thing. Don't worry. What you're doing here won't get anyone in trouble so long as you clean up at the end."

"What?" Jaxson's nostrils flared. "Clean up?"

"Make sure... people can't tell it was vampires?" I played confused at his questioning. Focusing on the act wasn't quite enough not to hear the whimpering inside, but it kept me from moving to investigate. "Come on. We can't expose ourselves to humans. They'll destroy us. We *eat* them."

The whimpering became a man pleading, and I tried not to hear the words.

"Fuck the rules," Jaxson finally said, shrugging. "They'll never know it was us. We're immortal. We can't fucking die, anyway."

Oh, but you really can, and I can't fucking wait for you to learn that.

"Yeah, there is that," I agreed. "So uh... a family? I normally pick up one guy, feed a little, then move on."

"Really? That's fucking boring. You know the rush of having them in your power. You can do anything you fucking want to them, and you just pick a guy and feed a little?"

"There's no need to be wasteful, right?"

"Oh, you are a cute, innocent little thing, aren't you?" His lecherous smile made me feel sick, but the mouse act was working. "You never killed anyone?"

"No." I tried to be embarrassed about it.

"Then you aren't really living," he whispered, leaning in. I stepped back.

"I'm sorry. I have a... problem with my personal space." I made sure he remembered I had claws as I sheepishly rubbed my neck.

"Well, we'll just have to get you fed and see if that loosens you up a bit. Let's go." He grabbed my arm and pulled me toward the door. Before I could think of attacking him for touching me, Calvin reached out and grabbed my other arm. They pulled me inside, and the door closed again.

"You'll have to pay me back for this," Jaxson whispered in my ear before shoving me into the middle of the room.

I barely heard those words, my entire focus on the blood everywhere. The loud, fearful heartbeats of strong, healthy people.

And how fucking hungry I was.

31

CHAPTER THIRTY-ONE
ALEXIUS

A lexius found Everly's tracks first, seeing how light they were in the snow. She had still been running and doing things she had no control over based on the tracks. Her speed was pure instinct. Her lightness of foot was the same. He ran beside the tracks, following them until he found the inevitable. He skidded to a stop, his heart racing in a way it hadn't in a long time. He went to a knee and started inspecting the body, the snow around it red with the human's blood. He rolled her over, hoping to find the bite that killed her. The woman was young, probably only an older teenager, maybe eighteen or nineteen.

And the bite...

It was one of them. She didn't do this.

He was filled with unimaginable relief. This was their double-fanged throat tearer. He had never yet tried to teach Everly the differences in the bite patterns, knowing there was only so much he could teach on a case while they were fighting to catch up to a group of killers. Plus, he had little experience teaching this specific part of his hunting technique. It was easier to educate about bite patterns using photos of victims, memorization tests, and going over the little nuances in an office than it was to use real bodies covered in blood in the middle of a stressful situation.

With the four vampires they were hunting, there were four distinct bites. The double-fanged one always tore out throats, and Alexius could see tiny scratches from every fang before the penetration of the skin. He'd initially thought it was tentative, but he was leaning more toward a sadistic streak in this one. Tentative vampires weren't so precise and consistent. This one knew exactly how they wanted to incite fear and pain before claiming a life, repeating it with every kill except the first.

Elizabeth. That was her name. Kavik's great-granddaughter. She had been killed by this vampire, but there had been no scratches. I only know the kill was by this vampire because of the formation of the skin tearing.

Alexius stood up. This vampire had one thing against him. Double fangs were fairly rare and random, which made the bites even more identifiable.

But it wasn't Everly, which was all that mattered.

He looked around, seeing the tracks in the snow leading away from the kill. He looked back at Everly's tracks and saw how she had stopped, then walked forward. There were three clear sets of tracks leaving the kill.

She left with them, and I don't know why. There are too many possibilities. She probably didn't have a choice. She ran into them, and they would have been suspicious or aggressive if she had tried to run away. Or they coerced her to follow them, promising to kill her if she didn't.

Or they offered to feed her, and she couldn't say no because of how hungry she was. She hasn't killed anyone yet, though. I have to get there and stop her from being dragged down to their level.

Alexius started following the trail and saw how Everly had come onto the scene at a different angle than how they left. With that, he realized neither he nor Everly had passed the home where the victims probably lived and were still being kept. Alexius didn't need a reason this woman had been out in the woods. If the sadistic one enjoyed inciting a little fear before the feeding, this was just an escalation. There was nothing special or unique about the cruel hunting tactic to achieve the right flavor.

Alexius snarled, his entire focus on getting to Everly.

I'm coming. I was too late last time, but you've given me another chance. I won't be this time.

He realized werewolves were running with him at the last moment. A large wolf, massive compared to a natural grey wolf, jumped in front of him and snarled as Alexius stopped in front of it.

"Don't pick this fight," Alexius warned. "I will go through you."

It lunged for him as another werewolf came in from the side.

Fucking pack hunters.

He was faster, dodging the one from the side, which was the real attack. As it passed, he grabbed its fur. Using its own momentum against it, he diverted its leap through the air and sent it into a tree, cracking the tree in half as the body broke against the trunk. The tree toppled over as the werewolf lay whimpering on the ground.

Alexius turned and snarled at the first werewolf while more came through the trees.

"Kavik, Alpha of the Fairbanks Werewolf Pack, present yourself, or I shall declare you a coward," he snarled at the wolves. He saw the shadows behind them, his eyes so good in the dark.

Kavik, Janek, and another werewolf were still in human form behind their werewolves.

"The kills are ours," Kavik snarled, moving through the giant wolves. "I am going to destroy those vampires before you can whisk them away for questioning. See, while you were driving for Beaver Creek and my werewolves were looking for names, I was looking into you. You, Alexius the Hunter, sire of Jacob. He was the one who rehabilitates these types of murderers, wasn't he?"

"You talk of him in the past tense, so you know my son is dead," Alexius said, his body tense, ready to spring into action as another werewolf foolishly came for him. However, he was outnumbered. He could easily kill one, two, even three if they came at him in those small numbers. If Kavik sent all ten of his werewolves at once, Alexius would only be able to run or die. He'd take some of them out, probably four or five, which might help Everly...

It would also help the murderers she was with.

"Yeah, I do," Kavik confirmed. "We just want to stop you so we can take the kills. I want Jaxson to die by my hands tonight. I want all of them to die by my hands tonight."

"I need to know who Turned them," Alexius reminded the werewolf.

"If you try to interfere, my werewolves will kill you. I don't fucking care about that. I want justice for my little girls. And I don't know if you'd send them to someone else to fix them. They don't deserve to be fixed."

"The only person who ever *fixed* vampires was my son, and you know he's dead. I have no intention of letting any of them live, Kavik. I just need their information."

"That's too bad." Kavik started walking away, following the direction of the trail. "Where's your little... assistant? Everly."

"She tracked them ahead of me and was able to integrate into the group earlier, right before you announced your hunt," Alexius lied. He smiled when Kavik turned to him, surprised. "She has an incredibly keen nose for blood at her age. She's not intimidating, but she's resourceful and knows how to play along with people to make them talk. If any of them die while I took them into custody, won't give up the information I need, or anything else, I have information from her. Plus, she'll give me a better idea of what to put in my report."

"I didn't think she was that... ballsy," Kavik growled, shaking his head. "Stupid of you to let a little thing like her out of your sight. If she gets hurt, it's a lesson that she should stay out of things too big for her."

"Don't make the mistake of underestimating Everly," Alexius warned. *It's time to draw a line in the sand.* "If you think you're going to storm in there with her in the middle and risk her life further, then *you* are going to die tonight."

Kavik growled again, this time a wordless rage. Alexius let it finish so the Alpha could speak his mind. Or try to.

"Don't—"

"Isaiah and Corissa are coming to this town at midnight, in only a few minutes. Do you really want to test me? Isaiah and everyone who follows him will fight for me and for her. Corissa has been a little pissed that one of their Alphas has gone dark in the middle of this. Do you think she'll defend your choices?"

"How—"

Alexius charged, pushing off as quickly as he could, faster than the werewolves around him. He was at Kavik before the Alpha could react. He had the werewolf's throat and squeezed, forcing the werewolves to back off as they realized their leader was in peril, and they would end his life if they tested Alexius.

"I run this show," Alexius snarled. "And you intend to endanger someone that is important to me. You should have done better research, Kavik. I kill people who even *consider* that. The only reason you're still breathing is I hope you have a shred of sense, and we've never been enemies. We didn't even know each other before this. I don't particularly like having dealings with other supernaturals, so don't make this a troublesome one." He squeezed a little harder, making Kavik's face turn red as he cut off the werewolf's airway. He reduced the pressure and smiled viciously. "Oh, I forgot. *You* have to *breathe*."

"You..." Kavik snarled. "You killed everyone involved in your son's death. Give me that. Give me the ones who killed my girls."

"If you *behave*." Alexius knew he was asking for something that might be too difficult for the Alpha. They had a hard time bending when they were so emotional and personally invested. They were used to being in charge, guiding and leading, not following. "And I only got to my son's murderers because Everly handed me all the evidence I needed on a silver platter. I will not let you put her in danger."

Alexius kept his eyes on Kavik's, knowing the importance. Alexius wasn't intimidated by the wolf eyes staring back at him or cared about the wild energy swirling around them. One on one, he could kill Kavik without working for it.

That made him Kavik's better.

Kavik lowered his eyes first.

Alexius released him, knowing this battle was over.

"You've wasted precious time," Alexius snapped. "Keep your werewolves spread out. Have them surround the home to catch any who escape the building. You and I will enter. No one else. There may be living humans still in the building, and we can't risk them getting killed, Turned, or Changed. We don't need this to be any messier than it is, are we clear?"

Kavik's expression shifted to one of horror.

"Current victims, other humans... I didn't even consider..."

"That's why I'm in charge."

32

CHAPTER THIRTY-TWO

I couldn't stop walking toward the family. They were on their knees in their living room. One woman had mascara stains running down her cheeks. She looked older, and I assumed she was the wife and mother of the family. The other girl seemed much younger, which made me sick. Then there was the father, the one pleading. There were also two dead bodies. An elderly man and woman.

"Me. Kill me and let them go," the father pleaded.

I looked at him, then nodded. My bloodlust, my hunger... it didn't really care. It was just hungry. Really, the man had just gotten my attention and reminded me I had to feed, and he was... as willing as he could be.

"Okay, sure," I mumbled.

"Aw, that's no fun," Jaxson said.

I ignored him as I went to the husband, listening to his strong pulse. He hadn't been bitten. The others had been, but not him. He was the best meal. The healthiest.

I didn't go for his neck. I grabbed his arm and sank

my fangs into his wrist. My first pull and swallow was like water after being lost in the desert, so different from the bags of blood. There was something *alive* to it that the bags never had. It filled me with more energy than any drink ever had, and it was instantaneous.

And the warmth? Oh, I really understood now. I had always thought the warmed blood from Alexius was the sensation everyone meant, but this perfectly heated blood made me feel as though I was curling up next to a fire on a cold night.

This was *everything*.

Yet, it was strange being on the other side of this interaction. In the back of my mind, I thought about how to maybe make this guy feel better about this. I didn't want it to be painful. I didn't want any of that, but I also didn't know the magic Alexius once used on me.

In my head, a memory started repeating. Oscar attacking me, Oscar feeding on me as I pleaded for him to stop.

I ignored it.

I was just hungry. That was all.

I needed to fill that hunger. It was the top priority.

I took a second pull, my mouth filling with blood, but this time, I caught the bitterness and a hair away from being sour. It wasn't a strong flavor, but it was there. Swallowing still came easy because my stomach was empty for so long, and my heart was finally beating. I needed more.

I couldn't stop. My grip grew tighter on his arm. He groaned, and someone begged me to stop.

I continued to drink, each mouthful growing more foul, each swallow getting harder to keep down.

Then my stomach was full, and my heart was racing to keep up. I spilled some of the blood and nearly gagged on the taste.

It's fear. This is what fear tastes like.

I tried to swallow another mouthful and nearly puked.

I can't... I can't do this. This is awful. The taste is awful.

The shock of how bad it was and the curdling feeling in my gut brought me clarity.

If I don't stop, I'm going to kill him.

I can't kill him.

Alexius would be so ashamed of me.

My mom and Jacob would never forgive me if I don't stop now.

I'll never forgive myself. I won't be a statistic. Another new vampire and yet another accident. *I won't.*

I have to stop now.

Pulling my fangs out of him, I put my tongue over the punctures. I needed to heal him, or he was going to bleed out. I just didn't know how that worked. I licked it, trying to ignore the terrible taste. The bleeding slowed, and I yanked my head away from him, falling backward, breathing heavily.

The man fell to the side, but he was alive. His heartbeat was a little weak, but he wouldn't die.

Not to me.

I heard the others talking as I got to my feet and made my way into the kitchen. Leaning on the counter, I turned the sink on to wash the blood off my hands.

"Well, you aren't very much fun," Jaxson said, his voice too close to me. "Why are you cleaning up? The party is barely getting started."

"I don't like being a messy eater." I shook my head as I wiped my face off. "And I don't like that much fear in the blood. I like... other feelings. Every emotion releases different hormones, chemicals into the blood."

"Yeah? What feelings do you like?" Jaxson leaned on the counter next to me, invading my personal space again. I looked around and saw the mistake I had made. The kitchen was a U, and I was stuck in it with him.

"Sexual endorphins are really nice," I lied. I had no idea, but I remembered Alexius feeding off me and figured it was his favorite. It had to taste better than the vile shit I'd just swallowed. "I normally... woo men in clubs and bars, have a bite to eat while we both... finish, then wipe their memories, so they don't remember the love bite."

"Wipe their memories?" Stacy seemed interested in that. "We can do that?"

"With practice," I confirmed. "I've been getting lessons from an older vampire—"

"How's the older vampire dick?" Amanda asked with a giggle, and I flushed as my heart raced.

"He's my boss," I told her, still furiously trying to scrub off any drop of blood I could find on my hands and face.

"That's fucking boring," Jaxson growled. "Vampires have jobs? Fucking seriously? We're monsters who eat people, and there's ones out there with jobs. And rules and shit? Fucking ridiculous. People get all the power they could ever dream of, and they waste it on that human bullshit."

"We need money to survive," I reminded him. "Just like anyone else."

Jaxson was looking at me as if I had grown a second head.

"Sounds fucking terrible," Calvin said with a laugh. "Amanda and I are going to go have some fun." I watched him as he grabbed the young woman by the arm, who screamed and cried as he dragged her away.

"Look, why don't you go feed more? You're so uptight." Jaxson leaned closer, and I moved back, but this time, he followed me. "You've never killed anyone, huh? Then you don't know the rush. It's indescribable, Everly. It'll loosen you up." He smiled. "Unless you don't need to be loosened up."

I lowered my head, my eyes darting around for anything to get me away from him.

Alexius isn't here yet, so I'm going to have to protect myself. I'm just a shiny new plaything to Jaxson. He only wants to exert power and make me scared, make me compliant. Been there, done that.

Never again.

I wasn't scared. Jaxson was just revolting, a lecherous, tiny man who wanted to feel powerful. He was clearly in control of this group.

"Baby, you have someone to play with," Stacy said, as I heard her footsteps coming closer.

I saw the frying pan left on the stove. Maybe there was a knife block behind me, but I wasn't in the situation to turn my back on Jaxson. Shifting, I tried to get closer to the stove while Jaxson was distracted.

"I don't want to play with a used whore tonight," Jaxson growled. She stomped out of the room, heading somewhere else, hissing viciously and muttering. I heard a door slam.

"Now that we're alone..." Jaxson raised an eyebrow. "I just gave you free blood, Everly. You need to pay me back."

"I have cash."

"Come on. I've never fucked a redhead before. Do the curtains match the drapes?"

Go fuck yourself, Jaxson. Try a less tired perverted line.

Or stop trying at all. That would be nice.

He grabbed my waist with one hand, and my anger roared at the touch.

"If you want to stay, you need to know how this works," Jaxson snapped.

He tried to grab my neck, but I avoided him.

I grabbed the handle of the frying pan with my right hand.

Or stop being alive.

That would be even better.

I pushed him off with my left hand, catching him off guard. He wasn't used to people fighting back. Then I swung, the gong-like ringing from the frying pan slamming into his skull echoing in my ears for several seconds after the impact. I looked down to see blood pooling around his head, covering the kitchen floor as I stood there with the frying pan.

"That was for Elizabeth," I hissed down at Jaxson's

body. I was never a religious person, hard to be while knowing about vampires, but seeing the blood touch my shoes, there was a verse I had heard a few times, probably from movies or in books. Something about the righteous being avenged and the blood of the wicked.

If I could describe anyone as wicked, Jaxson would be at the top of the list.

"What was that?" Stacy said, running back in. Calvin and Amanda were next, naked and covered in blood. Amanda was the only one brave enough to come see what I had done. She threw her hands over her mouth as she fought a scream.

I knew I wasn't done yet.

Jaxson had the *audacity* to groan in pain.

Lifting the pan over my head, I swung down and kept going as they stared at me in shock. Every swing made him more and more unrecognizable.

I stopped swinging when I realized I was hitting tile. I straightened and glared at the other vampires in the room, now all in the position to see what I had just done.

"Lesson number one: You *can* die," I snarled.

"No... no, no, no," Stacy was staring down at Jaxson. "NO!"

She went to her knees as the others just stared at me, horrified.

"And you *will*."

I took a step closer, making Amanda fall back and scream. She scrambled away, heading for the front door, not the one I had come in earlier. She was out the door and running before Calvin thought to stop me.

Screams came from outside as he lunged for me. I

swung my frying pan again but only hit air when something else came flying in through the opened door.

Chaos erupted. I stood there with my frying pan as Alexius forced Calvin to stay down. Kavik was grabbing Stacy, pulling her away from the dead body at my feet. I heard howls outside as Amanda continued to scream. She ran back into the house, and I saw the moment she realized there was nowhere safe for her.

I heard a snap, and my eyes flicked back to the living room. Alexius had broken Calvin's neck and moved on Amanda. Kavik broke Stacy's neck next and dropped her body on the floor unceremoniously. Amanda didn't have a chance to run again. A massive furred wall shoved her farther into the house. It took me a moment to register that it was a werewolf.

I hadn't known they could get so big. It was the biggest wolf I had ever seen, and the only ones I had ever seen in person had been from a distance at a zoo.

Once Amanda's neck was broken, things turned quiet again.

I looked back down at Jaxson's body, then at Kavik, who was walking slowly into the kitchen, seeing the body at my feet for the first time.

"Did you..." Kavik met my eyes.

"Yes," I hissed in response, my grip tight on the handle of my frying pan. "You have a problem with that?"

Kavik stepped back as Alexius walked around him. Alexius looked at the body, nodded, then held his hand to me.

"The pan, please," he requested.

I couldn't move my arm and didn't want to give him my weapon.

"They're not dead," I snarled at him.

"They will be soon. Breaking their necks disables them until I let them heal. Then I can question them, and we'll kill them. The frying pan, Everly."

I snarled, and Alexius sighed in response.

"Pick one."

"Calvin." It could have been any of them, but Calvin was just the first name that popped into my head.

Alexius nodded to Kavik, who grinned and went to the vampire's body. He growled as he ripped Calvin's head from the rest of his body, blood spraying everywhere as the humans still conscious screamed. I was pretty sure they had been screaming the entire time, but I had stopped hearing them.

As Kavik howled, even though he was still a human, I held out the frying pan. Moving slowly, Alexius took it, gently unwrapping my fingers, and put the pan on the counter.

"How are you feeling?" he asked once it was out of the equation.

"I don't know." I looked down, seeing the corpse I had created.

I had no idea.

.

CHAPTER THIRTY-THREE

"Janek and Lawrence would like to come in and help the humans," Kavik said, interrupting the long silence between Alexius and me.

"Bring them in," Alexius agreed with a nod. "We'll have to wipe their memories and stage a car accident to explain the deaths and their amnesia. That could work."

An eerie howl filled the night, and more voices followed. Kavik's head jerked into the direction of them, his eyes going wide.

"Corissa," Kavik whispered. "That's her howl and her wolves."

"I'll make sure she knows you ended up being more of a help than a hindrance," Alexius promised. "Get the humans out of the house."

I still hadn't really moved since I had tried to fight Calvin. Alexius stayed with me while Kavik helped his werewolves get the humans outside.

"They just took one into a back room," I said as they

looked at the bodies of the elderly couple. "A younger woman..."

Kavik nodded, and they went as a unit into the back. Kavik carried the young woman, her eyes wide with shock and horror, silent tears rolling down her cheeks.

Once all the humans were gone, both dead and alive, it was just Alexius and me.

"The humans will keep the werewolves occupied," he said, leaning on the counter.

"I keep wanting to think this is over, but it's not."

"No, it's not. I have to put them back together and question them, but first..." Alexius looked at me, and the endless darkness of his eyes held me captive. "Did you kill any of them? You've fed, Everly."

"Would you kill me if I did?" I asked in return.

"No!" Alexius shook his head, holding up his hands. I wondered if he felt guilty I would even think to ask. He was certainly surprised I did. "No... I want to be prepared for the fallout you'll have. If you did, there's no shame—"

"Well, I didn't." I felt sick, remembering the taste of the man's blood. "I fed on the man... made him pass out, but I tried..." I took a deep breath, collecting my thoughts and trying to find the right words to say. "I didn't want to kill him. His blood was soured and bitter with fear, and I could barely stomach it as I kept feeding. I tried to heal the bite when I was done."

"You fed on a human, as hungry as you were, and you stopped yourself. You should feel immensely proud."

"I didn't want to disappoint you," I whispered. "Or the memory of my mom... or Jacob. I didn't want to disappoint anyone. I would have been ashamed of myself.

I don't want to be a monster. I'm never going to kill a human. Never." It was a promise to myself. I wouldn't fear the possibility anymore. I would choose to die before I put myself in the situation of killing a human to feed my own needs. I would not lose my mind to the bloodlust ever again.

My control might be weak, but my conviction in that belief, that promise to myself, was strong.

Alexius nodded, then offered me his arm

"Fresh air?" he asked.

I took his arm, and he walked me outside through the front door.

"What took you so long?" I asked as we stopped on the porch. I watched the werewolves prowling in the trees and on the road. The neighbors had their lights on now.

"You had such a big lead, I had to change my tactic. I tried to catch the scent of blood you did and followed it as I called Isaiah to tell him what had happened. I was on the phone with him when the girl died. I was following your trail to the house when the werewolves tried to get in my way. One tried to take me down, to incapacitate me so Kavik could get his revenge. I broke the wolf's back." Alexius sighed as my jaw dropped. "Threw him into a tree. Broke the tree, too."

"And Kavik?"

"Roughed him up, played the little werewolf game to get him to listen. He wasn't considering you or the humans caught in this mess. Thank you for integrating with the group for information, just as we hoped would work."

But that wasn't... Oh, Alexius, thanks for protecting me. Again.

"No problem." I rolled with it.

"I'm glad I wasn't too late again."

"I never blamed you for the first time," I reminded him.

More people and werewolves were coming through down the road.

"This is a shit show!" Isaiah yelled. He ran ahead of the others and up the steps, stopping in front of us. "A neighborhood? Really?"

"I didn't pick the family they attacked," I snapped.

"Figure out what to tell everyone and make it go away." Alexius reached out and patted Isaiah's shoulder. "I thought we could spin this as a group of serial killers trying to pin murders on supernaturals, so they tried to replicate vicious kills of werewolves."

"Pin it on werewolves?" Isaiah snorted. "Let me spin it a bit more, then throw it to Corissa. It can be the payment she makes for losing track of Kavik. Speaking of..."

"I got him in line while Everly integrated with the group."

"Did you?" Isaiah gave me an intriguing look.

"I try so hard to be a mouse," I repeated, batting my eyelashes and stunning him.

"Well... someone has come into her own," he said, nodding slowly as he took that in.

"Then she killed one of them, right as Kavik and I were surrounding the property." Alexius looked down at me. "That was why it took us so long. We positioned the pack to make sure no one could run if they left the house, human or otherwise. We wanted everyone accounted for."

"If you have a werewolf pack, might as well use it the right way," Isaiah said with a one-shoulder shrug.

"So you... heard some of what happened inside?" I asked Alexius, swallowing.

"Let's say I don't blame you for killing him."

"She killed one?" Isaiah shook his head. "You know what? I'll read the report. I have enough to deal with tonight. I'll put all the pieces together later."

Alexius kept me out of the way while the werewolves and Isaiah, along with a handful of other vampires, worked to clean up the house. They started spinning the story for the neighbors and the local police when they arrived only a few minutes later. Vampires did our best to pretend to be humans working with the supernatural. Not a big deal for me. I had once been a human who worked for the supernatural.

This was a supernatural incident, so the killers weren't handed over to the local authorities and would disappear. Corissa's werewolves grabbed them quickly and made sure they were gone before the cops arrived. The victims were already gone, Kavik's pack whisking them away, and I knew no one would ever find them again, not under their old names. Their memories would be wiped or altered, depending on the memory. They would be crafted new identities, placed under a geas, and moved somewhere else in the world where no one they once knew would ever find them.

That part made me a little uncomfortable. I understood and had helped keep the secret for a long time, but they had just been traumatized, and we were going to take their life away from them. It felt so unfair.

On the long walk back to the motel, Alexius offered me some solace.

"They won't know what they lost," he whispered. "They'll have no idea anything is missing. They'll have no idea they lost a daughter and sister. Or their parents and grandparents. It's an extreme protective measure. We don't use it often, but when the other humans woke up and realized what was happening, we had to bring out the extreme measures. Vampires can't be discovered. They'll never break the spells put on them, and they'll be happy. They won't have nightmares, and they won't live in fear."

At the hotel, I went in with Alexius glued to me. We were led to a conference room, and I was surprised to see Amanda and Stacy sitting there, already healed, their eyes wide with fear. Something was keeping them strapped to the chairs, but I didn't recognize the material. Part of me wondered if it was vines or something organic, which made little sense. The door closed behind us and locked. Only Alexius and I were in the room with them.

"You killed Jaxson! This is all your fault!" Stacy screamed. "Where are we?"

"Where's Calvin?" Amanda demanded, but there was a lot more fear in her question.

"Calvin is dead," I answered, sitting across from them. "Like Jaxson, except Alpha Kavik of the Fairbanks Werewolf Pack is the one who got to rip his head off."

"Everly," Alexius chastised softly, but I heard the humor. "We want them to talk to us."

"You have no right to keep us here!" Stacy screamed at the top of her lungs. "Who the fuck are you?"

"I'm Everly, and this is Alexius. We're vampires, like you, but with morals. We hunt vampires who break the rules." It felt so good to say that to them. I heard a few people chuckle, but they weren't in the room. We were being watched, and people were listening in. I listened a little closer to the people outside the room, now knowing the walls weren't soundproof.

"I have every right to keep you wherever I please." Alexius walked around the table, leaning over Stacy as she tried to look up at him. "You're completely uneducated, so it would make sense you don't know. You were Turned into a vampire. We have rules, ones that safeguard us from exposing our existence to humanity and keep our kind under control. You broke several of those rules, so Everly and I were asked to come identify you, track you down, and execute you."

"We..." Stacy shrank. "We didn't know about any rules."

"Werewolves have rules. All supernaturals have rules. You can't really be so stupid to think murdering entire families would be acceptable to anyone," I snapped. "If it wasn't us, it would have been the pack, tearing you apart limb by limb. If it wasn't them, it would have been human governments, and you would have exposed vampires everywhere."

"We didn't think about it like that," she admitted. "We were just having fun. We were told we could have fun."

"By whom?" Alexius asked softly, leaning over her.

God, I hated how close he was to her. I wanted ten

349

feet between them. I wanted to put myself in the way and make sure he didn't get any stink on him.

"Jaxson," she whispered.

"Like Jaxson knew anything!" I shook my head in disbelief.

"I loved him," Stacy snapped. "Calvin was his best friend. We believed in Jaxson."

"You..." I looked at Alexius. "Can I have a minute alone with her?"

Alexius shrugged and walked away from her. I was happy to see the distance. Someone opened the door for him, locking me in after he left.

Leaning across the table, I stared at her and tried to understand why I hated her so much. She was being abused by him, and it was a bad take to be shitty to an abuse victim.

Elizabeth.

"He didn't love you," I explained. "You were a tool he could hurt and control. Normally, I would pity you."

"Good. I don't want your pity. I was going to have him after all these years. He could be good, great. He was mine," she hissed as tears rolled down her cheeks.

"Was he worth your best friend's life?"

Stacy smiled, tilting her head to the side. It was such an odd expression. The tears still wet her face, stains of makeup, but the smile was fake, taunting, playing innocent.

"What best friend?"

"Elizabeth," I growled. "Kavik's great-granddaughter. Jaxson's ex. *Your* best friend."

"Oh. *Her.* I put up with her because she had him. She

was desperate for normal friends. He wanted to make her one of us," Stacy explained, her smile growing. "Just like he made me, Calvin, and Amanda. I made sure that didn't happen. It wasn't hard. She had already pissed him off and paid for it. It took little to convince him to kill her and leave her dead."

The cut...

As the last piece fell into place, I lost control of my deep, undying fury, not just with Stacy but with everyone like her. Every Edwin and Claire, every Oscar, every Jaxson. Every fucking one of them.

I lunged across the table as the door swung open behind me. I had my claws in her throat and took a piece with me as I was hauled away. She was left stunned as blood poured out of her neck, and slumped as her eyes glazed over while I was dragging from the room.

Alexius dragged me out of the room as I screamed with fury. The room was locked again as Alexius held me in the hall, arms tight around me while I shook with rage. Isaiah came into view, shaking his head sadly.

"Damn, that's cold." Isaiah sighed. "Well... Everly found out the one thing we needed to know."

That made me cool down just a little. I realized the hall was actually full of people, and they had been watching from a two-way mirror that had been behind me. People were looking at me with abject shock and awe. I relaxed more, but I wasn't embarrassed by my outburst.

Stacy deserved it.

"Who is she?" someone whispered, and Alexius stiffened.

"She's his protégé," someone else answered. "That's what everyone else has been saying. An Orphan at that."

Well, I was warned I would be considered interesting.

I ignored them, looking at Isaiah as he eyed the ones whispering.

"I did? What did I learn?"

"Jaxson Turned the other three... and Jaxson is dead. That means we won't be able to discover who Turned him. Not yet," Alexius explained, his hold not loosening. "You made the best call you could in that house. There was no way to know the person who Turned him had taught him the process, but nothing else. Logically, it made sense if they were all Turned by one person. They added a layer of protection to their identity, and it worked out for them."

"The mystery continues." Isaiah nodded to another vampire. The door was opened, and that vampire, with a walk that reminded me of something more feline than human, went into the room. Amanda screamed until I heard the sounds of her head being torn off.

Stacy couldn't scream.

34

CHAPTER THIRTY-FOUR

"We'll add this unresolved mystery to the others," Alexius said. He didn't let me walk as Isaiah walked away. He lifted me, carrying me as Isaiah led us through the halls. Isaiah made no comment about it. There were a lot more people around than there had been when this started with that meeting. Some looked at us in shock, but I did my best to ignore them, trying not to be embarrassed. I knew Alexius was carrying me because he didn't want me to lose my temper again.

It was fine. Not having to walk and hold back from going back to make sure Stacy was really dead gave me time to think.

Isaiah locked us in his office, and Alexius put me down. He reached out and grabbed my wrist, and I went wide-eyed to see I was still holding the piece of Stacy's throat. He took it from me, went back to the door, and handed it off to someone outside the office, then leaned on a side table, crossing his arms as his expression turned thoughtful.

"I think this is connected to what happened to Jacob," I declared, with no evidence to back it up.

"Me, too," Isaiah agreed, as he sat down behind his desk. "We just need to figure out what the game is."

I was stunned by his agreement. Looking me over, he opened a drawer, pulled out a package of wet wipes, and put it on his desk, making it clear I had some cleaning up to do.

"Yes," Alexius chimed in while I pulled out several of the wipes and started cleaning my hands and wiping down my face, making sure nothing had sprayed on me. "It reminds me... of something. There are other possibilities to keep our minds open to, but it's a disturbing sequence of events."

"The dark times."

It took only a second to click.

"When you tried to make laws for vampires, and some of them fought back, right?" When Isaiah gave me a surprised look, I pointed a thumb at Alexius. "I asked him how he started doing this work for everyone. He told me about it while answering my question. I don't know the full history or anything."

"Yes, those," Isaiah confirmed. "What else did you tell her?"

"My history and introduction to Jacob, including how it ended. About early vampires, our... control and ways of life. How we were different from you, her, and even the murderers we were chasing. And about the ones we found up in the wilds a few centuries ago. There was a lot, but the trip was highly educational for her."

"It was, but let's get back to the situation." I found a

seat. I wanted to talk about this more. "It makes a lot of sense, right? Jacob helped by making sure new vampires back then learned control. Jacob isn't around anymore. Someone set up his death and put Edwin in as the fall guy. Now, Alexius gets a postcard to go to Alaska, where someone Turned a sick asshole, who then made a group for himself. No education, no trying to tell them anything at all. Jaxson was surprised to even see me. I didn't think he realized how many vampires really existed. He didn't *know* he could *die*. Someone just released him into the world... to cause chaos." I looked at Alexius. "Didn't Jacob's letter back then explain he was trying to help other vampires created for the same reason?"

"It did. He was trying his best to keep up. We're talking only three to four a year, but that's a lot of new vampires to teach."

"A young, out-of-control vampire can be a weapon of mass destruction, as you've learned. We didn't have any technology at the time, either. You expedited this process for us immensely." Isaiah put his feet on his desk.

"Someone else would have done it," I said, trying not to swell with pride.

"Certainly, but you were on the ground, able to communicate with Alexius directly. I could never send a stranger with him to do anything you did, and there wouldn't be a vampire capable who would *want* to. I can't force people to do a job against their will... sadly. I certainly wouldn't send my own family to do it. None of them are right for the work. When I help him with information, we often lose contact for days in large areas like the one you had to cover."

"Rupert and I have the same problem," Alexius added. "If this turns out to be a resurgence of those ideals, we'll have to change the way we do everything. They've had time to adjust to us, learn our habits, learn how we work, even our strengths and weaknesses."

"Is this it? Are we heading into another period of the dark times?" Isaiah asked, and for the first time since I met him, he looked genuinely worried.

"I think there's no way to tell until we have a more evident pattern. This could be someone with a grudge against me, using those who hate me, Jacob, or even possibly you, against me. I need more for a pattern. I don't disagree with the theory, and I will continue to be on the lookout for further evidence. I will also be on the lookout for evidence of other possibilities. If this is someone trying to get to me, I will make sure it's handled before they can do anything more devastating."

"We knew who the ring leaders were in the dark times. The ability for people to remain secret now is going to be an issue," Isaiah pointed out. "Shell corporations for money laundering, anonymous online accounts."

"VPNs," I added, and they frowned at me. "The most common use of a VPN is accessing region-locked content. You get a VPN, and it will trick websites and services that have region-locked content into thinking you're from a certain area in the world so you can access the content. If something is only available in Canada, you can watch it in the United States using a VPN. Could be used against IP traces, making it difficult to track where someone is emailing from. Someone sends you an email with a threat from somewhere in Asia, and you think it's from Europe. That's just the most basic stuff, available to anyone who wants to pay for it. Professional and experienced hackers can do a lot more. I'll have to do some research and brush up my knowledge on what people are doing now, the latest, most cutting-edge tricks of the trade." I crossed my arms. "I like hardware more than software and code. I can do it; it's just not my favorite."

"I have people who know how to do much of that," Isaiah said. "If it's necessary, I'll put you in touch with them, and you can exchange information. As it stands, I don't believe any of us know where to start."

"I never got to look over Edwin's computer again," I pointed out. "I would love to."

"I had my people do it. Nothing went anywhere. I have it in storage, where I would like it to remain. It's the core intelligence we have. I'm sorry." Isaiah even gave me a sympathetic smile. "But I'm certain I can ask someone to copy the hard drive and send it to you for you to look over it in your free time."

"Of course. That would work for me."

"We should try to find a weak point—Edwin or Jaxson. Kavik will probably agree to gather information on Jaxson and who he might have met recently. One of them could have been the vampire who Turned him. Or we could find out all of Edwin's contacts and shake them down one by one," Alexius said, pushing off from the table.

"Edwin was friends with a couple of ancients, Alexius. I've already spoken to them, but if you want to..."

"When is the next gathering?"

"May in New York at my nest. I love hosting everyone." Isaiah glanced at me. "You should come. We don't let younger vampires attend unless they're new offspring of an ancient attending. You might not be his offspring, but everyone would understand if that rule was bent for Alexius to bring you."

"You want me to be there because it would make things interesting."

"Absolutely, but it's your choice... and his." Isaiah jerked his head at Alexius. "Alexius, if you miss this one, you'll have to wait for December, and that one is being hosted by Maria. Hers are never as casual as mine."

"I'll get back to you. With Jacob no longer attending..." Alexius sighed.

"Yeah, I know. Just consider it." Isaiah pulled his feet off the desk and stood, stretching before he started pacing. "There is one difference between this event and the ones we faced all those years ago, Alexius."

"What is that?"

"Our least favorite moon cursed, the werewolves. Involving other supernaturals. The Tribunal hadn't formed at the time. Everyone was focused on themselves or killing another supernatural that encroached. There were no overarching laws for all or any sort of political connections between us. The only two species that really interacted frequently were the moon cursed, and their issues are their own."

"It's unlikely anyone cares about the Fairbanks pack," Alexius said, sounding like he didn't care about them himself.

"But Jaxson might have been targeted because it rattled the relationship we have with them," Isaiah countered. "Not Kavik and his pack, but Callahan and Corissa, the two most powerful Alphas in the world."

"Implying we might not be the only ones who will fall if this is a resurgence of those types of vampires?" Alexius groaned. "Politics."

The more I thought about it, the more I needed it answered.

"Jaxson was the boyfriend or ex-boyfriend, depending on when he was targeted. No one could guarantee he would kill Kavik's granddaughter and great-granddaughter. He might have just had the right sort of personality for the vampire to want to Turn him. Someone who could be cruel, someone who would find it easy to kill if it made him feel powerful. These were... wicked people. I don't think any of them had a moral compass."

"It wasn't really about who he was or who he would kill. You're right. Jaxson was probably just the right type of human." Isaiah giving me that one piece of the agreement told me he was about to give me a lesson. "It was the city it started in... a werewolf city. No other supernaturals live in Fairbanks, aside from the possibility of a handful of witches that don't make a fuss. If this had happened in Atlanta, that wolf pack would have gone to the nest in Atlanta and discussed it. Boston, Phoenix, any of those." Isaiah shook his head. "But it was in Fairbanks, Alaska, where the only thing Kavik could do was reach out to those above him who could get vampires to investigate. Callahan and Corissa, on the Tribunal. It was done in a place that sent it straight to the top, and it got everyone's attention." Isaiah pointed at Alexius. "And whoever schemed it made sure it got his, too."

I understood.

"Now, I'm going to send you two home," Isaiah declared. "We have a lot to think about, and you both probably need long showers and some rest." He eyed Alexius. "Maybe not you, but she does."

"She does," Alexius agreed.

I wanted to roll my eyes. I was feeling fine.

Isaiah went to the second door in his office and opened it, revealing Alexius' study.

"I never went back to my nest. Once things settle down here, I'll come back with your bags. I'll sleep through the day at your home, then be out of your hair by midnight, old friend. My nest was annoyed that I didn't return while this was happening."

"Did you go through my things?" Alexius asked.

"No, but I went through hers," Isaiah said, smiling when Alexius growled, and I hissed. "I'm messing with you. I slept in my room and left everything alone."

I went inside first, and Alexius followed me, closing the door behind him. We stood in his study in silence.

"You did amazing," he finally said.

I looked at his portrait with Jacob, then at him.

That was when it hit me.

I killed another vampire. I ripped out a girl's throat.

I did both, blinded by rage. Rage that had been born by my experience in Portland, Maine. I had thought it was gone, but it had come roaring back, stronger than ever.

"I lost my temper."

"There's nothing wrong with that. You need to learn to embrace it, not bottle it up until the pressure is too much."

"I've never been like that before. I didn't stop until..."

"You had a temper, as you want to call it, when we met. You screamed at me on the phone. You spit in Edwin's face. You have been forced to see the full depth of what you have inside yourself."

"No. I wasn't like this as a human. I wasn't capable of killing a man."

"Incapable or unwilling?" he asked. "Incapable, I can agree with. You weren't strong enough physically to do it. Unwilling? Did you never look at Edwin and wish you could kill him?"

"I..." I had wished for Edwin to die but knew I couldn't kill him, so I wished Alexius would. Anyone, really, but Alexius had been the weapon I had.

But if I could have done it on my own... I would have.

"Don't feel guilty. I'm the last person who will judge you for losing your temper."

"Because you're a berserker," I whispered, remembering that word from Edwin.

He went wide-eyed.

"Where did you hear that?"

"Edwin said it when he realized you were coming to kill him, but I didn't see it. I died. And I haven't seen it from you since. I trust you, so it doesn't really matter. Even if you had gone a bit crazy and killed them, I mean, they had a hand in killing your son. How was I going to judge?"

Alexius leaned on his desk, studying me.

"All these years, people have feared me because of what I am capable of, and the ones who don't fear me because they follow the law, they fear me for the day I lose control," he said eventually.

"Yeah..." I shrugged. "You don't really scare me. Sometimes, I'll think you're scary, but I don't live in fear you'll kill me." Maybe at some point, I did, but I didn't anymore. I was more worried about making him ashamed of me than I was of him killing me.

"Why?" He was genuinely confused.

"I see all the little ways you protect me. Like telling Kavik you sent me in as a plant. You knew if he understood how I really ended up with them, he would think I needed to be put down as well. You put your body in the way when powerful people look in my direction. You purposefully move to make them keep their attention on you, not me." I chuckled as I realized something more. "Thinking about it, it's the same way I tried to protect all of my friends in Portland. I made sure Edwin looked at me. I made sure he trusted me and left them alone. It didn't work all the time, but it worked most of the time." I smiled at him. "We have a lot in common."

"Apparently, we do." Pushing off his desk, he opened his study door, and I saw the familiar hallway. "I need to tell the staff we're back. You should get some rest. Take a hot shower or soak in a bath, then put on fresh clothes. I was thinking of reading in the garden with a bit of tea if you want to join me."

"I could do with a soothing drink." It sounded like heaven.

We met there an hour later and decompressed after the nightmare in silence, not saying a word more about the case or the future. It was the sort of silence you share with someone who knows you well. There's no reason to talk.

It was exactly what I needed.

35

CHAPTER THRITY-FIVE

THREE NIGHTS LATER

"Alexius!" I called out an hour past sunset.

With no response, I started my hunt.

I'd fed myself when I woke up, and he'd asked me to meet him but didn't tell me where he would be. I checked his study, not bothering to knock, then went to his room, where I knocked but got no reply. I checked the small sitting room and the large one. On my way to check the gym and library, I had to walk past the garden, which gave me a chance to look in.

There he was. Alone in the night garden, hands in his pockets as he waited for me.

Damn, he's so good looking. Straight out of a magazine, still acting like a god in his domain.

It took me longer than it should have to realize there were four heartbeats in the garden. I grinned as I opened the door, realizing what was about to happen.

"Happy birthday!" everyone yelled.

I laughed as Rupert jogged up with a tiara and forced it on me. I didn't fight back. Alexius kept a straight face, but one of the staff laughed. I knew them all now. Rupert, the butler who ran the house, was still the one I knew the best, but I finally had a real conversation with Shania, the housekeeper. There was also George, the groundskeeper, but oddly, he told me he only worked on the grounds upstairs. The last member of the staff was Harriet, the one who handled the blood supply. She was a nurse who had connections Alexius needed. George and Harriet were married, with three kids and seven grandchildren.

"George, you don't need to laugh at me."

"Oh, but look at you. Our vampire princess," he said, touching my shoulders. "Locked away for so long by the Dark Overlord and now allowed to bloom under the..." He looked up. "Moon?"

"I'm not a princess." I couldn't stop laughing.

"You don't get to make that decision," George told me, taking my free will right out of the equation.

I shook my head at Alexius, who started chuckling as he turned away.

"This was your grand plan for my birthday? A surprise party with old people who might as well think of me as their grandchild?"

"No, but..." His shoulders shook.

"We wanted to do something special for you," Shania said as she guided me to sit at a small table they had set up. There were a few presents on it. "We know it was hard for you to be down here for so long. After the recent events, Rupert decided we should have a bit of fun with it."

I was forced to open every present, something I had no qualms about. They were all somewhat comical gifts, vampire-related as if they had raided a novelty store, but I loved every one of them. And I laughed a lot. More than I really should have.

I blew out candles on a cake I couldn't eat, but that didn't bother me. It only added to the ridiculousness of the entire situation. As they ate the cake, I got up and went to Alexius, who was hiding by the bar he kept in the garden.

"You are laughing at me over here in the corner, and I do not appreciate it," I said as he sipped on his drink.

"If it's too much, I'll tell them to scale it back for next year," he promised. "Send gifts, but no party. Whatever you would like."

"Oh, this is fine," I said, shrugging. "You just aren't getting involved, and that's unfair. I would think my partner would join in on the fun of my birthday party."

"We are not partners," he reminded me.

"Not yet," I fired back.

George heard and went, "Oooh..." Alexius only smiled over his drink.

As the party drew to an end, he and I helped clean up. It went faster with us doing it, then we bade the staff farewell. I would see them later, but they didn't spend all night downstairs. Alexius and I felt good about my control, but it was all still supervised.

Once we were alone in the garden, I turned to him again.

"For weeks, I've wondered why the garden is the centerpiece of the house. You know, Corban called it infamous. I think I've finally figured it out, but I don't have any evidence yet."

"Oh?" Alexius put his drink down and crossed his arms. "What is your theory?"

"It's your garden," I said, smiling. It suited him, being a gardener. He did a violent job, but home was his shelter, his place of rest, and this garden was a thing of beauty he cultivated and cherished, something he could do with hands that killed more than they created.

"Yes, it is," he confirmed. "Which you would know if you ever left your room. I tend to it for at least one hour every night."

"I haven't been doing that since we got back from Alaska, but you haven't worked on the garden."

"I've been waiting for something. It arrived today while we slept, along with a good number of other things. Come with me. You'll want to see this. Not what I've been waiting on for the garden, but the other things."

I followed him, curious.

"This is my birthday present to you," he explained as he led me to the door upstairs. Following him into the main house above ground, I saw dozens of boxes in the living room. He reached for something on the wall and held it out to me.

I took my car keys, mystified.

"This is all... my stuff,"

"That's right. Isaiah and I can lose track of time, and we had when it came to bringing your things down here. We wanted to make sure anything relevant to Jacob's nest was properly handled, and... I just didn't think. This place couldn't be your home until you had your things. Now,—" he waved out to my stuff, still boxed but ready to be unpacked "—my home is your home, for as long as you want it to be."

Grinning like a fool, I looked into the boxes, seeing family photo albums, little knick-knacks, and everything else I had gone without. Some boxes had my entire wardrobe.

It was my entire life before meeting him, before becoming a vampire.

"Thank you," I said as I looked up, seeing him waiting on the outer edge of the mountain of boxes.

"No need to thank me."

"I'm going to need days to unpack all this," I said, edging between crying and laughing.

"I'll help."

"Will you?" I started getting out of the mountain. "Seems like a really boring thing for you to help with."

"I have to do one small thing first, then we can get started tonight," he said, chuckling as he lifted a small box.

"What are you doing?"

"Well, it could wait for tomorrow, but Isaiah sent me something I needed for my garden. I wanted to get it done as soon as possible."

"You didn't answer the question," I pointed out as I hung my keys up. There had to be six or seven car keys, and mine looked cheap at the end of the row, but they were there, which meant a lot to me. It was a piece of freedom I knew I would get back, something to look forward to.

"It's... fertilizer. You can watch if it interests you."

Alexius frowned. "Or you would find it very boring or strange... or disturbing, actually." He seemed nervous.

"Really? Is this why it's infamous?"

"No, though I do despise that Corban thought to call it that. I know Isaiah has spoken of my garden to some, but he would never tell anyone about this. Many would never see me as a gardener and that's what makes it infamous. Not this."

But I do.

I followed him back down to the basement and the night garden. He opened the box and revealed several black jars.

"These are... vampire ashes," he explained, lifting a jar. "Vampires I've killed. I don't get the ashes of all of them, but there are some... I feel I carry in some way. So, I spread their ashes in the soil here and let them go. These vampires took life, so much of it needlessly, and I use them to create life. My garden reminds me I have fought, survived, and turned the wasted into something better. Admittedly, it is morbid." He looked at the jar in his hand. "Some of them have waited some time. I wasn't sure what to do with one of these, which kept me from claiming any of them."

He put the jar down on the bar, and I saw a label.

Edwin.

"It's a little morbid," I agreed, taking the jar as he watched me.

"Go ahead if you like," he whispered.

I poured Edwin's ashes around the garden and put the empty jar back on the bar.

The next one Alexius put on the bar was even more surprising.

Jaxson.

I didn't say anything as I poured those ashes as well. Eventually, Alexius started, then we worked the ashes into the soil together. It didn't change the garden for me. The flowers were still beautiful, and the mood was still serene.

In fact, I understood what Alexius meant.

I survived, and this garden would now always remind me.

"Let me know when you're going to do this again."

"Of course."

"I'm going to take a quick shower before unpacking."

"I'll meet you in an hour," he said, wiping dirt off his hands.

I showered, then took a moment to check my computer. I had an email waiting on me and thought it was from Isaiah or even Kavik, who had emailed once to check in. There weren't many people who knew my email.

MISS EVERLY ABBOTT,

LEAVE the employment of Alexius the Hunter or find that his enemies become yours as well. This is your only warning.

. . .

I LEANED back in my chair, considering the message for a couple of minutes until I knew what to say. Typing my response quickly, I smiled as I hit send.

To Whom It May Concern

(Also known as the cowards who can't put their names on their emails)

Go to hell.

I WAS STILL SITTING THERE when Alexius knocked on my door.

"I thought we would meet upstairs," he said when I opened the door.

"Yeah, sorry. Lost track of time reading an email." I let him see it. He read over it, then looked at me. He was silent as he pushed away from my desk, offered me his arm, then led me out of my bedroom.

"Nothing to say?" I said softly.

He stopped walking, looking down at me as I stopped with him.

"Does it scare you? The threat?"

"A little, but I don't care."

"Are you sure?" He spoke with more concern now, that worry written all over his expression.

I wasn't entirely okay, but that email wasn't going to scare me off. It wasn't telling me anything I didn't already know, which was the fact that this job was dangerous. But the idea of danger didn't scare me as much as it used to so I tried for a little humor to make sure he knew it was okay.

"They're asking me to leave, and I really want to unpack. I don't want to go house hunting."

"Then you gave them the perfect response. Now, let's finally get you settled in."

Keep reading for more information about the next release, special news, and more.
Or sign up for my newsletter right now!
https://knbanet.com/newsletter/

DEAR READER

Thank you for reading!

People are threatening our main charactyer? What's a little Orphan to do?

Well, we'll see if she thinks of anything in the next book.

(Alexius, stop licking her)

EVERLY ABBOTT BOOK 3
COMING SEPTEMBER 2022

This time frame may change thanks to an elbow surgery I have coming up. At the latest, it might be a mid-late October release if I have to push it back. There's nothing to be done about it. I normally have a preorder up right. There isn't one.

If you want to follow for updates and catch the preorder when it's live, you can try these three things: my website to read my blog, sign up for my newsletter, or join my Facebook group.

Newsletter

https://knbanet.com/newsletter/

Facebook Readers Group:

https://www.facebook.com/groups/banetreaders

I also have a Patreon, where I write a monthly short story or novella. You can check that out here:

Patreon.com/knbanet

And remember,

Reviews are always welcome, whether you loved or hated the book. Please consider taking a few moments to leave one and know I appreciate every second of your time and I'm thankful.

THE TRIBUNAL ARCHIVES (EA)

The Everly Abbott series is set in the world of The Tribunal. Every series and standalone novel is written so it can be read alone.

For more information about The Tribunal Archives and the different series in it, you can go here:

tribunalarchives.com

ABOUT THE AUTHOR

KNBanet.com

Living in Arizona with her husband and 5 pets (2 dogs and 3 cats), K.N. Banet is a voracious... video game player. Actually, she spends most of her time writing, and when she's not writing she's either gaming or reading.

She enjoys writing about the complexities of relationships, no matter the type. Familial, romantic, or even political. The connections between characters is what draws her into writing all of her work. The ideas of responsibility, passion, and forging one's own path all make appearances.

facebook.com/KNBanet

instagram.com/Knbanetauthor

bookbub.com/authors/k-n-banet

amazon.com/K.N.-Banet/e/B08412L9VV

patreon.com/knbanet

ALSO BY K.N. BANET

Servant of the Blood

Blood of the Wicked

Tribunal Archives Stories

Ancient and Immortal (Call of Magic Anthology)

Hearts at War

Full Moon Magic (Rituals and Runes Anthology)

ACKNOWLEDGMENTS

Every book is hard work from the beginning to the end. Thank you to everyone who helps me get through them. My husband, Nick. My editor, Sandy Ebel. My proofreader, Michelle. My dear friends, Leigh, Becca, and Erika, who all provide love and support. My PA, Andi.

And you. The reader.

www.ingramcontent.com/pod-product-compliance
Lightning Source LLC
Chambersburg PA
CBHW050906250626
47155CB00001B/129